Praise for *We Begin Our Ascent*

"Joe Mungo Reed has the sort of triple-barreled name that often comes attached to a certain kind of disheveled country music star . . . But scratch all that. Reed is young and English and . . . based on the aloof, punishing control he displays in his small, tight bud of a first novel, *We Begin Our Ascent,* he doesn't appear to have a disheveled bone in his body. . . . It's one of the indices of Reed's talent that you hotly flip this book's pages even when there's not a lot going on, when it's just another hilly day on the tour. . . . This novel derives its power from its limited focus and direct language. There are no adipose, word-glutted sentences. Reed is mostly content to give us strong silk thread, absent pearls . . . This novel's darkness, like heart disease, sneaks up on you. . . . Like a racer, Reed carefully husbands his resources in this ruthless little sports novel. He enlists our mind in Sol's project as an athlete. He sees the madness in it as well."
—Dwight Garner, *The New York Times*

"Joe Mungo Reed's unforgettable debut novel, *We Begin Our Ascent,* introduces us to a powerful new literary voice—as riveting as DeLillo's or Morrison's. On the surface, this is a book about doping in the Tour de France, but it's really about marriage and masculinity, competition and loyalty, and a sense of aspiration that blooms a person open and simultaneously shuts him tight as a clamshell. I read it cover to cover in a gulp. Bravo!"
—Mary Karr, author of *The Art of Memoir* and *The Liars' Club*

"A dazzling debut by an exciting and essential new talent: fast, harrowing, compelling, masterfully structured, genuinely moving. Reed is a true stylist and has, like James Salter before him, a gift for making a physical world that is very naturally imbued with rich metaphorical meaning. This novel is a heartening reminder of what happens when a keen intelligence is applied to a rarefied subject."

—George Saunders, author of *Lincoln in the Bardo*

"A quick and enjoyable read, perfect for a summer weekend before the Tour. Reed's pacing is expert, slowly drawing you in and then driving you ever faster to the crux of the story and its quick, quiet denouement. And Reed's powers of perception and turns of phrase provide small delights throughout. . . . Its main draw . . . is Reed's voice, which even in this debut novel is already strong and will continue to rise to the top. . . . Reed also demonstrates piercing clarity about the sport's larger truths . . . [his] most potent observations mine the sport for broader meditations."

—*Outside*

"As meditative as it is thrilling."

—*Vanity Fair*

"Joe Mungo Reed propels readers through the fascinating competitive sports world of the Tour de France . . . with a humorous, philosophical lens. The narrative is richly poetic and smartly suspenseful, with themes of sacrifice, loyalty, and morality."

—*Christian Science Monitor*

"Exceptional . . . Reed's first novel lives squarely within Don DeLillo's sphere of influence . . . but Reed relies more heavily on plot than DeLillo, and the effect is remarkably successful: Alongside the ideas and the jokes, there is real suspense and human drama. . . . Fast and smart, funny and sad, this is an outstanding sports novel, and Reed is an author to watch."

—*Kirkus Reviews*, starred review

"This novel will hook you . . . and haunt you. Embroidered with a sly humor—and insider details about the cycling world—the novel explores the sacrifices we're willing to make for our dreams, climbing steadily toward its stunning climax."

—*AFAR* magazine

"Riveting . . . A beautifully written story of the consequences of the choices we make."

—*Good Housekeeping*

"*We Begin Our Ascent* is a brilliant debut novel, as affecting as it is smart. It gives us the particular life of competitive biking in all its fascinating complexity, delving into the visceral thrills of the race and the painful vagaries of the body in equal measure. Joe Mungo Reed writes dazzling sentences that veer from philosophy to absurd humor to childlike wonder. His mesmerizing and inventive engagement with his subject brings to mind another great sports novel, Don DeLillo's *End Zone*."

—Dana Spiotta, author of *Innocents and Others*

"*We Begin Our Ascent* is a book for anyone who has ever wanted something a little bit too much. Joe Mungo Reed's complicated characters have moved a step beyond the right thing, and they linger at the precipice. This is a story for our time."

—Kyle Minor, author of *Praying Drunk*

"From page one, Joe Mungo Reed will make you a cycling convert with his ability to convey the often quiet beauty, struggle, and competition of the sport. While the stages of the Tour keep the wheels of the plot spinning, it is the portrait of two ambitious people trying to work through the shades of grey in the choices they make in the pursuit of their dreams and the unfolding of their marriage that will keep you turning the pages."

—*The Daily Beast*

"With cool, unerring prose, Joe Mungo Reed provides a richly detailed—and, at times, comically absurdist—exploration of the

Tour de France that also functions as an extended metaphor for other long-term endeavors requiring stamina, ritual, and erasure of individuality for the greater good: marriage, parenting, work, life itself. Even if you don't know pelotons from pedals, *We Begin Our Ascent* makes its athletic microcosm vivid and exciting, and Reed is equally adept at dissecting the conflicts of the cyclist's taxed yet enlarged heart."

—Teddy Wayne, author of *Loner*

"*We Begin Our Ascent* is a nonstop heart-racing ride and a sneaky-smart tour of twenty-first-century labor relations. If you've ever worked hard enough to vomit just for a shiny sticker, this is the book for you."

—Malcolm Harris, author of *Kids These Days: Human Capital and the Making of Millennials*

"A fascinating, darkly funny look at doping in professional cycling.... As the team's problems go from bad to worse to disastrous, Reed's wryly profound narrator uncovers insights into groupthink, dependency, and the dangers of mixing personal and professional lives."

—*Booklist*

"Strong, lean, compact ... With its taut, unsentimental prose, Reed's novel is both an exciting depiction of the prestigious bike race and an intimate portrait of a couple coming to terms with the cost of pursuing difficult goals and determining whether they're worth the price."

—*Publishers Weekly*

We Begin
Our Ascent

* * *

Joe Mungo Reed

Simon & Schuster Paperbacks

NEW YORK · LONDON · TORONTO
SYDNEY · NEW DELHI

Simon & Schuster Paperbacks
An Imprint of Simon & Schuster, Inc.
1230 Avenue of the Americas
New York, NY 10020

Copyright © 2018 by Joe Mungo Reed

First Simon & Schuster trade paperback edition May 2019

SIMON & SCHUSTER PAPERBACKS and colophon are registered trademarks of Simon & Schuster, Inc.

For information about special discounts for bulk purchases, please contact Simon & Schuster Special Sales at 1-866-506-1949 or business@simonandschuster.com.

The Simon & Schuster Speakers Bureau can bring authors to your live event. For more information or to book an event, contact the Simon & Schuster Speakers Bureau at 1-866-248-3049 or visit our website at www.simonspeakers.com.

Interior design by Paul Dippolito

Manufactured in the United States of America

1   3   5   7   9   10   8   6   4   2

Library of Congress Cataloging-in-Publication Data

Names: Reed, Joe Mungo, author.
Title: We begin our ascent / Joe Mungo Reed.
Description: First Simon & Schuster hardcover edition. | New York, NY : Simon & Schuster, 2018.
Identifiers: LCCN 2018014606 (print) | LCCN 2018018173 (ebook) | ISBN 9781501169212 (ebook) | ISBN 9781501169205 (hardcover) | ISBN 9781501169229 (pbk.)
Classification: LCC PR6118.E4547 (ebook) | LCC PR6118.E4547 W4 2018 (print) | DDC 823/.92—dc23
LC record available at https://lccn.loc.gov/2018014606

ISBN 978-1-5011-6920-5
ISBN 978-1-5011-6922-9
ISBN 978-1-5011-6921-2 (ebook)

For Jenny

Chapter 1

We come from our rooms and stand in front of the elevator. We assemble quietly, treading slowly over the thick hotel carpet in our flip-flops. We breathe lightly. We do not talk. We watch the progress of the elevator in the illuminated runes above the door. We do not consider the stairs. *Do not walk unnecessarily.* This mantra is not merely practical but ideological. Energy is to be expended in only one way. "Sleep and cycle," our *directeur sportif*, Rafael, likes to say. "Sleep and cycle."

We enter the lighted, mirrored cabin when the doors slide back. We take our places, facing forward, a loose formation, which cannot help but bring to mind the grouping we will make on the road. We think about racing of course, finding life in cycling, cycling in life. We are preoccupied with thoughts of the day ahead. *The fear is always worse than the thing itself*: another mantra, its truth debatable, its usefulness clear.

When the doors of the elevator open, we step out and turn a slow left toward the private dining room of the hotel. We are in a lobby, the floor under our feet tiled now. Other guests notice us. We are grown men in matching sports clothes. Mostly, people know our business. It is the middle of the Tour. Roads are closed, press vans are on the streets, messages of encouragement adorn local shops. Perhaps these guests recognize us as individuals; more likely they know us merely as participants in something larger. The Tour is the real star of these days.

I have done speeches at sporting events, even opened a few bike shops. Whenever I do, whoever introduces me always says that the Tour is the hardest sporting contest in the world. I am just an artifact, proof that it is done by men. I am something which it has happened to, like a bolt fallen from a disintegrating spacecraft and recovered from a cornfield after the event, to prove that all that motion and brutality really existed. I accept this perspective, because this ennobles the activity, dignifies the fact that I am aging and breaking myself in doing it.

We eat our porridge, our omelettes, and our pasta quickly. We are, if nothing else, men of good appetite. I sit next to our team leader, Fabrice: a sort of privilege. He is a neat man. He has good table manners.

"How did you sleep?" he says.

"Normally," I say.

"Did you dream?" he says.

"No," I say. "You?"

"Oh yes," he says, "very richly."

Fabrice is crazy for Freud and Jung. He analyzes the products of his many hours of sleep. He has built an interest on the routine of his days.

"I dreamed of fathers," he says.

"Yes?" I say.

"They loomed."

"Loomed?"

"The fathers."

"What does that suggest?"

"In short, that I was anxious."

"Yes?"

"There are, of course, undertones, overtones, histories."

2

Fabrice's specialty is going uphill. He's a climber. Tours are most often decided in the mountains, where a small number of men are able to kick away from the rest of us. Fabrice is one of these men, or aspires to be. He has little weight to carry. He, more than anyone, is a creature connected to his bicycle. His proportions are three-quarters of those of a normal human being. He has a thin, bony face. His hair is dark, shaved on the sides and back in military style. His chest is large though, and his eyes painfully big. There are hopes for him in this tour, grand enough to be seldom vocalized: a place on the podium, a shot at first place, even.

"Any premonitions?" I ask.

He has peeled a banana. He carefully slices it, laid out on its turned-open skin. "You misunderstand," he says. "I'm not in the business of premonitions."

After we have eaten, Rafael rises to speak. He, like Fabrice, is a short man. He wears built-up shoes to increase his height. His role as directeur sportif places him in the team car following behind us riders on the road, threaded into the action by the earpieces we wear. He picks our team, plans tactics, relays information. He jokes that he does everything for us but the pedaling. His is the voice that echoes around my skull, encouraging greater effort, greater power output, greater commitment.

We have done twelve days of the Tour already. We have eleven more days of riding, and two rest days to come. Rafael is acutely conscious of our place in the schedule, in the country, in his plan for things: a knowing beyond knowing, like that of a pianist in the middle of a piece, unreflectively aware of the keys they are touching and will touch next, a perfect form of the music in mind, awaiting realization.

Rafael takes his time to look around the table, to check that all eyes are on him. "I'm not going to tell you how wonderful, how able, how loved by your papas you all are," he says. "To me, you are each capable of outputting a steady three hundred and fifty watts. I ask you to do that, okay?" His hair is thick, black, and short-cropped. He brushes one hand through it as if seeking to clean his palm. "If you do that, I give you a pat on the head. If you don't, I think you are a bag of shit and maybe you don't get a contract next year. All right?"

The bovine slowness of our nodding exemplifies our commitment to conserving energy, maybe also our reluctance to agree. Though he is in his late forties, Rafael is boyish. The perma-tanned skin of his cheeks is smooth. His neck is thin. His hair is still glossy. His dark eyebrows are thick and teased into a monobrow by a causeway of bristles arcing over the bridge of his nose. "Today is a mountain finish," he says. "Obviously, you are supporting Fabrice. Shield him from the wind, bring him water, give him your bike if he punctures. If it makes you happy, make an inspirational speech about how much you believe in him and slap him on the bottom." Rafael won eight stages of the Tour when he was a younger man. Once he rode so hard up to a mountaintop finish that medics strapped an oxygen mask to his gasping face as he crossed the line. "I will be more specific in the race briefing," he tells us. "None of you fuck up. I hate it when you fuck up."

We pick at the food that remains on our plates, then return to our rooms to rest.

* *

Before we leave the hotel, I call my wife, Liz. I am married, and even though this has been the case for nearly three years, in the midst of racing, this fact still sometimes hits me with a strangeness. We have a boy now also. He arrived last autumn with the simian face of a new

4

human, lying in his crib, clasping at the air with chubby hands, his palms nearly creaseless.

When I am on tour, Liz takes care of our son. She is a research biologist, a postdoc. She breeds and dissects zebra fish relentlessly, looking at their spinal cells, seeking to fathom the workings of specific genes.

She picks up after the fifth ring. She knows it is me, even on our old home phone without a screen telling her so. That is a feature of our third year of marriage and our first of parenthood: it is inevitably the other of our partnership making contact.

"How are you doing?" she says. I can make out the sounds of our kitchen in the background: our son gurgling in his high chair, a kettle coming to boil, the radio on low. I feel a nostalgia for the routine I left behind just weeks before. Yet I know, also, that it is a pleasure I should resist, like a warm bed on a cold morning. The thought of that kitchen is a comfortable one, and I do not want to diminish the leaden-bellied feeling that I have come to associate with proper preparation for a race.

"I'm good," I say. "Normal. Fine. Ready."

Our boy is called Barry. This was Liz's choice. A tribute to a favorite uncle, who died before I ever met her. She had been keen to name our child before he arrived, and so I ceded her this right and accepted a middle-aged man's name for our new baby. I cannot yet extend myself to think of him as Barry, however, and have called him B in this first year of his life.

I tell Liz that we will leave for the start line soon. There is not much for either of us to say, beyond acknowledgment of our activities, our consciousness of each other in the world. "We've got things to do today," Liz says. "I'm off to the lab, but perhaps we'll watch you on TV in the afternoon."

"Or the group," I say. "My head bobbing among other identically dressed men."

"I'm like one of those farmers who can recognize specific sheep," she says. "Somehow I always manage to pick you out of a crowd."

*   *

The silence on the bus is heavy. As we drive to the start line we reflect upon our bodies, conducting an inventory of aches, of tiredness, of places of strength. The curtains are partly drawn. We sit mutely, the same few scenes, concerning or hopeful, vying for supremacy in our minds. It is when one is racing that it is easiest to believe in one's power: when one is enclosed within the peloton, between those other bodies, part of a mass, rolling amorphously along the road like a drop of water down a pane of glass.

When we park, Tsutomo's fan is waiting. Tsutomo is Japanese. He is a *domestique* like me, another man riding in support of Fabrice. He seldom talks and never offers up his dreams for examination.

Shinichi follows Tsutomo around. He wears a battered windbreaker and cycles part of each day's route himself. He waves a Japanese flag. Tsutomo is entirely uninterested in him.

"Hello, Shinichi," I say, when I leave the bus. I speak to Shinichi because Tsutomo will not. I wonder if this isn't a small act of treachery.

"How is Tsutomo?" says Shinichi.

"He is well," I tell him.

"Not sick?" says Shinichi. "Eating good?" Shinichi is chubby. He has a robust jolliness entirely lacking in his hero. Tsutomo is wiry, slightly distant, handsome, the only asymmetry in his face the slight leftward lilt of his nose, broken in a past race.

"Very fit," I say.

Shinichi beams. He rubs his hands. He wears replica gloves and, under his windbreaker, the jersey of our cycling team. I wonder what it must cost, what Shinichi must go without, to follow Tsutomo around France each July.

"So," he says slowly. "Do you think today he will win?"

"Oh," I say. This is the dirty business of talking to people, of talking to fans. "Tsutomo will do what's best for the team. Perhaps he will help Fabrice win."

"Will you win?"

"I will help Tsutomo help Fabrice win."

That is largely true. We are competing only to get our team leader, Fabrice, across the twenty-one stages of this Tour in as little time as possible. This cumulative time, the criteria on which the winner of the Tour is judged, is all that matters to us. Our own results are not important. We shade him from the wind, pace him, will give him our own bike if he punctures. These measures have just small effects upon his time, yet this is a sport of fine margins—decided by differences of seconds after days and days of riding—and so small advantages, wrung from our fanatical assistance of our strongest rider, offer our team the best chance of victory. We only think of the ever-rising time it takes Fabrice to make his way through this race, how that time compares to his rivals', how we may act to lessen it.

The mechanics set up a headquarters around the team bus. Our bikes are mounted on stationary trainers to allow us to warm our legs. We are encouraged to drink a mixture of sugar syrup and caffeine. I spin on a trainer next to Fabrice. He is at ease in these mornings. He smells of Tiger Balm and saddle cream. His eyes are shiningly alert.

"A pedestrian steps off the pavement one day," he says, "and is run down by a cyclist."

"Right," I say.

"'You're lucky,' says the cyclist to the pedestrian."

I nod.

"'Why am I lucky?' says the pedestrian. 'That really hurt.'" Fabrice raises a finger, holds the pause. "'Well,' says the cyclist, 'I normally drive a bus.'"

I smile.

He laughs himself. "It's a good one," he says. "Don't tell me it's not a good one."

The PA system is blaring over by the start line, playing the greatest hits of the Police. Above us, a broadcast helicopter flies around, taking in the city, testing the thin morning sky.

Rafael comes over. The starting paddock is a small village, and Rafael has been walking it like a local notable, greeting journalists, organizers, other directeurs. He takes a moment to watch us. "Raise the tempo," he says. Fabrice's expression becomes stern. He shifts his weight to the front of his saddle. The hum of the trainer's flywheel rises.

I think of Liz saying that she will try to watch us on TV this afternoon. Last year one of the other teams' riders broke away from the pack and rode ahead of everyone for three hours. He was alone and riding hopelessly into a headwind. The peloton, with all the aerodynamic efficiency of a large group, caught and overtook him easily before the finish. He never really had a chance of winning.

Questioned afterward, he said it was his wife's birthday. He knew that if he rode off the front she'd get to see him for three hours on her TV screen. Also, his sponsor, a manufacturer of household cleaning products, saw its logo displayed upon his sweat-soaked race kit for most of the day.

We Begin Our Ascent

* *

When we start, we start slowly. Spectators cheer and blow air horns and we press down on our pedals and roll gradually up to speed. On the road something loosens inside us, because we are no longer dreading anything.

We are people who understand each other. We talk together. Cyclists from other teams often pull alongside Fabrice to ask him about their dreams. Teeth, I am led to understand, are powerful and recurring metaphors.

Tsutomo and I fall back to the support vehicle to collect water bottles for the other riders. Most often, this is what our assistance entails.

We roll through alpine foothills. We are on a highway cleared by gendarmes who now stand to the side of the road watching the crowds.

Our team surrounds Fabrice as we ride. We try to keep him near the front of the pack of riders, ready to chase down any competitors who might sprint off ahead.

Rafael shouts all sorts of technical details through our earpieces: speed, wind direction, projected wattages. He says, "I'm happy. Let's not fuck this up."

* *

Cycling is about moving through air. There are technicalities—distinctions like "turbulent" and "laminar flow," for instance—but really it is that simple. To push alone through the air is so much harder than moving along in the slipstream of another rider. The peloton—the group composed of the majority of riders, moving close together, sharing turns at the front—is much more efficient than any solitary cyclist. Victory in a tour is about staying with the peloton first of all, and then breaking from it to gain time when other factors, such as steep gradients, crosswinds, conflicts, or confusions, temporarily diminish its capability. The role of myself and Tsutomo is to keep Fabrice ensconced safely within the group for most of the race, to leave him enough energy to push ahead when the rest of us falter.

I still remember explaining all of this to Liz for the first time: the pleasure she took in it, and the satisfaction I took in turn in her engagement. She has a biologist's interest in adaptive strategy, in hidden motives and cooperation. We were in a coffee shop. She listened intently, leaning forward, fiddling with a sugar packet which eventually tore, spilling brown grains of sugar onto the wooden tabletop. "It's kinship selection," she said.

"Sorry?" I said.

"An evolutionary concept. You're like a honeybee, giving up a chance to breed for the queen."

"Yes?"

"The best strategy for your own reproductive success is to assist another who shares your genes," she said. "Speaking figuratively."

"Right."

"'Genes' in this case being your team, your sponsors."

"A maker of chicken nuggets," I said.

"Exactly," she said, laughing.

It was flattering to be considered in this way, to have my dedication regarded as something worthy of inquiry. Until I met Liz, I thought of charm as a proactive quality, something one deployed upon others. And yet she is charming in the opposite way, finding interest in the lives of those she meets, drawing out their stories.

Presently, she has turned her earnestness to B. She doesn't just observe his actions as I do but considers them in the context of his development. She hides a toy and speculates on whether he knows it hidden or considers it destroyed. She builds a narrative of his growth, threads events into a rich story, which, to my discomfort, currently advances forward without me.

* *

Lunches are canvas bags thrust out into the road by team helpers. We catch them as we move past, hook them temporarily over our shoulders, pick out energy gels and rice cakes.

There is an alpine river thundering along beside the highway, a railway on the other side. We roll past the outskirts of a town, past its supermarkets, lumber yards, and warehouses.

We leave the straightness of the highway. We begin to climb more steeply up a thinner, winding road toward some ski towns. Here the crowd is deeper. The spectators are attracted by the gradient: the chance to see us slow, suffer, begin to exhibit our differing capabilities. They have waited, written messages onto the road in whitewash. As the slope steepens, the peloton is less effective. Air resistance becomes a smaller portion of what holds us back. Riders start to tire, dropping gears, grimacing.

Fabrice is concentrating. Discussions of dreams ceased long ago. Tsutomo and I ride ahead of him, pushing hard, seeking to keep up with two teams, one sponsored by a northern European banking group, the other by a French manufacturer of farm machinery, who are raising the pace. People break from the lines of spectators at the roadside and run beside us. They bellow, wave their hands wildly. A fat man wearing lederhosen and a cowboy hat jogs at a speed one would not expect his build to allow, shouting into Fabrice's ear.

Pedals creak on their spindles. Some riders stand, some sit and spin, their bodies rocking in the saddle. Fingers dig into handlebar tape. "You're into the red zone, Tsutomo," says Rafael over the radio. The red zone means that Tsutomo's pulse is high, that he is exerting himself in a way that cannot be maintained. There is so much data taken from us that it must be returned simplified into a color-coded system. From the car, Rafael has access to our pulse rates, our speed, and the power we push through our pedals. Tsutomo slows and drops behind me and Fabrice in order to recover. I look back and realize that we have broken from the majority of riders. They are strung out behind us, down the switchbacks of the mountain, their progress assessable by flashes of their brightly colored kits and the activity in the crowd as they pass.

I am nauseous. We have to summit this hill, descend, and then summit another before the day's finish. There are forty kilometers to go. I try to give myself to my pace, convince myself of its inevitability. The bankers and the agricultural machinists have lost riders too. Our group is now forty or so riders strong. I think of my feet making circles. I try to imagine these circles as being independent of me, mechanical and necessary.

Two kilometers from the top of the climb, Tsutomo passes me and settles in front. He seems to have energy back but his pacing is erratic. He surges and slows a little. I see his forearms quiver with the effort.

"Very good, boys," says Rafael into our earpieces. "Let's keep this."

I stand on my pedals and glance back at the other riders, at the road falling away behind us. To my rear, Fabrice just holds his head down. He offers no hint of his condition. We crest the peak in the same group of forty. We begin to descend. As we start to freewheel, we do the zips of our cycling jerseys right up. The road dips away and we crouch into our bicycles. Having been unable to separate from each other, riders now work together, stringing out into a line. The wind rushing past chills us. Our sweat-soaked kits quickly become clammy. The air tears through the insubstantial lycra to our skin. There are few fans on this side of the mountain. The action is too fast to really appreciate. The only sounds are the wind and the buzz of our wheels against asphalt. If things are going right in a race, there is little pure fear. Instead, the experience is vivid, consuming. Fear is not quite fear if it does not have time to settle, but an energy, a strange quality of attention. My real anxiety comes to me in the evening, when I reflect upon past descents and anticipate new ones.

On the lower slopes of the mountain we enter a village. Shouts and clicks of gears echo off the walls of houses. Out of the village, the road levels. The riders bunch together into a group, two riders wide and twenty deep. We take turns to ride on the front, pushing into a crosswind. The detente which has prevailed during the descent will soon be broken. We anticipate the last climb: the thing that will decide the stage, determine the day's beneficiaries and victims.

Through our earpieces, Rafael reads out our pace, the distance to the finish line. Tsutomo and I need not make it to the finish with this group, many of whom are team leaders, favorites to win the Tour. We must simply pace Fabrice for as long as we can bear, then we may slow and grind toward the end with the stragglers.

In the flat of the bottom of the valley, hay is being harvested. The air is filled with the rich, peppery smell of cut grass stalks. People stand on the edge of ditches, between the fields and the road, calmer than the crowds on the hillside. They hold up signs or simply applaud.

Gradually, the road tilts into a climb. As a group, we keep pushing, though we know the pace to be unsustainable for all but a handful of us. At times like this I feel it is hardly worth breathing. Something is escaping from me and all my sucking in of air will not return it. My vision closes to encompass just the space in front. Now that we are back on an upslope the crowds are all around us, a blur of replica kits and banners and sunburnt skin. "Concentrate," says Rafael in my earpiece. "Ten kilometers left." Tsutomo is behind me and I can feel him faltering. I hear the click of Fabrice's gear shifter. Fabrice moves past Tsutomo and settles at my rear wheel. We ride a few moments longer and when I look back I see Tsutomo off the back of the group, suddenly just a man cycling up a steep hill alone.

As we go on, other riders begin to drop. Soon there are few more than thirty of us. Someone in the crowd sprays us with water. Spectators are forever proffering water. One may pour it over one's head, but it should not be drunk. It has been decided that the crowd could contain any number of psychopaths with any variety of designs on our insides. The water could be poisoned, unsanitary, tainted with substances that would interest the dope testers. "You are accountable," Rafael likes to say, menacingly, "for what goes into your bodies."

One of the members of the banking team stands on his pedals and attempts to stamp away from the group. The rest of us are alert, however. The group lurches, and draws itself around him.

The life has gone out of my legs. The pace is a machinery greater than any one of us. I feel I am being dragged into it, like a Victorian unfortunate caught in a factory apparatus.

Heroes, here, are made in ten-second increments. I tell myself, *Ten seconds more*, and then when those ten seconds have elapsed, I tell myself the same thing again. If you can put off your collapse long enough, there is no reason you can't take everything. However, in the moment, it all feels as rigged as a game at the fair. These increments just get longer.

Then I just drop. Fabrice gives me a nod as I seem to slide backward down the hill. I wait for that slower pace to calm me. I wait for my legs to return. They do not. No pace is slow enough. I pedal in hollow, aching strokes toward the line.

* *

The finish plays out over the radio. Rafael's exhortations go from encouraging to disappointed and then to slightly threatening, the tone ever detectable through the static. One of the leaders kicks ahead in the final few kilometers, and Fabrice can do nothing to stay with the man. He loses time.

As I approach the line later, Rafael addresses me through my earpiece. "One more kilometer," he says, "you lazy piece of shit."

I just keep pedaling. Everybody is passing me. Who knows how many have passed me. Soon, perhaps, a clown on a tiny bicycle will come squeaking up the hill.

Tsutomo, even, is gaining on me. We need just to cross the line, however. Fabrice is the racer; we are his assistants. The fans don't concede or even seem to know this. They are still hollering, urging us on, trying to hook into some submerged sense of pride. The last kilometer is cordoned off. They lean forward and beat high notes on the bars of the metal barricades. They seek some residue of spectacle, some desire, some fight in our eyes. They don't get it.

* *

The leading riders, those who haven't been packed off to massages, podiums, or interviews, roll back down the course warming down, spinning their legs idly. That's how we recover from cycling: more cycling. I keep my head down and continue to pedal. I pedal and I live in my little increments, endure these blocks of time, and eventually I am across the line.

At the finish, we fight through crowds and trail back to the bus. We reassemble easily because there are no commitments for our riders, no prizes to collect. Fabrice does a couple of interviews. He is curt, visibly disappointed. In previous days he has been doing well, staying with the major contenders in the race, building what Rafael calls a foundation. Today the television people get none of the sunniness, the sly pleasure and jokes that they have become inclined to expect from him.

People push food into my hands: protein bars, rice cakes, recovery shakes. Our bus is parked on the backstreets of the alpine town. Here the barriers and cordons which separate us from the crowds are largely absent. We are protected by the banality of our routines. We take off cycling clothes. We flannel our faces. Mechanics spin the cranks of our bicycles, spraying oil and adjusting bolts. We wait for the bus to move. An elderly couple watch us from a balcony coolly, the man smoking, the woman holding a small, yapping dog as if it were a child.

I eat a protein bar. The next day begins the moment we finish the last, we are told. So much of our success is built not on what happens on the race course, but on what happens before we start. "There is no fuel," Rafael says, "like the thought that you have done something in preparation that the other guy has not." He has never needed to sell any of us on this notion. We came into this team having marked ourselves out from so many other aspirants. We each knew what separated us from all those riders who fell away into amateurism. In our early careers, we all outpaced our competitors with the confidence that we had woken earlier than they had, that we had tuned our bikes more comprehensively, that we had trained whatever the weather, that we had been out riding on Christmas morning. Rafael's dictum has two aspects: positive and negative. We seek to do what other racers do not, and we do not neglect to copy gains our competitors make.

As I walk to the steps of the bus, I see Shinichi. He moves around the tour with some efficiency. Presence at both the start and finish is impressive. He sits on the pavement of the small street, his own bicycle resting beside him. He still wears his team kit and nods at me as I go over.

"A bad race," he says, shaking his head.

"I suppose," I say, "a little disappointing."

"Tsutomo was *very* tired," he says.

"We're all very tired," I say.

"Yes," he says, "*everyone* is very tired. Very tired is no excuse."

I shrug in reply.

On the bus, we pass around a little bottle with an eyedropper lid. Two drops on your tongue: that is the formula. It's a tiny dose of testosterone, enough to aid one's recovery, so small as to be undetectable by the drug testers. It is very important to feel that there is something within oneself doing good, fighting the insurgency that one's muscles and joints mount in the evening. "The ancient Greeks used to use testosterone," Rafael said to me once. "They used to eat ram's testicles before a race." He was overjoyed by this tidbit, wherever he had heard it. There is clearly some great justification in finding the roots of an action, any action, in antiquity. Perhaps I could have told him that the ancient Greeks used to own slaves and bugger children; maybe that would have been the smart reply. However, on tour we have no need for smart replies. I took Rafael's comment on board, and now when I use the dropper I think about the lineage of the act.

We pass the bottle covertly. Though it is our own team bus, there is a need to contain these activities. A couple of the new riders on the team are, as I was until nine months ago, yet to be ushered into the program. Though they might have made certain assumptions in light of their teammates' abilities, there is no need to offer them such evidence without good reason. The bus driver, for all we know, thinks us the most principled athletes to have walked the earth. Rafael has even taken care to keep our team doctor in the dark. Marc is only recently graduated from medical school. He has taken a pay cut to do what he says is a unique and fascinating job. He is a lanky, awkward guy in a perpetual quandary, it seems, about how to hold his body. He is balding in way that is painful to witness. His role is confined to the treatment of grazes and saddle rash. More illicit activities are performed by other members of the team staff and by doctors hired from outside the team. The era in which teams doped and were found out en masse has passed. Rafael has taken care to hire a doctor who can be shut out: "a useful buffer of ignorance."

The bus moves into the center of town. The vehicle swims in the glass front of an office block.

When I turn on my phone, I have a text message from my wife. "We watched the finish," it says. "We saw you. Good. Black socks and white shoes though?"

At first Liz's friends called me "The Cyclist." "What kind of adult," she reported one of them saying, "worries about how fast he can ride his bike?" Liz found this funny, and it was, though perhaps a little close to my own anxieties. She has always been an advocate of my career among her friends, however. She has learned to talk about the tactics, communicate the nuances of the sport. "You're missing out," she tells friends who watch football or tennis or nothing at all. I am grateful for the advocacy, though also aware that, among her friends, it has caused me to be solely defined by my profession. I have read that when Minoans first encountered mounted horsemen, they came up with the myth of centaurs to explain what they had seen. To Liz's friends, I think, I am at least half bicycle.

I sit next to Fabrice. He huddles against the window, the corner of his forehead resting on the glass. He watches the town stutter past us. "No one is getting a wing today," he says.

"No," I say. Wings are an invention of Rafael's. Performances in which members of our team do their jobs beyond all possible reproach are awarded little stickers of wings. We attach them to our bicycle frames, like kills marked on fighter planes. There is debate about the symbolism. Some on the team suggest that a wing means we ascend like birds; others argue that it is to do with our sponsor, a manufacturer of poultry products. We covet them, anyway. Rafael, more than anyone, knows what we should be doing. A reward from him is never given without good reason. No one, so far, on this tour, has acquired a wing. We are all eager to be the first to do so. Fabrice has four for the season, Tsutomo two. I, so far, have none.

Fabrice closes his eyes. He lets his head roll against the window with the movement of the coach. He is not sleeping. "Tomorrow," he says. "Tomorrow will be as smooth as cream."

Chapter 2

At the hotel I move slowly, conscious of my need to recover, cued by the rush of racing to enjoy the stillness of the dim hallways. I make my way to the small room I share with Tsutomo. A dirty kit lies on the floor, two energy bars beside it, as if remnants of a very exclusive rapture. He has been and departed already. He is having his massage elsewhere in the hotel. The room is quiet. The curtains are closed already. I sit on the bed. My phone connects. "Hello," says Liz. We talk for a while, go over the same things said earlier. I hear B in the background. His voice rises and falls in response to the activity of someone else, of his grandma.

* *

I met Liz by chance. I do not like to think about that, because to do so invites the consideration of alternatives, draws me into visualizations of different lives. My training and inclination make me a believer in necessity and causation. I need to be convinced of the efficacy of preparation, of the sure reward of my conditioning. If I were to truly attend to luck—to how easily a puncture or the crash of a rider in front might ruin a race, or how much my successes rely on the misfortunes of others—then I would struggle to prepare, to get myself out on the bike on winter mornings.

We were both flying back to London, making connections in Barcelona. It was a Sunday evening flight, and it was delayed at the last minute because there was a problem with the fluid that they were using to clean the plane. In compensation, the airline issued passengers meal tickets to be redeemed in any of the airport food outlets. We both joined the end of the line to receive these. I sensed Liz's prettiness beside me, some force outside my field of vision. She was tall. She had straight brown hair, hooded eyes that gave her glance a steadiness. I remember that she was dressed smartly, in a jacket and black jeans. I noticed this because though I wear team tracksuits often, I still try to dress up to fly. I have always felt the need to reject the clothes people wear in airports, the denial implied by such outfits: the elasticated sweatpants, the soft shoes, the neck pillows they wear hung in place as they pace the concourse, as if any sense of the speed and distance of a flight is only something to be blocked out.

Liz looked at the fifteen-euro voucher when it was handed to her. "I can spend it on wine?" she said.

The flight attendant didn't look up. "You can spend it on what you want," she said, "but alcohol is very expensive in this airport."

"Yes?"

"Believe me."

Liz looked at me as I received my own voucher. "You want to go halves on a bottle of red?" she said.

We ate in a counter-service pizzeria, in a seating area roped off from the echoing belly of the concourse. We had a bottle of wine, two plastic cups, and a small pizza on a paper plate. The sun was setting and the glassy corridors were full of soft light. Mr. Torres Pereira was missing his flight at gate twenty-seven. The announcement of that fact came again and again over the speakers. From the table, we could see out to the runway, to planes taxiing, made insectile by the expanses of glass and steel and tarmac around them. I was coming back from a training camp, she from a conference. We were unlike the others, I realized, because we were both glad of the delay. I felt this myself, and I sensed Liz's concordance. She had green eyes, and a funny way of holding her finger just beneath her chin as she talked. We were both busy people with hectic schedules, and suddenly here was a gap in our days for which neither of us had accounted. Perhaps we each knew, from the pleasure we were taking in this break, that there was no one waiting for the other at home. I asked her about her work, and she told me about her PhD: the zebra fish, the gene expression and breeding and lost-function experiments. "So what's the aim?" I said.

"To get my PhD," she said.

"The general aim?" I said.

She sighed. "You find the purpose of a gene in a fish."

"Suppose you do," I said. "And then?"

"Anything," she said. She kneaded the edge of her eyebrow with her fingers, looked at me. She wanted me to make the rest up for myself, and I recognized that desire. She had ambitions that she was reluctant to say out loud, and I knew this: the sense that you sought an objective rare enough that it felt too stark, almost childish, to simply say it.

It seemed so unlikely that I should find this woman, this feeling reflected back, in this airport, in all the drag of getting home. All meetings are chance, of course, but this one felt so especially.

* *

"You did well, from what I saw today," she now says over the phone. B gives a sharp cry like something being dragged across a polished floor. I ask her how he slept, what he ate. Liz gives answers of such scientific detail as would satisfy Rafael. We are that kind of parents now, though I do not mind this in the least. The sound of a vacuum cleaner comes from Liz's end of the call. Her mother is with her, giving a hand in caring for B. Liz will be going back to the lab in the early evening. We talk about her day at work, her return to it later. She sighs. "My students couldn't find the end of their own noses if I drew them a map," she says.

*   *

My first sense of her was that she made things happen around her. To go around London with her was like going on a treasure hunt of her devising. She had a gangliness that read alternately of girlishness and durability. She took me to a sushi restaurant above a barber in the West End with her friends, and it was good, so improbably so that I felt her due credit for its existence. When she went to the bathroom, her friends and I blundered on, like people trying to persevere through a power outage. I wondered how she came to be with me. I looked at those around the table and thought that they must have despised me for my good luck. She and I were both only children, and both had a similar sturdiness, a self-sufficiency born of that fact. She had something beyond it, though. She could pull others into her plans, bear them along in a way I could not.

We went to museums. Though I lived so close to the city, I had not done that much before meeting her. It is not that I had not thought museum going a good thing to do, but that I had not opened myself to it. The city offered so much that seemed a distraction, and so I was used to passing up experiences which would have been perfectly pleasant. Liz was different, in this respect. The thought that someone took interest in a subject she knew nothing about would unsettle her. She would return from parties and click through Wikipedia articles until late into the night, researching things she had talked to others about, learning more about the careers of those she had met. She had a deep desire to be rounded. She played a continual thought experiment: "Imagine

24

you were sent back in time four hundred years," she said. "How much of the modern world could you describe and explain?"

In Tate Modern, we walked through the bright rooms. She watched me examine the paintings. I strained to identify them. I would look at a picture and try to guess the author of the work from the limited cast of names I knew. I would consult the label, then, to check my intuition. When I had failed too often at this strategy, I tried to guess only the nationality of the painter. "They're not flash cards," Liz said, when we sat in the café on the third floor, a light rain hitting the windows. "Take a moment with them. See what really works for you."

The implication that some of them might not "work" for me was surprising. Here were paintings worth many millions of pounds, and Liz was suggesting that it was possible, simply, to not like some of them. I wouldn't have been more surprised if she had said that I could reach out and run my fingers across the pictures. Still, it was difficult to proceed with this knowledge, to stand and look, with Liz all the while seeking to gauge the authentic effect of the works upon me.

In one of the upper rooms there was a brass sculpture: a figure striding forward, the specifics of its body lost in stylized whorls and dashes of teased bronze. *Unique Forms of Continuity in Space.* I read the caption, about motion and futurism and the Nietzschean super-man. "It's you," said Liz. "It's a man totally dedicated to his motion through the air."

I shook my head. The likeness did not strike me as true. This fig-ure was so substantial, so defiant in the way it bore itself forward. The superman was bold, fleshed out. My teammates and I, however, were skinny, unique not in capabilities we had gained but in those we had chosen to jettison. The figure seemed to confront the wind, while we, I said, sought only to slip past without its noticing.

She was pleased with this. I felt her satisfaction in the way she turned away from the piece. We rode down through the building on the escalators. I suppose that I had cheated a little, achieved a victory on familiar ground, but I did not think of it that way then. It was exhilarating to meet her challenge.

* *

We end the call, and I leave the hotel room and walk down the corridor. Pictures of sailing boats alternate with sconces along the hallways. I round a corner to see Fabrice sitting on the carpet, his back against the wall. He fidgets, jogs his knees. He is thinking of the end of today's stage, I am sure. He and I are the same age—nearly thirty—and yet I am younger to it all. He has been racing since he was thirteen. There is still some of that teenager in him—his bounce, his fidgeting, his Kafka ears. One gets the sense that the real world has had little chance to make its mark upon him. He has had some good results in his past: one-day victories, stage wins, and a top-ten finish in this race two years ago. He has struggled for consistency, though. His promise is thought yet unfulfilled. There have been fewer comparisons to past champions in the last year, more mentions of those who flared and were forgotten. This tour is a chance to reinvent his potential, to bounce his story back into its former groove. I lean against the wall, slide down until I am seated beside him.

"Seeing the Butcher?" I say. He nods.

The Butcher is what we call the chiropractor. If he were really a butcher, however, he might be compelled to clean his equipment. The massage table holds a history in its complicated odor of sweat. "What's the difference between a chiropractor and an osteopath?" says Fabrice.

"Is this a joke?" I say.

"No no," he says. "It's a what you call it . . . an inquiry."

"I think that it's something to do with the intensity."

"Right," he says. "That sounds correct."

Fabrice goes before me, and when I see the Butcher, he is weary himself.

"You guys wear me out," he says. He is Norwegian. In mannerism and personality, he is more of a carpenter. He presses into my back. Parts of me crunch and readjust. He takes my neck and he cracks it left and then right. I don't like people cracking my neck. My impulse is to resist it. However, I am extremely good, and I do not joke here, at submitting to things which I do not like.

* *

Outside the Butcher's room, Rafael is waiting for me. "Solomon," he says. He uses my full name always, he and my mother only. "How did the Butcher do?" He stands close, furrows his heavy brow. He sucks aniseed drops constantly, and his breath is thick with the smell.

"Well enough," I say.

"Good," he says.

Rafael has been distant since the race finished. The result of each stage, for him, is always material from which something can be built. Sometimes he is triumphant, sometimes self-justifying, sometimes incensed. Never, though, is he resigned. Rafael's success is based upon a fierce blindness to chance, an ignorance of the limits of his influence. He closes one eye and rubs at the lid. He looks tired, dangerously so.

"There were issues today," he says.

I nod.

"You." He nods back. "You were not totally shit."

"Thanks," I say.

"Other people *were* totally shit. Other people let you down."

"Maybe."

"Yes. They let you down. Aren't you angry?" He looks at me expectantly.

"Raging," I say, feeling a need to placate him.

He raises his eyebrows.

"Inside," I say.

He shuts his eyes now; he resets himself. "A flat day, a flat day, a hilly day, the rest day," he says. "Then the last week, the mountain stages and a time trial." He does not need to spell out the plan for coming stages. The days with gradients are days on which Fabrice will seek to make time, the flat days are days to be endured. Each night Rafael pores over route maps, makes tallies of where gains may be made and losses limited. He inputs the data of the past day and works with it until he sees a path to the results he desires. I think of a shopkeeper recounting his takings again and again in the hope that his next calculation should make the cash and the receipts match.

"We'll do our best," I say.

He nods, cautiously satisfied, and moves away. I walk slowly down the nautical corridor. My muscles are loose, my vision clear. The light seems to flicker. The boats shift on lapping seas.

* *

Liz is close to her mother, Katherine. Katherine is clever, slightly spiky, grand in her manners. Liz's father, a professor of political economy, died in a car accident when Liz was very young, and Katherine is remarried to a man called Thomas, who owns a building supply warehouse in East Anglia. The two of them traveled down to London on the train four months after I had first met Liz, and we greeted them at Kings Cross. Katherine was tall like her daughter, with a straight nose, dark hair subtly dyed and held implausibly in place. Thomas was a broad, neat man with a mustache that I sensed he had worn for years. "So this is him?" Katherine said, and looked at her daughter for a steady second. We went to a grubby Chinese restaurant, which surprised me then but would not now. Katherine's terror is not dirtiness but mediocrity or inauthenticity, and the place was better on those terms than all the nearby Italian restaurants with columns around the doorways and tall pepper mills. She asked me questions about cycle racing that were pointed, as if the racing could not possibly be an end in itself but merely a way of attaining some other higher thing, which she expected me to articulate. "People like to watch this?" she said. "They understand it? They concern themselves with the details?"

All I could say was that people did watch my sport. It was Liz who came to my defense. She talked about tactics and psychology and the vicarious desires of the fans. Katherine nodded like she appreciated her daughter's effort.

"She's not keen on my career?" I asked Liz on the train home that night.

Liz exhaled in a way that signaled disagreement. "She just wants to be told why it consumes you. She wants to be sold on it."

"Yes?"

"A meaning," she said. "A sense of the story you tell yourself."

*   *

After our team dinner, I am not in the mood to sit and read or watch TV, and it is not yet late enough to sleep. I risk Rafael's wrath, then, by walking slowly around the hotel.

In the lounge, I find some of our team sitting between the plastic plants. The lounge is unpleasant—badly decorated and with a view of the hotel car park—and thus a perfect place to congregate.

No self-respecting holidaymakers would spend a minute of their vacation here, so it is ours. Johan lies on a pleather sofa. Sebastian sits upright in an armchair leafing through a magazine.

Johan is our sprinter. His job is to compete for wins in flat stages, those in which riders finish en masse. He pulls from the wind shadow of the peloton and thrashes for the line at the last minute. He is trained to ride in others' tailwinds until the final meters. While the rest of the team work for Fabrice, Johan competes to win individual stages in the sprints, seeking prizes, publicity, and acclaim for the team in this way.

Sebastian is Johan's minder. As we domestiques tend to Fabrice, he tends to Johan. He offers him shade from the elements and leads him into position for the finish. On days like the one just past, in which Johan has no chance of victory and must simply make it up and down the mountains within the elimination time, Sebastian paces Johan all day. I have seen neither of them much in the past twenty-four hours. While I was trying to help Fabrice, they were grinding along far behind.

"How's the boss man?" says Johan, meaning Fabrice. Some other teams concentrate fully on their sprinters, ignoring the overall race. Johan would, of course, rather be on such a team.

"Okay," I say.

"Didn't quite get the finish he wanted?" says Johan, the pleasure with which he says this ill-disguised.

"Uh-uh," I say.

"Flat tomorrow," says Sebastian.

Johan is wearing shorts and I can see him flex his quadriceps in response to mention of the coming stage. He is an abbreviated, muscular man, a different creature from the rest of us. He has longer hair, tied back in a small ponytail, and a goatee beard.

"It'll be your day," says Sebastian to Johan. Sebastian is the son of a famous cycling champion. Where his father was well-proportioned, though, he is stringy and awkward. Where his father pedaled with a wonderfully smooth style, Sebastian stamps through his strokes. Where his father was handsome, he has a big caricature of a face, a large nose and heavy jaw. It is hard to carry the diluted genes of a champion, and he probably would have done better avoiding the bike overall, getting a real profession. Theories on the causes of these differences between him and his father have been discussed at length. "It's the difference in nutrition in the modern age," Fabrice has said in Sebastian's absence. "It makes for larger people."

"His mother must be Amazonian," Johan has said.

"You know who else rides a bike?" Rafael likes to say. "The postman."

I take a seat next to Sebastian.

"In twenty hours," says Johan, breaking a silence, "I'll be kissing a podium girl."

"You know they only kiss the winners?" says Sebastian, and then laughs at his own joke.

"What would you know about that anyway?" says Johan. "The only time you've ever been on a podium is in your father's arms."

"He always used to take my sister, actually," says Sebastian.

Johan ignores his friend. He sits up and looks at me. "Have you seen the podium girls on this tour?" he says.

"I don't think so," I say. "We haven't had much cause to hang around the podium."

"Too true," says Sebastian.

Johan kisses his bunched fingers and lifts that same hand, opening it in appreciation. "Oh," he says. "Those girls . . ."

"Really?" I say.

"The best beauty," says Johan, "has a certain weirdness. Each of these girls is almost ugly. One has a pronounced underbite, another has a long forehead. These things allow you to convince yourself that others see them as unattractive. You feel you are the only one who truly appreciates them, really knows them. In this way, you can imagine such an intimacy without even having exchanged a word."

As I have said, one must find interests to stuff around one's days on tour. Johan is, above all, interested in chasing women. "There have been many eras," he told me once, "in which the things we value—money, politics, war, even cycling—were nonexistent or irrelevant. In no era, though, has sex been unimportant."

I told him that you could say the same thing about any other aspect of human survival: breathing or eating or shitting.

"I like those things too," he said primly. "Just not as much."

*　*

I have books in my room awaiting me: a small library carried in my luggage between hotels each day. Many are recommended by Liz, who despite B, despite the busyness of her lab, reads voraciously. I do not want to read now, though, but to be with these other men, in their studied idleness, in this small room, the traffic outside, the little TV above the door whispering the news.

I was struck when I first met Liz by the way her flat was so full of paper. There were the scientific journals she read, and the textbooks, but also piles of novels and newspapers and magazines. They spilled over the small desk in her bedroom, utterly obscuring everything. The third time I visited, I felt that I had to tidy the desk. It was too much to look at. I made four piles: textbooks, scientific papers, popular periodicals, and fiction. "You read all this?" I said. I couldn't imagine how she had the time, the inclination.

"I will," said Liz. She felt compelled to keep on top of it. She would do her work, which would occupy many more hours than most people's jobs, but she would also have an opinion on the books which had made the Booker short list, the artists who had been nominated for the Turner Prize, on contemporary political events and the quality of the coverage of them in the newspapers. She practiced the bassoon, an instrument she had learned to play to a nearly professional level in her teens. All this was certainly encouraged by Katherine, who had taken pains to send her daughter to a prestigious all-female school in the Cotswolds (sometimes, I suspected, simply so she could have this to hold over Liz forevermore). There was also the shadow of the dead father, who in death had been mythologized as an incomparable polymath.

In the first weeks of knowing her, I became eager to be able to stay with her and her friends in conversation. I read more widely, picked up books and newspapers and worked through them wondering how I would discuss them with Liz. It was hard to learn the dynamics of her group, the popular books they didn't like, the unpopular ones they did. When I got a handle on this, Liz met my competence with suspicion, however. "That's what Peter would say," she told me, when I described the drawbacks of a popular literary novel. She wanted something different from me. Sometimes one of her friends would say something high-flown and impenetrable and she'd laugh and look at me for a reaction, as if sure that it should naturally repulse me. I was awed by her friends though, by the breadth of what they knew, how they could talk.

"They are impressive, at first," she said. "They *want* to give you that sense. They think they can do anything, but none of them do."

"No?"

"Or they would be actually doing it," she said. She nodded at me, as if to prove her point, as if I embodied this doing.

* *

When I return to the room I am sharing with Tsutomo, he is already in his bed, facing the wall, apparently asleep, his side moving with the rhythm of his breathing. The room is illuminated only by light coming from the half-open bathroom door.

I quietly try to prepare for the night, stumbling in the dimness. When I make it into bed, I take time to think. I do not intend to sleep for these moments but merely to feel my body, to have some sense of my aches and pains. I am not always hopeful, but in this time I try to be. There are other men recovering in other rooms all over the city, thinking as I now am that tomorrow will be a better day than the one just past. The reality for most of us is that this will not be the case, and yet we will be on the start line tomorrow, and so we must disregard this fact. I stare at the ceiling. I try to think of what has gone well since I finished the day's stage, of the ways in which I feel prepared. I look up, visualizing these points of strength, trying to draw them into a constellation.

Chapter 3

The new day is sheathed in cloud. The light outside is dim, but the air is warm. This muted weather suits the care with which we leave the hotel. We load our bags onto the bus slowly and silently.

The day's stage will take us out of the mountains. It begins tending lightly downhill and then runs flat across the plains. None of the other team leaders will be able to make time against the fierce efficiency of the peloton in such circumstances, and so the game is to keep Fabrice within the mass of riders, trying to work against the contingencies—the falls, punctures, and miscommunications—which could see him caught out.

On the drive to the start, Rafael stands in the aisle and speaks, working hard for our attention. He does something with eye contact. There are rules, and he is as brazen in the breaking of these as any New Ager: holding gazes longer than should be bearable, really staring into us. "Be ready," he says. He indicates Fabrice. "Keep him with the other leaders. Be ready every moment." As he is finishing up, he looks at Johan. "Other than Sebastian," Rafael says, "we won't dedicate anyone else to lead you out in the sprint. Fabrice's place is too precarious. Do what you can. Follow one of the sprint teams' leadouts. Get in their space."

Johan nods reluctantly.

* *

Shinichi is once more waiting when we disembark at the start line. He waves a Japanese flag, part-bundled in his fist, when Tsutomo walks past. "Good luck," he says to me. I nod appreciatively but choose not to stop.

We wear running shoes when not in our cycling cleats: brilliantly colored, with reflective piping and technical flourishes rendered in different polymers. Provided by a sponsor, they're clumpy and incongruous beneath our tight shorts and shaven legs. We have no need for them, we who do not run or walk any great distance. Like the sneakers of the elderly, of young children, of Americans holidaying abroad, they accentuate our immobility. We cannot run, most of us. Our hamstrings have tightened to the minimal extension cycling requires. Our backs are used to being bent.

I have pictured my inflexibility when B will be bigger, when he will play in our back garden and seek companions in this play: the awkward, loping stride, the hunched way in which I will kick a ball.

Today's stage begins on cobbled streets, and our rubber soles squeak across the polished bellies of the cobblestones as we congregate outside the bus. The mechanics do final checks on our bikes, working in order. Fabrice's is looked over first, my own fifth. The Butcher comes by, pressed into another role: exhorting us to drink a concoction of electrolytes and syrup. Stationary cycle-trainers are assembled and we're summoned one by one to begin warming up. Fabrice and Tsutomo stamp into their cycling shoes and start to pedal. The increasing fluidity of their movements, and the rising zip of the electromagnetic resistance wheels, makes me think of something taking off.

Later, as I stand by the bus inventorying my kit, Fabrice wheels over on his bike. "Two men are in a bar watching the Tour," he says.

"Right."

"It's raining, and the riders are going up a mountain." Fabrice rubs at his hair and smiles. "Really filthy weather."

"I know the kind," I say.

"'Why do they do that?' says the first man. He does not understand. He shakes his head. 'The winner gets half a million euros,' says the second man." Fabrice waits. Watches me with a faint smile. "'I know *that*,' says the first man, 'but why do the *others* do it?'"

I laugh. "It's good," I say.

"Yes," he says, chuckling. "It has truth in it."

"Yes."

He winks. "Luckily I am the winner."

Rafael has been chatting with the directeur of the German banking team, over by their bus. He turns, laughing, finishing his own joke. He points at his colleague, smiles. "Be good," he says. He walks toward Fabrice and me. "Steady," he says. "No fuck-ups today." He stands over the front wheel of Fabrice's bike, slaps Fabrice's cheek playfully. Rafael has more faith in his team leader than anyone. Rafael discovered Fabrice, so the story goes, on a holiday to Corsica, coming across a skinny twelve-year-old coaxing a rusty mountain bike up a pass as he himself drove to a hunting lodge. He had his mentor, an ancient Italian, visit Fabrice to examine the boy and feel his legs. The mentor sucked his dentures, it is said, and declared Fabrice a future great. On Fabrice rests not just Rafael's hopes for the Tour, but the validity of Rafael's judgment and an uncharacteristic sentimentality: his belief in a lineage of talent conferred upon small boys in remote towns, as sure and unpredictable as the rebirth of the Lama.

Riders are making their way toward the start now. Fabrice clicks into his pedals, rolls off toward the line with a little push of encouragement from Rafael. I put on my glasses. I climb onto my bike, and ride off in pursuit of Fabrice, offering my apologies as I cut through the crowds, past vehicles. I stop behind the line among the tight press of other racers. I smell sunscreen, saddle ointment, washing powder. Riders ratchet closed cycling shoes, do up helmet straps, adjust the placement of cycle computers.

It is the period before the starting horn goes when to be still is harder than anything. We shift and fidget: energy spilling over into action, like water from a brimful glass.

*　*

When Liz and I had been together for a couple of months, she brought her mother and stepfather to watch a race of mine. It was an evening racing series in London: laps of a small urban circuit on the streets of Bermondsey. Sebastian and I did it without team support. It was nothing, a training session, but I felt as I rode a desire to do well. It was dusk, and there had been rain in the day. The air smelled of wet concrete, and the streets were slick. I pushed hard around the last laps. There were semipros who wanted the victory, for whom beating Sebastian or me would have been a great coup, and they were testing us, taking risks. On the penultimate corner, I went into the bend in first place yet skidded over as my front wheel lost traction. I lay in a crumple under a barrier as riders zipped past me.

I remounted and came home in the middle of the pack. I wheeled my bike over to where Liz, Thomas, and Katherine stood. I felt the burn of having wanted that small race too much. "You were close," said Katherine.

"It was just a silly thing," I said.

She nodded. "Of course."

"It was the cobblestones," I said. "They're lethal in the wet."

"Technically," said Thomas, "those are sett stones. They're worked stones. Granite. A nice job, I must say." Liz frowned at her stepfather.

She studied the bike as I leaned on it; it was undamaged but for some of the handlebar tape, which was torn and uncurling, hanging like ringlets from the bars. She shook her head. She knew that it was just a small race, an insignificant thing, and yet I saw that she had been seduced, as I had, by the thought that it was a chance to show her mother the seriousness of what I did.

It was a consolation, actually, to realize that Liz had felt the stakes too. I thought of something she had said about my career before: "It must be nice to be able to succeed so clearly," she said. "To have such definite parameters. Clear successes. No one is cheering me in my lab." That night, however, demonstrated the drawbacks of performing one's profession so publicly: the way in which expertise and preparation could be occluded by bad luck, the way that an expected success can buckle under the weight one has put upon it.

* *

Less than a kilometer after we begin, a handful of riders from opposing teams sprint away from the front. The peloton does not react to this but instead grinds along. Most of us are still finding what the day will be, trying to conserve and gauge our energies. We compete on each of the twenty-one days of the race, but there are unwritten rules, expectations and traditions which reach back to the men with their steel bikes, bad teeth, and muddy visages, to the stutter and shimmy of old newsreel footage. Not every minute of every day is heedless competition. There are truces and lulls, and moments of peace. Some of Liz's friends were disappointed to hear this, I remember, as if I were telling them that my sport was nothing more than professional wrestling. That is not the case though. The conventions observed among us riders do not contain the competition but channel it. They are flexible rules, liable to be shifted by resentments, disagreements, and alterations in fortune. We are governed by the will of the peloton, the mood of the mass, which is as changeable as that of any small village. On mornings such as this, on flat stages, we usually agree to make some progress before competition breaks out fully. We are content to sit together, to allow a few young men, back markers, to spend some time leading, in view of the cameras, taking the first applause of the fans. That is, as long as the men are sufficiently far down in the overall classification to pose no threat to any of the leaders, and providing that they have done nothing to offend the mass. The publicly outspoken, the gratingly showy will be chased down with pleasure. Local boys may be allowed down the road to enjoy the adoration of their home fans, until their lead gets too great and they will be brought back, swallowed up.

Today the seven men out ahead are adjudged unthreatening and inoffensive enough to be left to ride ahead. The peloton churns along steadily.

Tsutomo and I collect team lunch bags from helpers at the side of the road. We ride between our teammates, distributing them. Because he is the team leader, Fabrice is supplied, as is his wont, with a peeled boiled egg each lunchtime. He eats it like an indulged child. Though we're moving at forty kilometers per hour, he sits up on his bike and rides one-handed. He seeks to eat off the white first, until he has only the dusty yellow ball of yoke left. Then he squeezes this with his greasy fingers, exposed by his fingerless gloves. The yoke breaks up and, depending on the duration of the egg's boiling, either oozes or crumbles. The state of the yoke of each egg seems, to Fabrice, to constitute an important omen.

* *

Sometimes, I suppose, I have had too much faith in the arcana of my sport to engage and elevate me. The days before Liz had been smaller days, I now know. I had been racing, and thinking only about that. I was getting better, but I was also feeling the limits of what I did. I had assumed, when I became a professional, that things would be more intense, somehow, more vivid and real. The reality, though, was that my life had become smaller. I prohibited myself from many things, set myself in a limited pattern of thinking. It is perhaps obvious in hindsight, but obsession does not give you more, but less. I had the routines and the inflexibility of someone already old.

Liz accompanied me to a race in Italy, on the Ligurian coast. It took some time to arrange: the time off for Liz, the travel, the permission from Rafael. When we arrived, I recced the course, then rested and made sure I was hydrated and properly fed. It was a minor race, a preparation for the real season. Rafael would not have contemplated allowing Liz to stay in my room otherwise. The four of us racing— myself, Sebastian, Tsutomo, and Fabrice—sought to maintain our good habits. We sat in the hotel café for most of the day preceding the race. We talked, when we did at all, about racing. Liz was there for much of the time. She was exasperated but also slightly in awe at how limited a day we could live, as if she were finding out that there were men who could subsist on only air. She wanted to stroll along the seafront promenade, but I couldn't bear to. I told her I didn't want to walk anywhere the day before a race.

After lunch she disappeared and then reappeared in the hotel café, wheeling an empty wheelchair. "You don't want to walk," she said. Fabrice and Tsutomo laughed at me, shook their heads. Liz kept looking at me, daring me. I climbed into the chair. "We'll be back in a couple of hours," she said to my companions. Normally, I would have been mortified to be wheeled around, but that day I chose not to be. Liz cackled delightedly. "I told you we could do it," she said.

It was spring. The air was warm but there was a breeze coming off the sea. There were sailing boats out on the water, tacking against the wind. Other tourists were stopping to take photos of the view, but we glided past them. I was silent for much of the time. I just listened to Liz speak. She had been reading her guidebook. She leaned down behind me to tell me the history of the docks, to point out the town hall, an old palace on a hill. I smelled her perfume and felt her breath on the back of my neck.

Rafael was in the lobby when Liz wheeled me back into the hotel. His presence struck me with a sense of foreboding. He looked at me steadily, as if deciding upon a response. As I waited for this, Liz walked around the chair and toward him. "You must be Rafael," she said. "I've heard a lot about you." Something about her approach—not the words but her firm assurance that he would greet her reasonably—seemed to weight the scales in our favor.

Rafael smiled at Liz. He was shorter than her, even in his special shoes. He looked up at her, put out a hand. "I have heard a great deal about you too," he lied. I rose from the wheelchair, treating others in the lobby to an apparent miracle, and walked over to stand behind Liz.

She gestured at the chair. "We were trying to have a good afternoon without exerting him too much."

Rafael laughed. "Wonderful," he said. I felt for a moment the boyish silliness of my fear of him. It was an eerie moment. He touched my elbow. "Why have you been keeping this wonderful woman from us for so long?" he said.

That night Liz and I had sex, utterly silently, the slow creak of the mattress merging with the whispering of a window pulled back and forth on its hinges by the night wind, my teammates asleep in adjacent rooms. There is a prohibition on sex before racing. Rafael believes that intercourse diminishes the body in critical respects, despite Johan's marshaling of scientific articles that apparently refute this claim. The thought that what we did was prohibited intensified it.

The race went well. I spent time out ahead on a break. I was in the leading pack when we went up the small winding ascent on which Liz was waiting. I came home in eighteenth place.

* *

We are close to halfway through the stage when the pace begins to ramp up. The cadence of the group rises. The feeling, emergent among us, is that competition may be put off no longer. We breathe. We sweat. Heat rises from us as from stock animals penned tightly.

We hear the time advantage of the leaders come down in increments as we exert ourselves.

I am taking my turn at the head of the peloton when we catch the men. We're on one half of a closed-off highway, which curves through the landscape. We come over a very gentle rise and I see the breakers strung into a short line, turning their heads as we approach. Warnings over radios and the passing of the motorcycle outriders who precede the peloton have already informed them that they are being caught, and there is something in their resignation that almost makes me sorry for the ruthlessness of the group I tow behind me. The peloton, really, is the thing: the center of the bell curve. We riders are defined by our presence within it or apart from it. The very best, the likes of Fabrice, desire to leave the peloton behind. Their dreams are rendered in opposition to the machine. The rest of us worry each morning that this might be the day that we can't keep

Joe Mungo Reed

pace. Our nightmares see us left in the wake, among the team cars, the journalists, the riders fixing punctures. If ever there was one, I am a peloton man. I am happiest within the mass. I do not flatter myself that I can kick away and do without it. It has been enough for me to get here, to find a small place in such a famous event. Only, occasionally, as when we pass these eager, exhausted young men, can I see it any differently: as an aggressor rather than as an ally.

We come up to the riders. The seams of their kits are bordered with fine lines of salt from their perspiration. They ride at the side of the road, heads down. Warnings are called out as the peloton contracts to pass them. Then, they are gone, back into the mass.

* *

I have been only once to Liz's lab, back when she was working on her PhD. It's a cool, quiet place. She and her colleagues hunch over the benches, performing tasks on a microscopic scale. They work with the embryos of zebra fish. The fish are quick to hatch, and they are transparent. With the right magnification one can see right into them. On my visit, Liz took a little petri dish and shook it. In the center was a cluster of what seemed like bubbles but were not. They were embryos, about thirty hours old. When I looked through the microscope, I could see them: their miniature, newly formed spines, curved in a C around globular, translucent yolks. At the top of the spine were the first hints of organs blooming, a skull being formed, and beneath this was a tiny heart, filaments of red where blood was beginning to enter and leave it, the slightest twitching as it beat.

In the lab, Liz and her colleagues perform what they call lost-function experiments. They work on cells in the fish's spines, on interneurons. They render different genes mute and seek to measure the effect of this on cell development. "It's as if you have a car,"

44

Liz explained to me. "And you're taking out different parts to see what happens. Can it still drive? Is it faster, even? Is it better at going around corners?" The cells are modified to contain a fluorescent protein from deep-sea creatures, so that when viewed under a microscope, their growth is writ in neon. Liz sedates the fish, puts them on microscope slides. The transparency of the fish means one can look into them to register the way their glowing axons are beginning to thatch around their spines.

As a teenager, I was drawn to riding because of the certainty it offered, the way a clear objective made stark the choices of when to train and when to eat and when to sleep. Liz's work is based in routine too, and yet the aims are different. I realized, on that visit, she was creating a system in the hope that expectations would be confounded, with the wish that something unbidden, inexplicable might arise. When I visited, she was coming to the end of her thesis research. She'd been studying a particular gene: the one she would continue to study in her postdoctoral work. She had hopes, supported by data, that this gene was operative in cell repair. "And so?" I wanted to know.

"It could teach us things."

"Yes?"

"How bodies repair themselves, perhaps."

"Which would be useful for humans too?"

"Maybe. Possibly the things you are thinking: disease prevention, cancer cures, that kind of stuff."

"You think this is likely?"

"The chance is what wins us funding," she said. "But we must still be lucky, of course."

"You don't like to trumpet your work?"

"The world doesn't lack for ambitious promises," she said.

"Right," I said. I thought of my own career: the managing of my aims, the focus on single steps, individual acts.

"I'm putting my energy into the actual project," she said.

"Of course," I said. "The doing."

She smiled. "The activity itself," she said.

* *

With the breakers caught, the racing begins in earnest. Teams coalesce into groups within the peloton, sprinters and team leaders are shepherded to the front. Everyone who surges out ahead of the group is chased down now. The pace lurches to absorb attacks. It is hard, even in the middle of the peloton, to keep pace. I ride in front of Tsutomo, who is in front of Fabrice. We are at the mercy of the most ambitious, the most nervous. "Keep your underwear on," says Rafael over the radio. "Keep in there. Stay calm." Out of the corner of my eye I see the flash of our team colors. Sebastian squeezes his way between other riders, Johan on his wheel.

We come into the town in which we will finish, hammering along. The peloton is beginning to shed riders off the back. It is a looser thing. There is traffic furniture to negotiate. The group stretches, and we slice around a roundabout. We rattle down these small roads like pebbles down a drainpipe. Our freewheels fizz as we cease peddling for a moment. On the outside, a couple of riders hop onto a curb, and down again. The noise of the crowd is intense. It is nearly impossible to communicate among the mass. The road kinks slightly up ahead. The riders in front of me judder together but stay upright. I glance my brake to avoid colliding with the wheel of the rider in front. A Slovak rider, a time trial specialist, goes off the front with five kilometers to go. He stands and sprints and then, when he has opened up some gap, he tucks himself into his bike and pounds the pedals.

The two teams holding the pace at the head of the peloton seem to be modulating the speed of this pursuit. It is very likely that we will get him easily, and his leading in the meantime discourages others from attacking. I see Sebastian ahead of me, though he is slowing, being passed by others. Johan is somewhere in the melee at the front. My own thighs burn. Fabrice is huddled down behind me. Exhausted riders are dropping from the group ever more frequently, and so we are at risk of colliding with those slowing. We travel at motorcycle speeds without the hydraulic brakes or leathers. I come up by Sebastian, nearly glancing his shoulder. My legs are agony. I feel my calves on the verge of cramp. I check right, move to the side, try to get out of the main flow. We hit a corner and I concentrate only on keeping my line. Tsutomo leads Fabrice now. They are both in front of me. The cramp in my calves arrives, fully, but I cannot stop in the middle of this group. The Slovak is hovering forty yards ahead of the rest of us; I see him over the heads of others at the top of a slight incline. People are still accelerating past me. I feel like I am being left behind a breaking wave. I pedal. I hold my pace until it is truly safe to slow, to make my way to the line in my own time. The head of the peloton has no doubt surged around the Slovak. The helicopter moves in a steady line up ahead, following the sprint finish. The noise of the crowd on the final straight is deafening. I let myself freewheel down this last stretch. I turn my attention to preserving energy.

I find Fabrice at the finish line. He's okay. He finished with the main group, lost no time. "It's a meringue of a stage," he says. "You'd never think so much energy would go into something so boring." He is happy. He wheels over to a barrier and signs autographs. He gives a brief and playful interview to a young reporter from a local radio station.

Johan and Sebastian are already near the bus when we arrive.

"It didn't work out for you?" I say to Johan. He scowls but doesn't answer.

"He had a *good* day," says Sebastian. "He came eleventh."

"Please don't brag about me coming *eleventh*," says Johan. "I have some dignity."

"Amongst this caliber of racer," says Sebastian, "that is not a small accomplishment."

Johan sighs and stalks off to cool down on the stationary trainer.

I cool down myself. I climb onto the bus. I retrieve my tracksuit, my phone, my wallet, my wedding ring.

* *

Liz and I married within nine months of meeting. The days of that first autumn together were swift, clipped days. Liz was busy in the lab, finishing a PhD, and I was training steadily. My landlord was putting the house I rented on the market. Liz's housemate was moving out. It made sense to live together suddenly, and that fact seemed to open other possibilities. We were living strange, unbalanced lives, our eyes on the horizon. It was a comfort for each of us to be with someone else who thought about the future, who weighed days ahead over wearying present routines. The similarity of our positions, of our needs, felt so uncommon.

I didn't know the register to propose in, how serious it should be. I felt that I was speaking a language that I only knew so well, in which I could communicate blunderingly or not at all. We were not those people, I hoped, who believed a wedding to be the climax or culmination of a life. We had objectives beyond the ordinary. I did not want to get down on one knee in a tastefully lit restaurant, to have others applaud as if we had actually achieved something, to have a bottle of champagne arrive in a polished stainless steel bucket. Still, I did not want to do it comfortably. It seemed important that the gesture should make me a little uneasy, and that I should endure that discontent. Doing it in privacy would have been a cop-out. I wanted to show the extent to which being with Liz had allowed me to step outside myself.

I asked her on the riverbank in the end. We had eaten an excellent dinner. It was a Tuesday night. We walked toward the river, close to the theater we had been to on that first meeting with Liz's mother. I stopped her at the edge of the river, near a closed gateway that led to a floating ferry landing. The dark water lapped ahead of us. The fittings clanked with the shifting of the jetty. I did not get down on one knee, which I regret now. It would have been a small thing. I took out the ring it in its box and placed it on the wall we leaned against. "Will you marry me?" I asked.

"Okay," she said, so lightly that I was disconcerted. Yet that was her, I thought: someone always ready for whatever came next. She sometimes seemed to know what I would say before I did. She was prepared for the world, forever set to meet what it would cast toward her. She smiled. She fingered the ring, put it on, took it off and played with it, put it on again.

Chapter 4

I wake to birdcalls, to sunlight seeping through the patterned curtains. It is still early, and the alarm has not gone. I lie back. Tsutomo is still asleep. I clear my throat as quietly as I can. I feel my soft palate as I do so, alert to a catch, to a tenderness that might presage a cold. There is not a morning of the past ten years that I have not woken and worried about my state of health. My airways feel clear though. I concentrate on my breathing, on the inhale and exhale, on the slight strain of an intercostal muscle that this reflection makes clear.

I cannot sleep. I know my alarm will go soon, that the day will commence. I lie and let my mind run.

The hotel room is neat, plain. It lightens in imperceptible increments. It is an antiseptic life, this. In a couple of hours, I will pack my small bag, vacate the room without more of a trace of my occupancy than the rucking up of the sheets. It is so different from home, with B, so many things spread across floors and tabletops. I think of Liz getting up far away, making her own way into the day.

At the breakfast table, I sit next to Fabrice. He asks whether I dreamed. I think back and find nothing behind the sensation of having woken, my slow thinking as I waited for the alarm.

* *

Once she had agreed to marry, Liz went into it with a velocity. Neither of us had the patience or the time for worrying about outfits and dances and table decorations, but we had a large meal, a party afterward. My mother came. She had recently retired from her job as a hospital receptionist, and she had just seen a retirement counselor who had told her that her life from that point on was her own. She was on her way to Spain to buy a house, an act of uncharacteristic resolve that I sensed was a gesture toward a new imagining of herself. My mother is a quiet woman, capable but diffident. She cannot place herself at the center of an anecdote but loses her way in detail and texture that she does not have the confidence to discount. She sat with Katherine and Thomas, and I was gratified and a little surprised by the patience with which Katherine listened to her stories.

Liz and I moved to the northern periphery of the city. I came south to this new house, Liz north. Liz had finished her PhD and begun her postdoc work in the same lab straightaway. There we were, suddenly with all of this: a summer ahead of us; a largely empty house; neighbors; a street of London plane trees; a route for me, up along the river, out into the countryside above the M25.

We saw Liz's friends when we could. We would meet them for dinner. Liz would come straight from the laboratory, and I would take the train into the center of the city. The friends were interested in our new lives, in our marriage, though, as a rule, not quite curious enough to make the journey to see us at home. We would barely have been in the house to greet them anyway. Both of us were busy then. I was riding better than I ever had, increasingly finding myself selected by Rafael for the bigger races. I wondered whether my new life, my new perspective, was helping. It was probably just conditioning, I told myself reluctantly: adaptation, development, the body as machine. The friends asked about my racing still, but it was hard to explain my advances. They expected, I think, when Liz mentioned my recent successes, that I should be winning races, appearing on television. They did not really understand the difficulty of making it into the ranks of truly world-class riders. They saw I was zealous, but not that this zeal could be surpassed by others, for whom racing meant even more. Liz could identify with this. She had similar problems communicating her own work with her friends. She had moved up in the hierarchy of the lab, and now the success of certain protocols, of essential parts of the study, rested with her. "If it goes well, it's like cooking," she said. "If it goes wrong, it's like a murder investigation." It was going well. She had good hands, an observant eye. Her results were regarded as reliable. It was patient work, systematic and unglamorous. I felt heartened to hear that she saw elements of her own work in mine, pleased by the sense that it drew us together. We were partners in our sense of isolation, in our preoccupations incomprehensible to so many. We both had our routines, our slogs, in service of single moments, possibilities. It felt noble, all this putting off.

*   *

On the journey to the start, Rafael rattles around the coach like a wasp trapped in a Coke can. Today is another flat stage, another day to simply make it through. Tomorrow is a day of low rolling hills. We are in what Rafael has dubbed the "maintenance" portion of the Tour: days during which no great gains are to be made and losses are to be precluded. He is agitated. The bus sighs to a halt. Rafael stands at the front and speaks before we disembark. "I am not getting the best feeling seeing you all today," he says. "You seem tired. You seem without interest." I can hear the public address system, the patter of words, the high-frequency creak of speakers. "Let me say, nobody outside this bus cares about you. Nobody out there requires that you race. You do this because you want to." Rafael sighs loudly and theatrically. "You care. I care. Otherwise everything is fucked."

Later I join Fabrice on the warm-up bikes. "A cyclist is riding in a race," he says, not looking up from his steady pedaling. "Halfway through, the race referee pulls up beside him. The race referee tells the cyclist that the car of his directeur sportif crashed into a tree half an hour before, killing everyone inside." He looks at me now, though he doesn't change his cadence. " 'Oh good,' says the cyclist. 'I thought my radio earpiece was broken.' "

"A good one," I say.

* *

That new house was a surprise in all that it seemed to ask of us. Liz and I had chosen it, of course. We had driven around the locality in the estate agent's branded car. It was what we could afford. It had good transport connections. I could travel easily to airports to fly abroad.

We had made the logical, forward-looking choices, encouraged by the man in his polyester suit. We were some way out of the city, and so we came to the understanding that we should be entitled to another bedroom, to a lawn. The garden was for the cat, ostensibly, but who would spend so much for just a cat?

Liz did not allow herself to settle too readily into this new life. She did not take her mother's prompts to decorate or get to know the mostly older neighbors. She was keen to hold off the routines and compromises of our new suburban existence, I sensed, and I was glad to see this but also worried by the sense that her wariness strayed into a wider feeling of dissatisfaction. The more she progressed with her job, the more it seemed a source of distress. Her colleagues marveled at her fluency, but in her actual accomplishment of the position she had built so long toward, she was truly faced for the first time with the scant effect of the work she had chosen, the world's apparent indifference to all her expertise.

It was not logical to think that the slow, steady science she was doing should have won her wide recognition, and yet we are not always logical in our hopes. I thought of all my slow progress in my career and the sense I used to have that others did not recognize the difficulty of all I did, that people around me did not take time to understand the milestones I was passing. I made a point to highlight her successes, to talk of what went well with her work. She was grateful but dissatisfied with the praise. I was partial, after all. It was not my role to offer the affirmation she sought.

For a while she exercised rigorously. She would borrow my turbo trainer after work, attach her own bike to it, and sit in the bike room, spinning, rubbing sweat from her forehead with a hand towel. She would go to the gym on her way into the lab. She jogged on the weekends when I went out to ride.

Liz had been a swimmer when she was at school. I could imagine it: the bleached-out hair, the loose walk, the smell of chlorine on her skin.

Her exertions seemed a way to channel frustration, to displace energy, and yet I also felt that there was some part of her that wanted to show that she could have, had she wanted, been doing what I did. I believed it. I did not deny that my work was more straightforward, that she would, had she really wanted to, have easily succeeded in my realm. My work was not the work of a lifetime though. There was that. It advanced more predictably, but then would be done so much faster.

We saw less of Liz's mother in these days. We worked. We steadily made the house more livable. Liz's friend Davina came around for tea. The two women had been friends since school, far longer than Liz had known the rest of her social group, whom she had met at university. They talked animatedly in teenage voices which they'd preserved somehow. She was short, Davina, chubby, fair, and loud. The contrast between her and Liz seemed somehow more explicable when I thought of the two of them together as teens.

Liz went to a couple of conferences. I went to continental Europe for weeks on end. It was still a surprise to come home. Settling in the place was less easy than I had anticipated. We were beginning the ordinary rituals we had put off for our careers, and yet in delaying these activities, I realized, we had taken them to be more thoughtless, more automatic than they were.

When one is cycling surrounded by others, one does not think of slowing, or speeding up, or stopping pedaling. One thinks only of behaving as the group dictates: leaning into corners at the same angle, pumping one's legs at a similar rate, marking the same parabolas around alpine turns. There is not, in one sense, a single choice to be made. In another sense, however, there are many choices: the hard and unending decisions made in the service of behaving uniformly, reliably, and predictably.

*   *

The start line is its usual chaos. I cycle slowly toward it behind Tsutomo. We weave between team cars, packed and ready to follow behind the race, past journalists and broadcasters mounting motorbikes in preparation for pursuing us. Some engines are running and there is a smell of petrol in the air. The television helicopter is up already, filming the gathering crowds. The publicity caravan—the parade of sponsors' floats from which promotional materials are thrown out to the grasp of waiting fans—has departed some time ago. Ahead I can see that spectators have massed to watch the start, clasping inflatable batons and wearing souvenir hats. As we approach the line, Tsutomo swerves to avoid the doctor of another team stepping out from behind the race referee's car. Tsutomo says "Bastard!" with the force of a sneeze, and the man holds up his hands, surrender-like, in apology.

There are times in a race of this profile when it feels we riders are lost within all the peripheral activity, like a rich man diminished by his large house. Tsutomo wheels toward the other members of our team, giving quiet warnings to riders as he negotiates his way past them. It is the race, of course, that takes us back to ourselves: the lurch of adrenaline as the starting klaxon goes, the return to our objectives, the need to hold the pace.

*   *

Liz and I conceived B in the first winter of our marriage. It seemed both logical and slightly mad to have a child. On the one hand was the desire we both had to add something new to our life, to advance together. On the other was work. "It's not normal so early in a postdoc to take maternity leave," said Liz. I would be racing throughout each spring and summer.

There was something about the assumption that parenthood should threaten our ambitions, however, that we were eager to disprove. The idea that now was not the time seemed to contain an implicit assumption that at some future date our lives would be halted by parenthood. Even to put things off was to buy into this. Our relationship was forged on pushing on, on noticing our own drive in the other, and so there was something fortifying in facing down this thing that people said would take us from our work.

He was a baby we would love, of course, a result of our love for each other, but the choice of having him when we did was determined also by a private assurance, shared only between Liz and me.

We went to a café and watched a couple twitching with anxiety as their toddler played quietly in the corner, and in a strange way this made the prospect seem easier because neither of us could imagine our way to being that kind of parent. Who were these people, so obsessed, so hollowed out by their offspring? Who acted as if the most enduring of human practices was the most impossible?

Everyone is an exceptionalist in relation to their marriage, and yet I felt we *were* remarkably diligent, capable, and tough. We moved toward the decision by contrasting ourselves against the wider world. In separating our partnership from others, we felt more certain of its solidity. We were stepping ourselves apart in myth, as countries build a nationality from the threats and deficiencies of their neighbors.

That February when B was conceived, I was sleeping in an altitude tent: an airtight little chamber that through the grumbling operation of a small machine mimicked the oxygen-reduced environment of a mountain top. The tent was set out beside the bed, a single mattress inside it. I would zip myself inside each night and sleep a fitful sleep of odd dreams in my little pocket of depleted air. Liz and I would have sex, and then I would get up and leave the bed, tucking down the duvet again and padding over the carpet toward the tent, where I bedded down on the small mattress, closing the door behind me.

I had to race that summer through Liz's pregnancy. The crimped time we had together at home was intense. We listened to the stories and the tips of friends who already had children, and afterward sat up in bed critiquing their accounts and the actions they had described. We prepared what was to be B's room. We sat on the sofa and leafed through catalogs and baby books. The coffee table in the living room became a heap of paper, just as Liz's desk had once been. The writing on this paper was so banal, though this banality seemed a challenge. Like a bank statement or a vehicle manual, the import of the parenting literature inhered in its impenetrability. We learned much that was petty and pointless, yet who could know whether we were still missing some crucial thing? There was a sort of ecstasy in giving in to it all.

* *

Once we have left the town, the weather begins to close in. It is a gray, windy day, piled cloud tumbling across the sky above us. It is the kind of day that makes sense of the complexions of veteran riders, that skin rippled and creased like bark. We huddle into our bikes, we turn our faces from the gusts, barely looking where we are going. We grumble and pray that the hours will just pass.

We move through a village, the buildings offering moments of shade from the wind that cuts in from the right. We round a fountain, the plume of which is blown into a mist. We leave the town again and speed through fields, a slightly sweet hint of manure in the air, copses of trees swaying around farmhouses.

Rafael is active on the radio. "These are the days where you earn your money," he says. "These are the days where we learn who you really are."

* *

Last autumn I went to a race weeks before B's arrival. I was eager to be done with the season, to be fully attentive to Liz. The race was important for the finances of the team, however, and a place where I could push my case for inclusion in major events over the following year. Rafael was already planning the next season. I arrived to the hotel in which we were staying to find that he had improvised an office in the basement. He had already, apparently, renegotiated sponsorship with a sports drink company and cut two riders from the roster. The office had been nicknamed "the Führer bunker."

The evening after the race, which had gone well, he called me to a meeting down there. I descended the rickety stairs with trepidation. He'd set out four chairs, a laptop, and a foldout table. Behind him was the Hotel Alpina laundry cart, situated under the laundry chute. The basement was illuminated unforgivingly with strip lighting. I took a seat facing him.

"Let's say," Rafael began, "that you're in a small village and you're chasing a girl." The only reminder of the day continuing above was the periodic dropping of linen, as vacated rooms were prepared for new guests. "This village we are imagining is small," he said. "There's not much for the other boys to do. You're going to have some competition." Pillowcases fluttered out of the chute like downed birds.

"What do women like?" Rafael said. This is not the kind of question directeurs sportifs usually ask their riders.

"Um," I said. Rafael looked at me very intently, raising his heavy eyebrows. "Some people date on the Internet now," I said, "if their job makes it hard to meet women."

"I'm not asking for dating tips," he said. "This is a metaphor, you bag of shit."

"Right."

"And if I were looking for dating tips, I wouldn't ask you."

"Sure," I said.

He squeezed water into his mouth from a team bottle. "You almost fucked my metaphor."

"I'm in a village, chasing a girl," I said. "I'm following."

"You are a married man, of course."

"In the metaphor?"

"In real life."

"Yes," I said. "My wife's about to have our first child."

"You never told me."

"I didn't think that sort of thing interested you."

"What do you mean, 'that sort of thing'?"

"Our families."

"Of course I'm fucking interested." I expected him to explain this assertion, but he said no more.

"I'm sorry," I said. "What were you saying about the village?"

"What do women like about men?" he said. "What does your wife like about you?"

"Conversation?" I said. He shook his head. "Commitment? Empathy?" He kept shaking. "Jokes? Cooking?"

"Okay, okay, okay," he said. "Perhaps all of those things a little bit, but what they like a lot is height. Of all the James Bonds only the new one, Daniel Craig, has been under six foot. And what is Daniel Craig?" He mimed flicking something off the table. "A little goblin."

"I like *Casino Royale*," I said.

"Of all the Bonds, only Roger Moore has the true British style." Rafael wrinkled his nose. There was a rattling from the laundry chute and a ball of towels shot out. "Women like height. So in the chase for this, how you say, 'hypothetical' girl in our village, height is important."

"Okay," I said, "I can see that."

"And it is man's nature to maximize every advantage."

"I don't see," I said, "how you could maximize your height."

"Not many people know this," said Rafael, leaning forward conspiratorially, "but I am only one hundred and fifty centimeters tall." He placed a shoe on the table with a thunk. It looked like a bowling shoe with a bath sponge glued to the bottom. "A built-up shoe," he said. "Nearly undetectable."

"Ah," I said.

"Now, imagine every man in the village goes and buys a pair of built-up shoes. Every man apart from you."

"Okay."

"A big problem, no? All of you—the men in this village—have natural charms, but your own are being obscured by something unnatural." He prodded the thick sole of the shoe. "By this rubber shit."

"I can imagine," I said eventually.

"Is this a problem for the other men? No! They all have built-up shoes. They are differentiated by other things. It is, how you say, zero sum. But for you, it is a problem. This girl is deceived in her view of you. What do you do?"

"Buy her flowers?"

Rafael banged his shoe on the table. "Don't fuck me around!" he said. "You go and buy some built-up shoes!"

"Okay," I said.

"You go and buy some shoes and you put them on and then you can try and impress this woman with your funny jokes or your gourmet cooking or your magic tricks or whatever you think is so fucking impressive about you!" He banged the shoe on the table again. "Everyone is happy! Everything is back to normal! The end!"

"I'm not sure I quite understand," I said.

"It's a metaphor," he said, "and I haven't told you what it's a metaphor for yet."

"Is it a metaphor for something to do with cycling?" I said.

"Of course." He raised his bottle again and sprayed water down his throat. A little liquid dripped from his chin, spotting into the table. "Suppose I told you some people were using"—Rafael made air quotes—"'built-up shoes' in cycle races."

"I don't follow."

"Suppose some people were enhancing their natural talents in a way which obscured yours. Would you be happy? Would you feel it was fair that they were making you look like a weak little Daniel Craig?" Rafael pointed at me with every *you*, as if tapping on an invisible window.

"No," I said. "They'd be cheating." Confronted with Rafael's intense, small-man self-possession I sometimes feel like a lumbering giant, overwhelmed, unable to swat him off. I don't know quite how to face him, where, as it were, to put my legs and my arms.

Rafael leaned toward me, shaking his head. "But what if it was the kind of cheating which nobody cared about stopping?" He stroked the toe of the shoe. "What if it was a harmless kind of cheating, a sort of open secret?"

"But if everyone thinks like that . . ."

"Yes?"

"If no one tries to change . . ."

Rafael hissed out a breath. "How many races have you won?" he asked. "How many stages?"

"I won a stage of the Tour of Colombia."

"Have you won a stage of the Tour? Of the Giro? Of the Vuelta? One of the classics? When you ride, are the fans shouting your name? Do you see your name written on the road? Who, my friend, is going to listen to you if you start talking about built-up shoes? Who is going to listen to me, even? I'd love to say something too, but I am just a nobody. People will just say, 'Oh, Rafael is old and bitter.' No one, my friend, wants to hear us talk about built-up shoes. They are being used and talking will not do anything to stop it. Do you want people to disregard your natural talents, your training, your excellent bicycle-handling skills?"

"No," I said.

"Then, as you British say, as Roger Moore might say, 'If you can't beat them, join them.' I have a totally safe kind of built-up shoe, the very kind that all these less-scrupulous cycling teams are using. Do you understand me?" He raised a thick eyebrow.

"It's becoming clearer," I said.

"Well," he said, "suppose a doctor visited you and he offered you this totally safe built-up shoe. Keeping in your mind that we have reached this conclusion—that there is no way to get around the fact that all of the opposition are also using built-up shoes. Could you offer any objections?"

"It's undetectable?" I said.

"Yes."

"What if it is not always?"

"That is a worry for later."

"You don't care about that?"

"I'm sorry," he said. "I think you misunderstand. The trophy presentation happens on the day of the race. You were born now. You are racing now. Maybe you hope the others will be disqualified in many years' time. Perhaps you want to win in the small print, be a little asterisk, but I thought you might actually want to cross the line first, hear the cheering of the fans." He stopped. He looked at me, a steady stare. "You have done the training already, and now this is one last push. You would get the full benefits of your many natural talents and we would all win a lot more races. Then perhaps one day, as a man of such excellent moral judgment, you would have acquired the necessary stature to speak and be listened to on the subject of built-up shoes and they'd be banned forever and we would have you to thank." He pointed directly at me and smiled, as if paying me credit. "And, by the way, if you didn't want to do things this way, I must say, it would hurt the team. Your talents would be obscured. We wouldn't want that, would we?"

"Of course not," I said quickly. I was taken aback by his sudden severity. He still seemed to want more of me. "Not in the least," I said.

"This team doesn't have room for anyone who isn't prepared to make full use of their talents, just to be clear."

"Right."

"Does that sound good? No? We will discuss the specifics: some painless injections, drops of a substance taken orally during stage races, and the collection of a couple of liters of your blood sometime in spring. Okay?" He took the shoe from the table and put it back on. He rose and proffered a hand. "You can go now." I shook and then moved toward the stairs. A series of duvet covers began to billow down into the laundry cart. He scuffed his foot more securely into his shoe. "Congratulations too," he said.

"Sorry?" I said.

"On the child," he said.

*　*

As we near the finish now, the pace of the peloton rises. There is a strong crosswind cutting into our faces. The various national flags held by spectators are pulled taut. We shield Fabrice and, as a team, seek the shelter of the middle of the group.

In a crosswind the power of the peloton is even more pronounced. Riders take short turns at the front of the group, dipping back into wind shade afterward to recover. Those at the front span across the road in an echelon formation, one rider furthest up the road and others shaded on a diagonal. This formation recharges itself with a painstaking switching of positions. Pressed so close and traveling so fast, riders move cautiously, call out warnings, dab brake levers, and swear emphatically.

The sprinters' teams are driving at the front, seeking to pull their men into the best position in advance of the finish line. A few of the other teams have sent their leaders up through the group too, trying to keep them safe by minimizing the number of riders ahead of them and thus the possibility of being taken out by a crash in front. Johan has already moved forward with the other sprinters. We should probably be dragging Fabrice up, but the road is clogged and the impetus escapes us. If Fabrice wants to go to the head of the group, he will tell us, I think. If it were so important, Rafael would be shouting it into our ears.

The road bends right, then left, then right again. The peloton flexes, quicksilver through these turns. Then there is a slight rise, and we are touching our brake levers to account for the slowing of the leading riders on this ascent. The riders at the front pick up speed again as they make the crest. This acceleration, though, comes like a jerk on a rope. The group ceases compressing, begins to stretch again. Each rider takes an instant to recognize the need to go faster. Suddenly there is more space between riders than ever. The wind cuts into the middle of the pack.

Some riders ahead of us stand on their pedals and sprint to keep up with those ahead of them. The road is congested though, and much of the group has been caught off guard. The riders at the front of the peloton, sensing the opportunity, are pushing their advantage. The group, we realize too late, is tearing. Around our team, people call out in frustration, urging those directly ahead of them to push on. Yet the riders on the point of the tear are surprised. They block our way. The front bunch churns ahead—five meters, then ten, then fifteen—taking its wind shade with it.

It is an emergent thing: some tiny glitch in the behavior of the group. And yet this small discrepancy has unloosed Fabrice's competitors, who advance into the distance. Their gain is still less than a hundred meters, but those are meters which are almost impossible to ride across alone. The feat would require effort beyond that made by the riders ahead, who so efficiently swap their places. The riders at the head of our new group are unready to push into the wind, unorganized. Fabrice could lose time on his rivals for no good reason, for no lack of effort or conditioning on his own part. We must organize our own group into some semblance of an efficient machine, work together to pull back the group ahead.

Rafael comes on the radio now. He offers only a crackly scream of rage.

He is understood. We ride to the front, leer into the wind, call to other teams to assist us. We try to pull Fabrice back across the gap. Recovering from an effort at the front, I find myself pressed in the pack next to him. His face is set. I pass him my bottle, which he takes and squeezes over his head. He pauses, frowns. "Sugar drink?" he says. "Not water?"

"Drink," I say. "Sorry."

He wipes at his face irately then, as if attempting to shake the stickiness off him, convulses his head and neck muscles, a vaguely equine gesture, graceful in the midst of all the chaos.

Our rump peloton does not make good time. The group ahead, populated by the more motivated riders—the sprinters still hunting for a win, the other team leaders looking to make time—stretches its lead. We are surrounded by riders simply seeking to make it through the stage: climbers saving themselves for the mountains and domestiques who have already performed their water-carrying duties. Some of these riders take turns at the front but our pace is forever dropping off, requiring one of our team to return to the front to try and pull it back up. Fabrice sits pedaling sullenly.

"You're losing time," says Rafael in our earpieces. He gives us the precise numbers, the time checks. He plots the trend. He tells us the kind of level at which we need to work. He is sinking into a sea of static. As sometimes happens, the radio is not working well. His voice is shrouded increasingly by fuzz, until what he says becomes indistinguishable. I look around and see that my colleagues have removed their earpieces, which now hang from their collars, swinging in the high wind.

* *

I returned from that last autumn race and that basement conversation with Rafael on Liz's second day of maternity leave. B was due to arrive in four weeks, and she had left the lab with reluctance. She was settling uneasily into those days of waiting, walking the house slowly, sore and heavy-footed.

I meant to recount Rafael's persuasions straightaway, but instead I was overwhelmed by the emptiness of the time, the sudden stillness after my season, after Liz's work, before all that was to come. We slept late in the mornings. They were exquisite autumn days, dry and warm, presided over by a steady yellow sun. We were close and quiet. She had given up coffee, but I drank so many cups. She read more seriously than she had for many years. She considered playing the bassoon. "It will do something terrible to the baby in the womb," I joked. It was a strange time of waiting, and I came to think the fineness of those days to be a form of improbable balance: a suspension bridge, a chemical molecule, an archway in a church. I didn't want to bring anything else in. What Rafael was asking of me churned in my mind, but I held it off, tried to lose myself in the vividness of the period, the acute sense of time moving past. But then treatments began coming in the mail: packages of vials and glass bottles addressed to "Timothy Dalton" that needed to be explained.

In the baby room, I recounted the conversation I'd had with Rafael. Liz and I were assembling a bedside table. She sat and I stood. I talked as she worked. "In short," I said, "I'm being asked whether I don't want a little chemical assistance."

She winced. "Spare the euphemism," she said.

I waited for more. She screwed a leg into place with a small hex key.

"What do you think?" I said.

"I don't know," she said. "Is it dangerous?"

"In what sense?"

"In any."

"It's undetectable," I said. "They do these things in hospitals. The transfusions. Hormone supplements."

"Yes," she said, "but all sorts of drugs are used in hospitals. It depends on the context."

"There is a doctor involved. He has many years of experience."

"And there's no way you can do without?"

"It's hard to progress otherwise," I said. "Do you remember the oxygen tent?" I had taken the tent down in late spring.

"Yes," she said. "Of course."

"This is five or ten times more effective than the tent." Rafael would have pushed here, asked whether sleeping in an artificially altered environment was qualitatively different from an injection of a few hormones, but I waited.

She had paused her work on the table. She closed her eyes, rolled her neck back. It crunched. She looked back at me. "Okay," she said.

"Okay?"

"If you won't get banned or killed—that much we owe to the baby—then I guess that's okay."

"You're sure?" I said.

69

"Give me some credit," she said. She picked the table up again. Set to work on the second leg. "Did you not imagine that I'd considered this a possibility?"

I had expected her to be angry, but suddenly I was the one who felt wronged. She had accepted in moments something I had wrestled with for days. "I don't *want* to do this," I said.

"Of course not."

"Have you not thought that I might hold out?"

"You're committed," she said. "You're serious."

"But this is not the main measure of seriousness."

"Sure," she said. She spoke with exasperated disbelief. "But you're not going to give up your career because of it, are you?"

"No," I said. Yet I felt defensive, wounded that she hadn't considered the possibility of my choosing otherwise. Had she been waiting for this moment? Did she take it as evidence of my professional progression?

"I've worried about the idea a lot," I said.

"Of course," she said. "That's why I'm agreeing. Assuming you've thought it through. Trusting you."

"It's not simple," I said.

She nodded in agreement. "The others are doing it, right? If every X does Y and you are an X . . ." She sat back, a hand on her stomach. "Let me understand. Don't put a face on for me."

* *

Eventually, the spires of the town in which we are to finish appear, like catches in the stitching between the sky and the flat horizon. We speed through the outskirts, around roundabouts, into the final, cordoned section of the course. Briefly I replace my earpiece but find it still to be transmitting only hissing. We hear the public-address system at the finish broadcasting a commentary. The commentator is counting down the time we have lost, a count which only concludes as we cross the line. "Ooh, ooh, ooh," he says in sympathy.

As we find our way back through the crowds to the bus, however, something strange happens. People congratulate us. "You must be pleased," says a rider from a competing squad, a Dutchman I hardly know. I look at Fabrice. He shakes his head.

Miguel, a former colleague of ours, now riding for another team, wheels through the crowd toward his own team bus. He stands on one pedal of his bicycle, scuffing himself along with the other foot. He sees us, smiles. "Nice," he says.

Craning my neck to look around the finish, I see Johan, surrounded by a crush of journalists and cameras, sitting on a stool.

"I think Johan won the stage," I say to Fabrice.

Fabrice looks at me and laughs mirthlessly.

* *

We have to wait on the bus for Johan to finish with his podium duties and interviews. Rafael for once is confused as to how to react. He is apoplectic, of course, regarding those of us charged with protecting Fabrice, yet at the same time he must consider the great coup of Johan's stage win. Johan, we have learned, jumped from Sebastian's wheel and infiltrated the sprint preparations of another team, hung behind their man, waited, and then took off at the last minute, passing the rider just before the line. By Johan's account, this passing was simply the result of his superior power. Others have suggested his opponent was slowed by a near collision with another rider. The sponsors are happy anyway. Johan has collected prize money. Television replays show slow-motion footage of him crossing the line, sitting up on his bike, arms raised above his head, his mouth agape.

There is a myth, born somewhere in the pelotons of the past, that air-conditioning after a hot stage is likely to cause riders respiratory difficulties. Rafael is nothing if not heedful of the traditions of racing, and so we sit on a sweltering bus waiting for Johan.

When he finally gets onto the bus, Johan raises the stage winner's bouquet above his head. He looks at us, challenging us to share his success. We call our congratulations through the heavy air. Fabrice raises his voice to say good work. Rafael comes up the bus steps behind Johan. The driver starts the engine and we begin the journey back to our hotel.

As the bus lurches through the tight city streets around the finish line, Johan walks slowly down the aisle, deciding where to sit. There is a seat free next to me and he studies me for a second before taking it. He gives a sigh of pleasure. He flaps his bouquet idly. "I told you I would win," he says.

"It was yesterday's stage you said you'd win," I say, but he ignores me. I point to the bouquet. "Aren't you supposed to throw that into the crowd?" I say.

"That's at a wedding," says Johan. "It's called a winner's bouquet. It's for the winner." He thinks a little more. "There's no class in throwing away what you've just been given." He picks at the flowers. "Also—who knows?—someone in the crowd might have had allergies." He looks at me. "I wanted it," he says finally, as if I've persisted in questioning him. "I've always wanted to win a stage." He lapses back into a tired silence.

I know what he means. We own so little for our efforts. In those flowers are represented many sacrifices: hours of training sessions, dietary restrictions, nights of staying home, even Johan's acceptance of unregulated pharmaceutical assistance. It is nice to hold on to something. It is a guarantee against the threats too. There are journalists who will talk down his achievements, testers with their needles and mass spectrometers. To hold an object in his hand, a thing they will never demand back, is a reassurance.

As we pull onto the motorway, Johan becomes alert again. "Who's going to have a glass of champagne with me tonight?" he says loudly. Rafael, three rows ahead, rises from his seat and looks back. "You and I can have some champagne, Johan. The rest of these idiots get a squirt of lemon in their water."

Later Rafael arrives with the leather pouch and the small scissors. He presses the wing sticker into Johan's palm. Johan closes his fingers tightly around it.

Chapter 5

It is the most beautiful evening, as if the weather is seeking to prove the pettiness of our displeasure. The wind has blown itself out, the air is warm, the colors of the landscape sharp. We are in the same kind of hotel as usual: a functionalist box with a large car park in front. The mechanics are set up on a small space of asphalt between the bus and the hotel. The team bikes are arrayed on a long rack. A radio plays techno, the thrust of the music lost in the open air.

I walk out and fetch my bike. I have had my massage and still feel the warmth of the Butcher's hands in my back. I retrieve a workstand for the bike, clamp it into place. The two mechanics acknowledge me silently.

Of course, I do not need to do my own work: the mechanics will do what is needed, and the bike is running well besides. But I like to occupy my hands. I've been running over the question of how we let Fabrice get dropped, and I seek some escape from it.

I flick through the gears of the bike, spinning its pedals with a hand. I test the rear brake. The parts hiss and click to my satisfaction. I undo the quick-release levers on the rear wheel then, and lift it out of the frame. I wrench off the rear cassette, then grease the freewheel mechanism. I take a cloth and carefully rub at each sprocket of the cassette.

The first thing I loved about cycling was the machine. I saved to upgrade from my child's mountain bike to a proper road bike. I spent months researching that first purchase, and then when I had it, I attended obsessively to maintaining and upgrading it. I loved the efficiency of the model I bought—all that had been shorn from it—and I worked to make it even lighter. I got a slimmer saddle, thinner handlebar tape, special latex tubes. I took a drill and drilled small holes in the aluminum of the rims. There was always something more one could be doing, other reductions to be made. This sense of progression, the feeling that even the tiniest changes could build toward something, was not one I had encountered elsewhere. I took it into my training when I started in earnest, losing myself not just in the riding but in the planning of it, in the joy of paying such meticulous attention.

My ringtone sounds from my pocket. I put down my cloth and wheel. I pinch my phone in my palm, trying to avoid grasping it with my oily fingers.

"Hello," says Liz.

"Hi," I say. I walk to the other side of the bus. I have been waiting to talk to her without knowing it: cued by habit, yet dulled by the stupidity that tiredness brings on.

"That was tough," she says. "I was sorry to watch it. You should have moved Fabrice to the front of the pack before the break happened."

"Don't I know it," I say. "You are in agreement with Rafael, though more composed."

"Yes?" she says. She laughs. "I'm getting ready. I'm getting ready to come and see you."

"I know," I say. "I'm pleased. I'm excited." I'm too tired to summon the necessary life in my voice to underline the truth of this.

"I'll pack tomorrow," she says. "And then the day after we go at four thirty in the morning. I've done the calculations. That is the latest we can go."

"That's tough."

"Do you want anything? Do you want some white socks?"

"I'm good for socks."

She sighs. "It's going to be a nightmare: traveling with a baby and then all of that."

"It's going to be tough," I say. I scratch my arm, leave a stripe of grease against it. "I wish I could be there to help."

She gives a weary laugh. "If you were traveling with us," she says, "who would we be going to see?"

"I don't know," I say. "Perhaps we'd be taking a holiday."

"Like normal people," she says.

I laugh. "Yes. Like normal people."

* *

Fabrice raps on my hotel door after dinner. I have been lying on the bed, snoozing. He inclines his head. "We have a team meeting," he says. He puts an ironic stress on the words.

We walk down the corridor together. "I'm sorry we let you down today," I say.

He frowns. I see the recollection of the stage play over his face. He shakes his head in disagreement. "I need to be in charge," he says. "I need to be in control on the road."

We enter Rafael's room. Rafael is there, the Butcher, Tsutomo. The Butcher is seated, digging around in an open holdall placed on his lap. Rafael meanwhile examines the room suspiciously. He peers out the window through the closed curtains, as if expecting to find a face pressed up against it. He looks under the bed.

"Where's Marc?" says Rafael. "Where's our team doctor?"

"Don't worry," says the Butcher. "He is well out of the way. He's downstairs in the lounge, playing Ping-Pong with Sebastian."

"Ideal," Rafael says.

Fabrice sits on the bed. The Butcher indicates that Tsutomo and I should take places next to our team leader. The Butcher digs around in the holdall and brings out syringes and a clinking cooler bag of vials. He kneels in front of Fabrice and kneads at Fabrice's arm. He locates a vein on his inner biceps, above his tan line: a place that will be hidden by his racing jersey. He fills the syringe from the vial, inserts it carefully into the vein, briefly pulls back the plunger to check for the swirl of red that indicates he has hit the bloodstream, then steadily pushes in the contents of the syringe. Rafael and the Butcher call this microdosing and seem to enjoy all the connotations of this name: the sense of convenience and finely wrought intelligence. The Butcher gives Fabrice a cotton pad to hold to the needle mark. The Butcher sets about Tsutomo and then me.

"All done," says Rafael. "All gone."

We are just getting hormones for now. In seventy-two hours, on the coming rest day, we will be reinjected with a half liter of blood taken earlier in the year. It was harvested at the height of our training, all those lush red cells, healthy and ready to carry oxygen. Our own blood is now dilute, diminished by all the trauma of racing. It will be refreshed.

* *

Before a preseason race, I found myself waiting in a motel. There were lamps with mustard-colored shades, an old TV/VCR, an airbrushed painting of a woodland cottage at dusk. A doctor knocked on my room door. "I've come for your blood," he said, mock-Dracula.

We were in a roadside bonk motel, in one of four rooms rented for two hours. Rafael had hired prostitutes—four of them—to offer some ostensible reason for our short visit. They sat with Rafael in an adjacent room, flicking through magazines, waiting to be dismissed once the medical man had done his stuff. "I vant to suck your blard!" said the doctor, growing into the role.

I let him into the room and sat on the bed. I was the last of our group to be seen.

"You're going to feel a little prick," said the doctor, kneeling on the floor, seeking something in his leather doctor's bag. He wore a shiny gray suit but his glasses were old-fashioned and large. He was bald and he wrinkled his long forehead as he searched for the necessary items. He was a comforting classic of his type: the backdoor dope doctor, a man with some deficiencies to kick against. There was the sharp pain of the needle and the long ache of the drawing of blood. He tapped the filling bag. "Got to get this on ice."

"How do you freeze it?" I said.

"On the move," said the doctor.

"You've got a portable freezer?" I said.

"The whole deal," he said.

When the bag was full, he took the needle from my arm. He dropped it into his plastic box of sharps. He fished around in his bag and took out a paper hat and blue-striped apron.

"Why are you getting dressed now?" I said.

"My cover," said the doctor. He pointed out the window to the rainy, windblown parking lot. Between the cars stood an ice cream van. A plastic anthropomorphized ice cream cone, with arms, legs, and bulging eyes was suspended on a pole above the van, ready, I supposed, to rotate with the movement of the vehicle. It regarded the hotel maniacally.

"It's got freezers," said the doctor. "It plays music. It's got everything."

"Great," I said.

"Do you want a lolly?" he said.

79

* *

The week before B was born, I waited at home with Liz. It was October, an unseasonal warm snap just before the clocks changed. I had been scheduled to attend a team meeting on the continent, but Liz was due. I stayed with her, happily neglected my training schedule. B was five days late. We had prepared, and now we just anticipated B's arrival. We were close in those days. It was a pleasure to close ourselves off from the world so completely. I recalled our meeting, in that airport years before, and the way that both of us had been able to find each other in the midst of a delay, in time we hadn't accounted for. When Liz's labor started, I drove her to the hospital. The labor was long but without complication. Then he was with us.

I had been ready to overstate myself, to humor those attending to us, but I did not need to. I remember holding him and feeling scared by how much I wanted to give him, as if he were a hole hundreds of miles deep that I must somehow fill by hand.

I called Rafael three days after we had returned home to catch up on the team meeting. I told him B had been born, that all had gone well. "Did you ride that day?" he said.

"What?" I said. "No. My boy was being born."

"Of course," he said. "Just know you'll be racing men who would have."

* *

There is something about our injections that makes us lonesome, as if we fear our association after the event should make our activities suspicious, as if our contemplation of what we have done might resonate between us, become detectable in the air. Fabrice and Tsutomo retreat to their beds. I sit down in the lobby of the hotel, reading a newspaper, watching people coming and going, keeping an eye on a cat that parades through the flowerbeds outside the front of the hotel. I go to the café and drink a mint tea. The sun sets. I pad back along hotel corridors when it is finally dark.

In the room, Tsutomo is already asleep. I lie on the bed. The curtains are slightly open and light leaks from a streetlight outside. My eyes adjust slowly to the gloom. There is a small piece of string hanging from a tack pushed into the ceiling. Something was hung from it once, I think: a balloon, likely. Someone celebrated an event of consequence in this little hotel room.

From his bed, Tsutomo makes a strangled cough. Covers rustle. He turns, seeming not to wake fully. I am restless. I go into the cramped bathroom. I decide that I will have a bath in the small plastic tub. I set the water running and begin unwrapping the tiny soaps from their hotel-branded packaging. I squeeze a couple of the mini tubes of shampoo into the water, hoping to make bubbles. This is my life on tour, this hotel life, furnished with small things intended for single uses. There are those who like the hotel rooms—the neatness, the fresh sheets and towels—and those who do not, who still miss home. Rafael and Fabrice are towel people and always will be. I have found a comfort in the regularity, the frictionlessness of these days. Yet I have also begun to identify a sadness in them, gained a guilty sense that I should not be so easily pleased.

Chapter 6

I wake and put on my tracksuit in the dim room. Tsutomo is gone.
I slept for hours without dreaming.

Liz and I joke that races are where I go to rest. There is no wailing
child to disturb me, only the smallest sound of Tsutomo's breathing,
the tiny creaks of his bed frame as he shifts in his sleep.

We read the books about infant sleep patterns. They are piled
at home in the living room, torn strips of paper marking pertinent
pages. We decided on a CIO method of helping B sleep. "Cry it out"
is what the initials stand for. When he first wakes, we comfort him
after five minutes of crying. If he wakes again, we go to him after ten
minutes, then fifteen after that. The idea is that he should learn to
sleep alone. There is some flexibility in the theory. We worked together to choose those precise numbers. We made endless cups of
tea and talked about it. We read blogs. There was so much literature,
and yet there was not consensus. When B arrived, though, in those
first months he never seemed to stop crying. When we tried to put
our plan into practice, it was impossible. We wondered whether it
was because we hadn't been more consistent or whether our assumptions were wrong. We read more. We did not want to credit chance,
to throw up our hands so early in this process. We wanted only a right
way to do things, a sense of control.

I remember looking into his eyes when he was crying and feeling
a vacancy there. He was uncomfortable, and all else of him had fled

83

behind that fact. I felt shatteringly unable to protect him, though I held him right there in my hands.

We were more rattled, more concerned, of course, than we had thought that we would be before becoming parents. Friends told us that couples were either lucky or unlucky in these things, that some children just struggled to sleep. I could accept this logically, but it was hard to hear B cry and believe it. Liz and I spent hours on the Internet, pouring our concerns into search engines: rashes and drowsiness and splutters he made when he awoke. I remember that in this period Liz read in a magazine that web searches used a significant amount of electricity because servers somewhere had to rev up each time one typed out a query. "We must be burning whole forests," she said. "Whole seams of coal."

Katherine was eager to be involved. She came down to London just after we had brought B home. She slept on our sofa, saying that she wanted to be near, to be of use. She watched us as we went about our tasks. She walked about the house, picking things up and inspecting them: books and ornaments and toys. She was quiet, but there was an acuity to her gaze. I felt Liz eyeing her mother whenever Katherine came into the room. On the third day of Katherine's visit, the tension came to a head.

"I appreciate it," Liz said. "It's nice to have you here."

"What?" said Katherine. She could hear the *but* coming and wanted to cut to it.

"We can do this ourselves," Liz said. "Or we'll learn."

"I brought you up pretty much alone," said Katherine. "I have a lot to pass on."

"It's important for me to do this myself."

"There are limits," Katherine said. "You do not have endless energy. You need to choose what to focus on. You have to establish your priorities."

"I know," said Liz.

"You do not act like you do."

"They're *my* priorities," said Liz, "not yours." She shook her head, said nothing more. The two of them looked at each other for some time. They stopped there though. It was as if they had waded too far into a swamp and wanted to go no further.

Later Liz said, "I feel like I'm a model soldier, and she's a general pushing me around a large map." I felt for her, yet I also wondered whether she would truly have it any other way. I had never had such an advocate as Katherine. My mother was kind. She drove me to races when I was younger, stood on verges to the edge of suburban lanes smoking Lambert and Butler menthols and waiting for me to race by, but there was not that sense of fierce calculation that Katherine gave off, the feeling that each action was so critically important. To be pushed around the map, to have some sense of the campaign one was supposed to wage, did not seem to me such a burden but instead something that I would have liked, that I might wish for our own son.

*   *

I hear a noise in the corridor. I open the door of the room.

"Oh," says Rafael. "What a coincidence. Just the man I was looking for." He is into his stride already. "Breakfast is under way," he says. "I am supposing that you will be making your way down."

"Of course."

"Perhaps we could take a walk before."

"A walk?"

"Get some of the fresh air of the garden."

Out of the back of the hotel is a small lawn, littered with cigarette butts and dog shit. Rafael walks across it, placing his feet with care. We stop at the hedge. He peers through a gap in the foliage to the adjacent car park. "Yes," he says. "A nice day. A good time to talk."

"Okay," I say.

"You are well?"

"Yes. Tired, but okay."

"Good," says Rafael. "Your wife is coming for a visit on the rest day."

"Yes," I say.

"How nice."

"Yes."

"I have a little news," Rafael says.

"Yes?"

"Things are, as they say, totally fucked."

"Oh," I say. "The break? Us losing time yesterday?"

He shakes his head. "Not that," he says. "Not *only* that. This is more to do with strategy. The doctor . . ."

"Marc?"

"The other one. He has run into some difficulty. He is in trouble."

"They found him out?" I say.

"Not in relation to us, thanks to God."

"How? Other teams?"

"Other needs." Rafael shakes his head. "Housewives. Prescription drugs for housewives. The problem was that they were skinny. He was making deliveries in his van. Why, the neighbors asked themselves, can these women eat so much ice cream and stay so thin? The neighbors became very envious and looked into the situation. Everything unraveled. Female envy is very dangerous. I am glad, when I consider this, that I have not married."

"I'm sorry to hear this," I say.

"He has, because of all this, just been put out of commission. We were due to resupply tomorrow. We were due to give you some of your blood back on the rest day."

"Yes."

"There are more mountains coming up. We need to recover a little time."

"Okay," I say. "Why are you telling me?"

"The supply chain is broken," says Rafael. "I thought you could help."

"I'm racing."

"Of course." Rafael throws out his hands, laughs. "I was not talking about you doing it yourself."

"No?"

"Your wife will be driving along the E17?"

"No," I say.

"She will not be taking this route?"

"No," I say. "She will. She will not do what you are suggesting."

"I have suggested nothing," says Rafael. "I am only asking a few innocuous questions."

"You are preparing to suggest something."

"Of course," says Rafael. "She makes a stop on her trip down the motorway, meets a contact of mine, picks up the shipment. It is very easy."

"No," I say again.

"Think about it."

"She is coming with my son," I say.

"Perfect," says Rafael. "That will be a good cover for the operation."

"He is not a cover," I say. "What are you saying?"

87

Rafael looks at me with a surprise that suggests I have spoken more forcefully than I usually do. "That was a poor way of phrasing," he says. "Of course, your son is a small human being."

"Yes," I say. I shake my head.

Rafael holds his hands in a position of prayer. "I was making my point with force," he says, "because I am so eager for you to have a little talk with your wife." He gives an unsteady laugh, a laugh that suggests he is on the edge of some other emotion.

"She is not part of this," I say.

"Come," he says. "I am not making her team doctor."

"That is my life. My real life. My home life."

He laughs again, bitterly. "Everything is your life. You have one life," he says. "Be honest. You are not a cat."

There is the sound of voices from the car park. We both look through the hedge. It is the mechanics, beginning to load the bikes onto the trailer behind the bus. Rafael watches in silence for a minute, alert to any errors of protocol. He turns back to face me, reluctantly satisfied. "You know," he says, "you are genuinely good at something—world class—and yet now you act like this is nothing, like this is something to throw away."

"There are limits," I say.

"Sure," he says.

"You want her to carry bags of our blood?" I say.

"That would be very useful," he says.

"It would be crazy. How would she hide it? How would she keep it cool in the car? What would she say if she were caught?"

"What about hormones?" he says. "Some little vials? Not so hard to hide inside the spare tire space. That is better, no?"

"No."

"No? You will be substantially remunerated."

88

"That is not the point."

"No. But it is still something. With a child. With things you must buy. The big chairs people push their children in. The balloons shaped like the cartoon sponge. Your wife might like the money."

"For doing this?" I say. "No."

"You are so sure," he says. He looks at me as if curious. "Do one thing for me: make sure. Only that."

"No," I say.

"I am persistent," he says. "Remember."

"Yes," I say. He is not wrong.

"Where's your phone?" he says.

"In my room."

"Go and get it," he says. "Just some vials. Put the proposal to her. Is that so dangerous?"

I nod. I move away across the lawn. He watches me as I retreat.

I take the elevator back up to my room. The phone nearly rings through before it is picked up. "Hello?" says Liz, a hard question mark at the end.

"It's me," I say.

"Yes," she says.

I could say nothing of my recent conversation, but I am a poor liar, and so I do what Rafael asks: just enough to have discharged my duty and to be able to tell him so. I explain what Rafael wants. Liz listens. I hear some screeches and croaks from B, but he does not cry.

"That's crazy," she says. Something falls to the floor. I hear her sigh, put down the phone, pick the thing up again. There is a croak from B. She lifts the receiver. "What will he pay?" she says.

"I don't know," I say. "I didn't ask."

"He's a strange one."

"You don't want to do it, do you?"

"Ask me."

"Do you?"

"It's not ideal. I suppose I could do it well. Who else is he going to get in a hurry?"

"But you'd be involved, and with Barry."

"Yes. You think I'd mess it up?"

"No. You're thorough. I think you'd do it as well as anyone could."

"Thanks."

"But there are risks."

"You said it was safe, undetectable."

"It is," I say. "In the blood. In the body. But in the world . . ."

"You don't have to let me help you," she says. "But if you decide not to, do it for the right reasons."

"Meaning?"

"Don't be squeamish," she says. "Don't underestimate me."

Rafael is waiting in a chair by the elevator. He sits back, taps his fingers on a small table beside him.

"It is arranged?" he says quietly.

"No," I say.

"No?"

"No."

"She says it?"

"I say it."

Rafael's lips flinch in displeasure. "You have been on this program and now you want to," he says, "make a, how you say, U-turn?"

"No," I say. "I never agreed to this. It's a different thing."

"Everything is a different thing," Rafael says. His tone has acquired a bitter hiss. He spits into a bowl of potpourri on the ornamental table. "You won't get your treatment."

"I'll go without."

He snorts. "You know where I grew up?"

I try to preempt him, to judge the narrative: "In a tiny shack?" I say. "In a dirty barn?"

He looks at me with distaste. "No. I grew up in a perfectly acceptable house, but that is not the issue. I grew up on the beach."

I concede the point.

"I grew up ten meters from the sea, and do you know what I dreamed of every day? I dreamed of the mountains. I wanted to go to the mountains, to see films about the mountains, to read about the mountains, to simply sit alone and think about the mountains. I was, to use your idiom, head above heels about the mountains. Why was that?"

"Why?" I say. He has his momentum and I resolve to endure.

"I was not in the mountains. I had the sea. I could go any day I wanted to the sea, but that was too easy. I wanted the mountains. There was probably some boy in the mountains dreaming about the sea, and why was that? Because he could not have the sea. Who likes to read about money more than the poor? Who likes to read about beauty more than the ugly? What are our favorite stories about? Flying, magic, living forever: the things we cannot do. There might be some planet where people fly around and never die and what would their favorite stories be about? Walking and death." He looks at me, one thick eyebrow arched. "And do you know what our most popular fantasy is? Do you know what is the core of every human story?"

I shake my head.

"Somebody changes," he says. "Somebody always changes. And you come to me and you say you've made a decision, as if that will make some difference to anything at all."

* *

91

Katherine and Thomas came to lunch for Christmas when B was two months old. They arrived with boxes of pristine, tiny clothes that he would almost instantly outgrow. I went out riding between frosty fields and returned to the smell of turkey. We were doing the meal properly, with all the trimmings. I ate a lot, which I seldom do. We had glasses for water and wine out. There was an ironed white table-cloth. We had provided different pieces of cutlery for each course. There was some polite conversation, the sense that we must all go about eating properly, tucking in elbows, chewing politely, as if we were all being watched. B was restful that afternoon.

I was pleased by it all. It was no real achievement, I suppose. Thousands of people were sitting down to comparable Christmas dinners, and yet this fact was one reason for my feeling of fulfillment: the sense of having done this ordinary thing well enough and finding pleasure in this doing.

The satisfaction of it stayed with me long after Katherine and Thomas had departed, through those muted days between Christmas and the arrival of the new year. I liked this time. I went out training on my winter bike, wearing my gloves and thermal tights. When I passed through the populated sections of my route, the streets were busy with those shopping, jogging, walking dogs. Most people were on holiday, and though I was still, in a sense, working, I felt a companionship with them. We were, all of us, sharing these dim, chilly afternoons.

Liz's restlessness in the period surprised me, though probably I should have recognized its source. While I drew solace from the suspension of these days, for her they underlined her idleness. The rest of the world was on holiday, watching TV, and drinking in the afternoons. Even the lab was empty but for a few of the technicians going in to feed the fish. Yet for her these late December days were indistinguishable from any others of the previous months. She was due to be returning to work after the new year, and she itched to do it. Her students had not been finding changes from the mutation the project was studying. "I know they're missing something," she said. "They're unobservant." One picks up a fluency in the lab, she told me. It was like unlocking a door, she said. Everyone's front door has a knack to it—a twist, a little push against the bolt—and yet people don't think for a minute about opening their own locks. "How do you describe it though, to someone who can't do it?" she said. "How do you make them do it right?"

She went back to the lab on the first work day of the new year. I relished her precise prettiness in her work clothes. I was envious that it seemed directed to others and not me. She was meticulously prepared. It was as if she dared the world to suggest that motherhood had diminished her appetite for work.

*   *

The other riders have finished breakfast when I reach the dining room. The waiters move around, clearing up dishes, carrying stacks of dirty plates into the kitchen. I am not hungry, but I load up my plate with what is left. The porridge is cool and set hard on top, the coffee tepid. Sebastian, the last rider still at the table, wipes his mouth with his napkin. I take a seat next to him. "I'm going," he says. "No offense, of course." He taps the giant red sports watch that, bug-like, grips to his wrist. I work to force my food down. He stands and lumbers out of the room. There is an hour before we will leave the hotel, but I feel caught behind, rushed. I look up to see a waiter watching me eat with an expression of distaste.

When I am nearly finished, my phone rings. I stand, walk out to the hotel car park to take it.

"I just talked to Rafael," Liz says.

"What?"

"He called me."

"He called you?"

"As I said. He made some insinuations."

"What do you mean?" I say.

"About his suggestion that I assist him."

"Right." I feel the breakfast in my stomach, the sour taste of coffee on my teeth.

"It's pretty critical," she says. "I think he really needs this. He's prepared to make things very difficult if we don't help him."

"That's my problem," I say.

"Why do you say that?" she says. "You earn most of the money. I know about all of this. You store your products in our fridge."

"What did he say?"

"Your job is on the line, I think."

"He's bluffing," I say. I exhale. I cough drily. "This ruins your trip," I say. "It turns it into something else."

"Perhaps that's not so terrible," she says. "He tells me he will pay for the hotels."

"I can't just do everything he says."

"That's true," she says. She is speaking calmly. "But this is not about what he wants. It's about you."

"We can't do it," I say.

"If your career is on the line?"

"Even then," I say.

She laughs as if in disbelief. "All these years. This trying. You won't let me give you a hand. This is just one little thing more."

"With him there is always one little thing more."

"Well," she says. "You know how it is. It's your choice."

94

She waits. There is an answer she wants, and I know why she desires it. I think of her nights of coming home from bad days at the laboratory, of her talking under her breath, reliving problems that I could not conceive of let alone solve. The vows of marriage have felt to me to be limited things at times, my ability to ease her passage through the world constrained by what little I know of her work. I think of waking in the night to find that she has not been sleeping, looking at her lying there in the dim streetlight that cuts through the curtains, her turning to look at me sadly, and the sense in her doing this that I cannot set her mind at ease, that she does not expect me to.

I remember heading out training on a winter day after B had been born, before Liz returned to the lab. It was a long, cold ride, sleeting throughout. The weather was so bad that I found myself perversely ecstatic. Just being out on the bike was a triumph. I was glad to have endured the ride, felt that this endurance augured well for the season. When I opened the front door with my numb fingers, however, Liz was still in the same place on the sofa she had been sitting when I left. She watched me come in without expression and asked with no particular expectation in her voice how the ride had been. I found that I didn't want to answer her truly and share the odd pleasure I had taken in the last three hours. I looked at my weary wife and at B rolling on his mat, and I felt with sadness that she could not take in the thoughts that had pleased me, could not imagine my petty priorities.

She exhales. I still do not speak. "Let me do this for you," she says.

Why have I not considered that she might feel about my profession as I did her work? Why would I not have imagined there was a hunger to be let in?

"You're sure?" I say.

"Of course."

"Okay," I say. "The vials. Just the vials."

95

* *

Later, in the starting area, Fabrice seeks me out. I am sitting on a chair by the bus putting on my socks and shoes. "Late to breakfast," he says. "Everything okay?"

"Rafael wanted to see me," I say.

"I see," he says. "The issue is all sorted out?" He gives no indication of whether he knows what Rafael has asked.

"Oh yes," I say.

He takes a seat next to me. He buckles his own shoes a little tighter, releases the buckles, tightens them again. He has just today's stage to make it through before the rest day, before he may recover a little, before he will have leisure to spend time with Rafael considering his gains, his route to victory. He sits up from fiddling with his shoes and looks at me. "A cyclist is visited by a genie on the day of the World Championships," he says.

"Okay," I say.

He slaps his thighs. His legs are newly shaven. "The genie says, 'I will give you a wish, with just one condition: that anything you ask for, your greatest rival will have double.'"

"Okay."

"'So if I ask to win the World Championships . . . ,' the cyclist says. 'Your rival will win it twice,' says the genie." Fabrice's index finger rises. "The cyclist thinks. 'Well, then I suppose that I would like you to push an uncooked baking potato into my rectum.'"

"That's good," I say.

"Yes," says Fabrice. "I have told it a number of times. It is important to specify a *baking* potato. A spring potato . . ." He shrugs, stands, and clacks off in the direction of his bike.

96

* *

We have barely gone a kilometer from the start when a couple of young riders from the German team sprint off up a short climb. Others in the peloton are unwilling to let them go, and so we are all thrown into a chase from the start of the day, stiff and grumbling and not yet broken into any kind of rhythm. Today's stage has a number of small inclines and descents that will hamper the efficiency of the peloton, so as a group we are eager to let no one get too far ahead. I ride next to Tsutomo, who shakes his head. "Assholes," he says. He turns and catches my eye. "They were prepared."

"Indeed," I say.

"The blond one was chewing his handlebars at the start."

* *

When I thought of drug taking before, I always considered it so simple. One would have a few injections, I thought, and become better at what one does. Rafael's program, however, puts a lie to this. "Making you shit bags better," he says, "is like trying to fix a wristwatch with a rock."

There are no rules, apparently. There is talk of "responders" to different substances. One man's wing is another man's millstone. "You are all unique," says Rafael. "Not in the way that I care about your what-is-called 'personalities'; in the way that the drugs always affect each of you differently." Our needs vary too. Johan, for instance, does not have so many of the endurance treatments. He cares about sprinting, and thus power, and takes growth hormone. I do not see the specifics of his treatments, but I witness him bulging at the seams in the season. The hormone makes his jaw grow, and he complains of dental problems all summer.

I went to stay with Rafael for training in early winter. B was still young, but I was assured the trip was important. Rafael and the Butcher live close together. I rode in the days, and Rafael and the Butcher followed me in their cars. Sometimes Fabrice, who also lives in the region, came to join.

There was a computer attached to my bicycle, logging my power output, my speed, and my heart rate. Occasionally Rafael asked how I felt. More often though, he and the Butcher simply consulted the data. "The mind is one of the body's least reliable parts," Rafael said to me when I told him that I was feeling tired. "The data, on the second hand, is almost always correct." He told me the data looked good. He urged me to push a little harder.

In these days, he tested my response to a few substances: for recovery, for muscle growth, for weight loss.

Riding with Fabrice on one of these days, I told him that I never knew my body had so many states. Fabrice nodded in response. "In their way," he said, "the two of them are artists."

Fabrice and I did two long rides sequentially, and before the second I was given an injection which made me ride like a man pursued. Fabrice and I rode next to each other up a switchbacking climb. I felt I had a spring in my riding that Fabrice did not. The hill sank beneath me with a thrilling inevitability. Fabrice shifted his limbs as though they were impossibly heavy. Each time I eased ahead it seemed less likely he would return to riding level with me.

At the top of the climb, the Butcher and Rafael were there to meet us, to debrief. Fabrice was unusually sullen. I was enthusiastic. "They can give me that stuff every day," I said, when Fabrice and I were freewheeling slowly down the mountain.

"It becomes less effective," he said. "It inhibits future growth."

"Still."

"Still it was you also."

"Me?"

"You think a drop or two of this or that can do so much?"

"I don't know."

"You have to think the capability is inside of you, do you not?"

We rode in silence for a time. We concentrated on taking the corners. The evening was setting in. Lights were on in the valley. "Just don't take too much," Fabrice said. "It burns you up."

I came, despite myself, to appreciate the danger of it all. I am cautious by nature, but some of the things I have encountered have made me wonder at our desire. I have heard rumors of a bovine blood extract smuggled around the world. People have talked in the peloton of a weight-loss drug pulled even from a testing phase, yet available through certain doctors. I marvel sometimes. We are doing all this for a bicycle race? It is almost magnificent. Fabrice thinks this too, I guess. Even in his regret there was a quantity of pride. His warning was in some way a challenge.

* *

The rolling nature of the stage takes a toll on my legs. We catch the first breakers, and then another group goes on the next climb. They are just four riders, down in the overall ranking, no real threat to Fabrice and the other leaders. We will pull them in slowly, however. The peloton is a twitchy thing today. The group is forever changing speed as the incline of the road alters. I am eager not to let our team get dropped as we did the day previously, and so I stand, I hang off the handlebars. I concentrate on the motion of those at the front of the group.

Fabrice sits silent behind me. He pedals in easy circles. He breathes through his nose. I reprimand those ahead who let the pace slacken. Tsutomo takes his turn ahead of Fabrice. I push forward.

I pedal at the front for a while and enjoy the sensation of cutting through the thick summer air, the sense of steering a great machine.

* *

As the spring began to approach, I started to have more commitments. There was a training camp; there were races to go to on the continent. B was so small, we didn't want to entrust him to a nanny. Liz's old friend Davina, who only worked part time, did a considerable amount of caring for B. For a couple of weeks, when I was away racing, she spent nearly as much time in our house as she did in her own. I do not think that Liz and I are selfish people, but we were good at blocking out a true sense of how much we were taking advantage of Davina's generosity. Occasionally a word or expression of hers would cause me to consider the reality of what Liz and I were asking. I would recall how I had thought of certain parents before the arrival of our own child, of how much I had been irritated by those who took up pavements with pushchairs, or refused to take their wailing child out of a crowded restaurant. I would look at B, though, and feel that we were not doing that. She liked him, I felt. It was inconceivable that she could not.

Eventually, Davina's patience just ran out. "I can't do this much," she said one evening when Liz had just got in from work, and when I had just flown back into the city from a race. We all knew this had been coming, I suppose. It was a relief, even. She was nice to do it then. I had ten days before I needed to travel again. We had time to come up with a new arrangement.

We interviewed for a nanny, found a skinny girl in her early twenties who was preparing to go to nursing college in the autumn. For some reason, she was learning Finnish. "I could speak Finnish to the baby," she said.

"I think that might be confusing for him," said Liz. "For you to be trying to teach him Finnish at this point."

The girl was pleasant. She wore a baggy cable-knit cardigan. She had flushed cheeks, gave the impression of someone trying very hard. It was when she left and we started discussing her rate of pay that we had doubts. "It's the transactional nature," said Liz.

"We can pay her more," I said.

"But the payment itself," said Liz. "So soon. So young for him." She pointed at B, who lay on his mat, who had been admirably quiet for the visit of the girl.

"But you need to be in the lab."

She shrugged. "Sure." She both wanted and didn't want this context, this encouragement of her own ambitions. I don't think she was yet inclined to concede that we had to choose between care for B and our work. "It's a *job* for this girl," she said.

"Yes."

"The secret of adulthood," Liz said. "Most people are bad at their jobs."

"You sound like Rafael," I said.

She laughed. "Does that make me wrong?" she said.

"Just scary," I said. I laughed myself.

I understood her impulse, I thought. I felt that the issue of care for B should never be resolved too easily. I have plenty of devices to measure my training, to track my power and distance and speed and heart rate. And yet what reassures me I am doing enough is the sense of pushing into discomfort, going outside of what I know myself able to do. It is the same with B, I think: there is the need to do enough for him, yet beyond that is a feeling that his care should cost us effort, that we should give him more than we think we can.

There was, of course, a relatively simple option, though it was not one we were easily inclined to take. Katherine was still eager for more time with her grandchild. Parcels of presents and clothes arrived every couple of weeks.

Liz was not keen on this option, but the idea of paying someone displeased her even more. I thought that Katherine would do a good job, but I knew also that Liz would chafe against her mother's regular presence. "She can wind me up," said Liz, "but I'm better with her now. I won't let her get to me."

When we asked Katherine, it was as if she had known we would. She came down the day before I was due to leave for a training camp and tidied up the spare room. She brought with her a box of baby things that had once been Liz's own. This exasperated Liz, who regarded them as old and dirty, but I was impressed by the care with which they had been packed away, by the fact that Katherine had stored them and retrieved them after all these years.

I didn't see Katherine as much as Liz did, because she was covering for my absences. She would arrive early on days on which I was due to go away, so well put together already, made up and smelling of Yardley's Lavender. She would even make me sandwiches for the flight.

At first Katherine followed the guidelines Liz had given her, but soon she was using her own initiative. Liz was staying later than she would have liked at the lab. She was struggling to improve the procedures. She came home to find that Katherine had made changes to feeding patterns, to clothes, to certain routines we had laid down. Liz complained about this on the phone, and I commiserated. However, in these first weeks of being cared for by his grandmother, B did become calmer. Perhaps this would have happened anyway. Perhaps his previous discomfort was just a phase. We did not begrudge Katherine this success anyway. We forgot all our former resistance. We were readier to renounce opinions than we previously would have been. We put less stock in coherence.

* *

I am in the middle of the pack when we reconnect with the second breakaway group of the day. However, as soon as we have done so, another handful of riders sprint off up the road. There is a quick panic around us as riders wonder whether any of the main competitors are trying to ride away. The men are just more back markers though. It is one of those days, of infernal attacks and countermoves. The idea that one rider, of all who attempt it, should get across the line first seems even stranger than usual.

I fall back from the peloton to the team car in order to collect water. Rafael buzzes down the passenger window. "How is Fabrice?" he says. The Butcher drives.

Rafael begins to hand me bottles but does so slowly. He offers the first one out the window and I grip it. He doesn't let go, however, but holds on, dragging me with him and the car, saving me from having to pedal properly. Every now and then, for the sake of appearances, I take the bottle fully and put it into my rear pockets, then grasp another one passed out by Rafael.

"Fabrice is well," I say. "Ask him on the radio."

"Literally broadcast it?" says Rafael. "Let other teams hear? Come on. Think."

"Okay," I say. "Sorry. I think he's feeling good."

"Excellent," says Rafael. "Tell him that he should be looking for a break in the last hour of racing. Tell him that I want him to try to make up time today."

"Okay," I say.

"These are my real instructions," says Rafael. "I will broadcast some things over the team radio, but they will be diversionary. Today we need, as you might say, the element of surprise."

"Okay," I say. The window begins to rise with a mechanical moan. Rafael lets go of the last bottle and I lurch back into purposeful pedaling. The car pulls ahead of me to offer some wind shade as I ride back to the peloton. Chasing back to the group, I always fear that I have fallen too far behind, regardless of how often I have performed this maneuver.

I nudge my way through the pack to Fabrice and Tsutomo. I hand them their bottles and discreetly pass on their instructions. "Good," says Fabrice. "I'm ready."

In our earpieces there is the fizz of the radio channel being opened. "Whoa, we're halfway there," sings Rafael. "Whoa, we're living on a prayer." When he finishes the chorus, he sings guitar and drum parts.

"He's serious," says Fabrice. "Even when he's silly, he's serious."

* *

One night in spring Liz came home furious. It was a warm day, one of the first of the year. I was home and had put B to bed. The windows of the kitchen were open, and I could hear traffic and the rhythmic clack of trains passing on the line half a mile away. Katherine was up in Norfolk.

"Things are fucked," said Liz. We were in the kitchen and she put her bag on the table, pushed away some baby bottles, sterilized and drying. "The results are fucked."

"Really?" I said. I thought of those dim rooms, the tanks of zebra fish, the grumble of all those machines.

"Yes," she said. "The gene we had hopes for. Lbx3. There is no coherence in the results, no apparent effects. Our hypothesis is off."

"So you're ruling things out?" I said. "You need to try a different route?"

"It's not like that," she said. She shook her head.

She and I sat opposite each other. I didn't know what to say.

"I don't even know if everything has been done right," she said. "If everyone has followed the protocol." She picked at a hangnail.

"You can start again?" I said. "Can't you study a different gene?"

"This is not a cake," she said. "This is years of work, huge funding checks."

I thought of my feeling after a bad race: the pain of the moment, and also the pang of considering all those days behind of training, collapsing into retrospective incoherence. To know her sense of desperation was not to know how to assuage it though. She stared at the table. I made her tea. I backed off and left her space.

* *

In the last fifty kilometers the route profile ripples like a child's depiction of the sea. These are not big peaks, but they have the potential to break the peloton apart.

The atmosphere is tense. Riders know that the stage is to be won in these minutes. Some riders become more silent, others chatter, seeking to put off those around them.

Rafael opens the radio channel again and sings the chorus of "Satisfaction" by the Rolling Stones.

"Okay," says Fabrice, beckoning Tsutomo and me to ride beside him. "One of you sticks with me, one of you goes off early as a decoy."

"I stick with you," says Tsutomo.

"You feel strong?" says Fabrice.

"Of course," says Tsutomo.

Fabrice looks at me. "At the beginning of the next hill go as hard as you can for a minute. Then expect to be caught. As soon as you are, then Tsutomo and I will go."

"A one-two," says Tsutomo. "Like we are boxers."

* *

I had to race two days after Liz brought home her disappointment. She was still going to work, of course. They had funding left. They were trying to salvage what they could. There was a weariness to Liz when she came home, however, even though she was back earlier than she would have been previously.

Katherine arrived before my departure and said she would take care of her daughter, "get her out of the dumps," as she phrased it—a promise that concerned me more than it reassured.

Liz called me twice on those days when I was away. She was keen to hear that everything was proceeding as I hoped, more interested than usual in my results, in my form.

The race did go well. The team was in good shape. We controlled the peloton for a time. The race was won by others out on a break, but amidst the rest of the riders Fabrice seemed able to churn away with an ease which suggested good things for the rest of the summer.

I returned to Liz and B and Katherine, apparently happy in the kitchen. Liz was throwing bread out the window, and the three of them were watching the birds alighting on the back patio to collect it.

Liz and I talked about the race, about the conclusions that could be drawn. "It was good," I said. "Rafael is very happy."

"Did you win?" said Katherine. She was tearing up crusts of bread, piling the crumbs on the table for her daughter to throw.

"I wasn't trying to win," I said. "That's not the aim for me." I looked at Liz. She smiled sympathetically but didn't step in. I was angered by Katherine's question, by the sense that this was in fact her intention.

"She hasn't learned," I said later, when Liz and I were in bed. "She doesn't know my aims. She can't understand success."

"She was picking at you," said Liz. "She does that."

"That doesn't make it not annoying." I had listened to Liz make similar claims about Katherine, and yet she was not in the mood to accept my protestations.

"Sure," she said. "It's a sign that she likes you."

"Really?"

"That you *matter* to her, at least."

"I'm not so certain." The window was open. I could hear wind through the leaves of trees in the garden.

"She wants you to do well," said Liz. "That's how she encourages."

"Encourages?"

"She expects a lot of people," Liz said. "You have witnessed this, surely?"

"And yet she lives with Thomas," I said.

"Thomas is fine." Liz turned to face the window. The mattress creaked.

"Of course."

"He's reached his potential. He's all he can be."

"And I'm not?"

"I didn't say that."

"But you implied it."

"Not on purpose." Her voice was quiet now.

"Still."

"She's difficult," said Liz. "That's the message."

"Do you think I could ever impress her?"

"I don't know."

"By my cycling?"

"Maybe," she said.

"What could I do?"

Liz sighed. "If you won a stage. If you were a team leader. If the ladies in her book group knew who you were."

"I can't just *do* that."

"I'm not saying she's reasonable. I'm not saying you should."

"What are you saying?"

"I'm answering your question."

"Do you think I'm trying hard enough?"

"What do I know about it?"

"What's your impression?"

She thought. We both lay there in the darkness. The sound of the trains was gone. "I think you're doing fine," she said.

* *

We reach the bottom of the next hill in the midst of countryside. I can smell the stink of rapeseed in the air. Horses gallop across a field, startled by the television helicopter. The road tends leftward as it begins to climb. It stretches up to a copse of trees a few hundred meters away. The peloton hugs to the left verge, cutting to the quick of the curve. I pull to the right, out of the main flow of the group, as if preparing to drop to the back for water. I feel a lurch of nervousness. I take a drink from my bottle and then throw it to the side of the road, where fans scramble to retrieve such a relic. I inhale deeply, change up a gear, and stamp hard into my pedals. I aim for the trees and think only of emptying my legs.

My strength is a surprise. The pace is unbearable, certainly, but it is a thrill to throw everything at the incline. The spectators call out, and it is strange in that instant to think that those shouts are intended solely for me. I count to ten and then count again. I am crouched into my handlebars as if in a position of prayer. It is only when I have counted to ten a third time that I allow myself to glance back—inclining my head downward, looking through the cage of my arms, beneath my left armpit—to see the peloton fifty meters behind me.

My pace is dropping, but I think that it is not yet time to submit. Perhaps today will be the day I earn a wing. The raw grating of my breathing is uncomfortable but no longer unsustainable. My thoughts glance the previous night's injection, the steamy room, a warm red feeling. Ahead of me a man strays into the road, waving a French flag at his side like a matador. "*Go,*" he shouts breathlessly, "*go.*"

Past the copse of trees, the road bends right and steepens. I cut into the corner, causing the fans to step back. I ride hard out of it and look back to see that I still have some lead on the group. I decide that it is not yet the time that I need to let myself be caught. My motions feel sprung, necessary. I take note, for the first time, of the motorbike ahead of me, its passenger turning in the saddle to level a television camera at my face. I try to catch up with it. I look up and see electricity wires strung over the road up ahead. I set my concentration onto making it past them.

Passing under the wires, I look with panic for another thing onto which to latch my gaze. The road tends leftward once again and there is another copse of trees on the horizon. I push for these trees and think I see the lens of the camera ahead winking: a reflection of sunlight or the result of a change of focus. The crowds at the side of the road get thicker as I ascend. Sometimes I make out shouts, facial expressions. I notice an old man, sitting back from the road in a canvas chair, eating a sandwich.

As I make the trees, something else looms into my line of sight: a stark chunk of color. I realize that I am seeing the summit of the hill and, marking this, an inflatable arch. I must have been riding for more than two minutes. We will descend for a time now, and it will not be possible, going downhill, for Fabrice and Tsutomo to sprint away and deliver the second blow of our planned one-two.

I stand on my pedals as I make up the final yards to the summit and wonder what I should do. As I pass under the arch, I look back and see no one on the section of road visible behind me. I fold myself down into my bike and begin the descent.

I take the corners as fast as I can. I fly out of the exits, no more than a couple of centimeters from the verge. The few spectators on the descent retreat from my frantic progress. The television motorbike does not try to keep pace ahead but follows me from behind.

At the bottom of the hill, I pick up a pedaling rhythm again. It feels natural, despite my growing tiredness. I wonder in the moment whether this could really be sustainable, whether this could be my day.

My radio coughs into life. "Get back. Get back," Rafael sings. "Get back to where you once belonged."

I keep my head down. I think that I will keep riding. I will take my moment at the front. They ask me to ride, I think. They would be foolish to rebuke me for riding too hard.

I change my grip on the bars; I move forward in the saddle. I shift up a gear. I suck my teeth. Then, however, the road begins to slope up again. I drop three gears. I concentrate on paddling the pedals around. I keep my shoulders steady. I clench my jaw.

We enter a town and I see the spectators looking past me, down the road. They are waiting for something else. I am not the actor but the thing to be acted upon. I look back. The peloton comes up the road like a wave. It sweeps up to me in seconds. It flows around me. I turn to see Fabrice. "You made us wait," he says, and it is hard to tell whether his rising tone expresses surprise or consternation. Then he nudges out to the right of the mass of riders and puts in a sudden burst of speed. Tsutomo follows. The fans jostle to catch a glimpse of it all, shifting and shouting, open mouths and waving arms.

With Fabrice out in front, I gratefully sink to the back of the pack, happy to watch the break make time. Reports among the riders say that a group of seven has coalesced around Fabrice. He is gaining on his rivals in the overall classification. Everything is going well. I remind myself that I have done my duty for the day. I will my legs around. I try to enjoy the respite of riding at the back of the group and ignore what only I know: that this recovery was not chosen but necessary, a humbling.

Chapter 7

I roll into the finish to find that Fabrice has stayed near the line to greet Tsutomo and me. He grabs me into an embrace while I am still on my bike. His race kit is soaked with sweat, clammy now that he has stood waiting for us to arrive. He came in in the first group, making time on his rivals. To Fabrice's side, Tsutomo stands over his own bike, his elbows resting on his handlebars, his head bowed. "My boys," Fabrice says. "My friends."

In the finish area, there is a crush of photographers, journalists, officials, VIPs, and men handing out water. A man in a fluorescent vest takes hold of Fabrice's arm and pulls him toward the mic zone, past fans leaning over the barriers and shouting, reaching out to brush their hands against us. Fabrice keeps hold of me. I step off my bike and am dragged behind him. We come to stand on a carpet in front of an array of cameras and microphones. Riders to our left give interviews. Arms extend toward us holding microphones and recorders. Red lights turn on. A monitor to our right plays footage from the stage finish. The road turned a sharp left and steepened in the final half kilometer of the stage, and now, on the screen, I watch Fabrice accelerating around this final corner, spinning away from the breakaway group with a striking smoothness. He had no need to fight for the stage win today. He was seeking time on other contenders in the group behind, and probably would have done better to sit and grind his way to the line rather than engaging in the bursts and fakes of riders setting themselves for the finish line sprint. I watch his mouth in slow motion, gasping air, his lips pulled back against his teeth. The fans are screaming, thrilled, banging against the barriers, all arms and eyes and camera flashes.

Fabrice sees me looking at the TV. "I got carried away," he says quietly, as the footage shows the other riders catch and surge around him, as we watch him tuck with great difficulty into their slipstream. He looks at the carpet. Shakes it all off. "It was a good day. I didn't need to do that."

I gesture at the fans leaning over the barrier. "That's why they love you," I say.

He smiles coyly at this, like a teenager paid a compliment. Then he gathers his resolve, turns to the journalists, his arm around me. "I brought a buddy," he says in a different, confident voice. The reporters look at me briefly, then back to Fabrice.

"A good result?" someone asks. The crowd shifts. The clump of microphones pressed in front of us bristles like a living thing.

"Oh," says Fabrice, "certainly. You know me. I just try to do my best." He lolls a tongue out of the side of his mouth in a pantomime of fatigue. "Luckily, today my best was good enough. Or wait." He pulls me closer toward him. "Me and my team's best."

Another journalist asks Fabrice how his tour has gone in general. "Ups and downs, my friend," he says. "I have been on the roller-coaster."

How come, a short lady with a sun visor and a Dictaphone wants to know, Fabrice has improved so quickly after the previous days' disappointments? "It is," she says, "pretty incredible." She gives full time to each syllable of the last word. The implication is not difficult to recognize.

Fabrice waits and then smiles. "Thank you," he says. "It is always nice to get compliments." There are some laughs from the journalists.

"I'm glad," says the woman, deadpan, matching him, "but I was also asking *how*."

"Oh." He sighs, suddenly weary, catching the eye of another journalist. Then he breathes in, smiles widely again. "You would like some tips." There are more laughs. He pauses to take a prolonged drink, taking care to display the branding on the bottle's side to the cameras. "I am afraid there is no magic formula," he says. "I have worked very hard this year. I have made small gains in many places. My training has improved. My race preparation has improved." He points to me. "My team has improved. I have made changes to my diet."

"What kind of changes?" asks the lady.

Fabrice points to the logo emblazoned across his racing jersey. "Chicken nuggets," he says. "Healthy, nutritious, and full of energy."

Those clustered around us laugh again, louder now. Fabrice raises a hand in farewell and we fight our way back through the crowd and toward the team bus. The journalists want to believe him. Fabrice's strength, his unlikely response to the previous stage, is the thing that makes the narrative today. You are allowed one piece of magic, no more, and he has been careful to not ask too much of their faith.

* *

In late spring I returned from a training ride to find Liz scrolling through a triathlon website. The important information about performance-enhancing drugs is easily accessible on the Internet, prosaic in contrast to so many other transgressions possible in cyberspace. Amateur triathletes are the ones who are truly uninhibited. Their Internet forums are extensive. They all seem to have day jobs in finance and bring their ruthlessness and asymmetric personalities to bear on their hobby.

They talk about how to grease their thighs to slip wet suits off faster. They debate the taste and digestibility of different energy bars. They touch upon many odd things, and in the midst of all this banality, they discuss methods of doping.

"It's fascinating," Liz said. She sat back and looked at me. "These people are so driven."

"They're nuts, triathletes," I told her.

She nodded. She wanted to stay serious. B was asleep in the room next door. He would wake soon, we both knew, and go through his routine of trying to reclaim his soft limbs from slumber, this body new to itself, reestablishing its bounds. She told me about an experiment some scientists in San Diego had done on pigs. They put the pigs on a treadmill and made them run. Through surgery, they loosened the pericardium membrane that surrounds the heart of each pig. The pigs were set trotting on the treadmill again, and with this membrane cut, their endurance was 30 percent better. "The heart's capacity *increased phenomenally,*" she said. There was probably some terrible side effect to slicing into this protective membrane, Liz said, but she thought someone would try doing such a thing in humans. "It's crazy," she said, as much in admiration as reproach. "Someone will try it, for sure."

I didn't linger too long on this kind of stuff. It felt beyond what I needed to know. Liz was surprised by my limited interest in the subject, almost offended. She was like a Victorian explorer, arrived on a volcanic island and perturbed to find the islanders using pumice and swimming in thermal pools but entirely uninterested in the geological phenomena that had produced such things.

* *

Rafael, sitting in a canvas chair near the bus, watches Fabrice and me approach. "That was racing," he says. "We showed all the fucking fucks." The mechanics come and take our bicycles. We stand in front of Rafael. "You know what?" he says. "Tonight my balls will not be aching. No one is chewing on them, no sponsors, no journalists, no other teams, no riders. You know what also?" We shake our heads. "Tomorrow is your rest day. You will have some recovery. Perhaps you will see your significant others." He winks at me.

"It's a good day," says Fabrice.

"Yes," says Rafael thoughtfully. "I am just a man like any other man, but it seems people are always trying to fuck me where I do not want to be fucked." He shakes his head happily, stands and slaps Fabrice on the back. He is in one of his moods of forceful geniality, of overbearing fellow feeling. He pinches my shoulder. Sometimes he descends from his position to move among us. He does so with the ease of an aristocrat in a pub: an ease born not of commonality but of an inability to distinguish the suspicion with which he is viewed.

I think of the middle of winter, on a preseason training camp, when Rafael joined Fabrice and me for a ride. We were in the Spanish sierras. I sat on a bench outside our accommodation, jogging my legs in the chilly morning air, enjoying the sun that had just risen at the head of the valley. To my surprise, Rafael appeared beside me in full kit. "I'm riding with you boys," he said.

Fabrice had arrived too. "Lucky," he said. "We're going slowly. Today is a recovery ride."

"Do you know how many races I've won?" said Rafael.

"You're retired," said Fabrice.

"True," said Rafael. "But remember what I retired from. I rode in the age of champions." He walked away from the bench toward the garage in which our bikes were stored. It was a shock to meet him at this hour, so close and intense. Fabrice and I followed.

"There are champions in any age," said Fabrice.

Rafael spat air. "But I rode in the old days, before the benefits you have: the new bikes, the doctors, the assistance."

There was a silence.

"Of course, that's the way it is," said Rafael. "That's just the way."

"You were so full of pills you rattled when you hit potholes," said Fabrice.

"God!" said Rafael. "And what good it did us? Have you ever raced on amphetamines? Yuck. You feel terrible, and what is the result? You ride like a crazy fool. You, my children, do not know how lucky you are."

In the garage Fabrice and I took our own bikes, Rafael Tsutomo's. The road was empty and we rode three abreast. "You do know," said Rafael, "that I don't want to do it?"

"What?" said Fabrice.

"The substances," he said. "All of that."

"Yes," said Fabrice. A car came up behind us. We didn't shift. Its engine changed in pitch as it dropped a gear, swerved around us to overtake.

"But it happens," said Rafael. "We have to make money. The sponsors have certain expectations. I do not want to wear a raincoat, but if it rains . . ."

"Yes," said Fabrice dully. "I understand this. This is how I work, knowing this."

"I think about it," said Rafael.

"I know," said Fabrice. He was uninterested in hearing more. I could sympathize. His disquiet was that of a patient faced with a doctor who insists on "laying out the options." He had ceded control, abdicated choice and the incumbent worries. He changed to a higher gear, stood on his pedals, and surged away. He idled and let us catch him. "It's a good day," he said. "I feel good."

* *

At the end of the camp, Rafael drove Fabrice and me to the airport. The whole team was being split amongst different cars, and he made an effort to pick us as passengers, as if he still had something to prove. "You're part of something," he said. "You both understand this?"

"Yes," said Fabrice. "Of course."

"This is your year," said Rafael to Fabrice.

We drove steadily down the mountains, toward the sea, the landscape drying as we lost altitude and then becoming verdant once again as we approached the ocean. We did the drive mostly in silence. Despite his knowledge of the Beatles and Bon Jovi, I have never witnessed Rafael listening to music. I have seen him take whole plane journeys simply sitting blankly. I am still unsure whether his mental life is immensely rich or utterly minimal. Once I offered him a newspaper during a flight. He looked at me surprised. "I am a patient man," he said.

We reached the coastline and turned south. "We're going to be early for your planes," said Rafael, looking at his watch. "I have somewhere I want to take you." The road ran along the top of a steep slope overlooking the sea. Little lanes plunged down to secluded beaches and coves. Above us steep hills, lightly forested with pine trees, built to a range of cliffs. Rafael clicked the indicator and turned off the main road, down one of the lanes to the sea's edge. We switchbacked down, feeling the muted winter warmth rising off the rocky landscape through the open windows of the car. "This is a treat," said Rafael. "A real treat for both of you." Asphalt gave way to a stony track and we crunched on toward a fishing village. "Beautiful, no?" said Rafael.

"Sure," said Fabrice.

"Come on," said Rafael. "Look at this place. Relax. What do you think is going to happen? We're going to see somebody, somebody great, and you're not even going to get poked with a needle."

Five or six houses huddled where the sea cleaved into a bay. There was a short concrete jetty and a circle of dust behind the houses on which four cars were parked. Rafael stopped the car and got out. Fabrice and I followed him. The air smelled salty. I could feel the moisture in the light wind. "What do you think?" I said to Fabrice.

"No idea," he said.

"His mother?" I said.

"I don't know," said Fabrice. "That would assume he was born of woman."

Rafael walked over to the back door of one of the houses. He knocked and waited. A cat appeared from around the corner of the building and brushed itself against Rafael's leg. He gave it a gentle kick. A woman, about the same age as Rafael, opened the door. "Rafa," she said. She hugged him. She saw us over his shoulder and beckoned us into the house. "It's good to see you," she said to Rafael. "We've been getting bored of each other here. I'm not going to say it's been easy." Her Spanish accent was thick, a little hard for me to follow. She beckoned us over. She guided us through the cool center of the building. It smelled of dried cat food and coffee. "Visitors are unusual these days, I'm afraid," she said.

Rafael shook his head. "How could I pass by?" he said.

She opened a door and stood at the threshold. "You've always been one of the good ones," she said to Rafael. She stroked the back of his head as he passed.

The room had a syrupy airlessness. Black-and-white photographs covered the walls. Between them, old woolen cycling jerseys were tacked up, their colors fading, their sponsors long bankrupted, re-named, or subsumed into other companies. An old man sat in a leather chair, his small body almost lost in its plushness. He looked at us through large glasses that sat on a tumorous nose. He smiled wanly at Rafael. Rafael pointed to him, then looked at Fabrice and then me, grinning. "Eh?" he said. "A dream come real, no?"

Fabrice smiled. "Oh . . . yes," he said. He moved to shake the old man's hand.

Rafael frowned. He looked between us. "You know, no?" he said. "The Crazy Hare, la Liebre Loca?"

A tiny hand reached from the folds of the chair to join Fabrice's.

"Remind me," I said.

"Jesus," said Rafael. "You really are just pairs of legs, you boys."

"He's familiar," I said. "I just asked for a reminder."

"*Today riders threw themselves at the Galibier like spiders trying to climb from a bath tub,*" said Rafael, projecting his voice from the back of his throat. "*The heat on the climb was intense, and the gradient shattered the peloton apart. Great climbs such as these are the domains of great riders and today a young man from the south of Spain, whom they call the Hare, staked his claim for consideration on these terms . . .*"

Fabrice released the old man's hand and the man's arm fell back to the chair as if it were something dropped. "Pleased to meet you," said Fabrice, "An honor."

"*L'Équipe,*" said Rafael. "I could recite the whole story if you wish."

I moved toward the man. I thought I should greet him. His skin had a disquieting looseness; in places it was cracked and chalky, at others glossily translucent. I have never done well with old people. I took his hand and he blinked. His palm was cold. "A pleasure to meet you," I said.

His left eye closed slightly. "Good morning," he began to say,
until the phrase broke into a racking cough. He jerked his right hand
out of mine, toward his face, but it reached a limit of strength or flexibility just beneath his chin and stayed there clawlike and shaking as
he coughed. His left arm remained at his side.

Rafael nudged me out of the way. He took a tissue from a box
next to the Hare's chair. He put his hand gently behind the old man's
skull, his fingers running through the greasy gray hair. He lifted the
man's head and put the tissue to his mouth. The Hare's fit reached
its conclusion. Rafael lifted the tissue from the face, a fibril of saliva
stretching between it and the man's lip, and dropped it into a waste-
paper basket. He put a hand on the Hare's shoulder and looked directly into his eyes. "All right?" Rafael said. He leaned in and kissed
the Hare on the cheek. "It's good to see you, old man," he said.

Outside the house, the Hare looked different. It had felt, walking
him slowly from his back room, that the coastal sunlight would rip
through him. In reality, it plumped him out, gave depth to his wrinkles.
In the manner of abandoned boats and old agricultural machinery, he
looked picturesque. Rafael held the Hare's left arm at the elbow and
gestured expansively with his free hand. "Quite a day," he said. "Eh?"

The Hare was warming up. "Yes," he said. "This is my weather."

Fabrice stood looking out to sea. "Fabrice," said Rafael, "this,
here, is a true champion."

"I know," Fabrice said flatly. "Those great days. The newsreels.
Don't think I don't know."

"This was his childhood home," said Rafael. "This is where it
all comes from. This man invented us." He breathed in as if the air
around us should contain some trace of the origin he spoke about.
"There is a line unbroken from him to you. Think of this. It is worth
very much to preserve, no?"

The Hare saw the car branded with our team's logos, its lurid fluorescent striping. He raised his right arm and pointed a bent finger. "The car," said Rafael. They walked toward it.

The woman had come out of the house and she stood next to me. "Are you his daughter?" I said. She nodded.

"I'm glad you came," she said. "Rafael is a good man. It's a shame he never became a father."

She looked at the others standing by the car. "The bikes," she said. "He'll want to see the bikes. You should get your bikes out." She shouted to Rafael. "The bikes, Rafa. Show him the bikes."

Having taken a bicycle from the car and reassembled it, we passed it to the Hare. He steadied himself by gripping the white-taped handlebars. Behind him, Rafael held both the Hare and the bike.

"You know," said the Hare's daughter, "I think he wants to ride. Let's let him ride."

"Really," said Fabrice. He looked at the Hare. "Do you want to ride?"

The Hare flinched in an attempted shrug.

"I'm not sure he'll be able to," said Fabrice.

The Hare frowned. "I can," he said.

Rafael and the Hare's daughter worked with the bike and the Hare. They took down the saddle. They radically inclined the bike to one side and lifted his leg over it. They clamped his hands to the handlebars and placed his feet onto the pedals. Rafael held him upright, seated now on the saddle.

The old man looked purposefully ahead. His daughter bent and quickly tucked his canvas trouser legs out of the way of the chain, into beige woolen socks. Rafael smiled. "Are we ready?" he said. "Are we ready for the moment of truth?"

The Hare's mouth turned down a little. The expression preceded, by a moment, his pressing on the pedals. Then his knees began to move slowly. Rafael started to walk with him. The tires of the bike crunched over the grit and dust. He was still leaning severely into Rafael as he rode. Rafael struggled to hold the small man with his own slight frame. The Hare began to pick up speed. He began to describe a circle around the parking lot.

They made a full turn before the holding got too much for Rafael. He gestured to me. "Swap me out," he said. "We need somebody larger."

I came over and took the Hare's weight. I clasped the handlebars where Rafael had been gripping them. The Hare's body pressed against me. I smelled his sour smell. I was so close to him that I could feel his limbs vibrating in their fragile, old-man tenseness. He started to push the pedals again. I was on the inside of the circle and he pedaled leaning in. He sped up a little. I trotted, and the pressure against me became less, though he was still unsteady.

The Hare grunted with the effort of it all. I had a sense, in the moment, of why we were there, of Rafael's intentions in bringing us to meet the man. The glories of his past were present to the Hare as he cycled. He was a better set of quadriceps and lungs away from being able to race as he had last done forty years ago. He grunted again: a hoarse, hollow sound, as if he were being emptied. We would have to stop soon. He was riding to his limit, tiring himself as he had when he raced, simply to do these tiny laps. He had time-traveled from his prime, from when things were last so vital. Forty years though, I thought. Forty years.

* *

I pad slowly through the hotel again. I have had my massage. I have eaten a snack. I wait for dinner.

The hotel has a roof garden: some decking laid down between architectural gestures. I go up and stand in the wind. Air outlets sprout fungally from the hotel roof. Cloud is striped in fine lines across a mackerel-skin sky. Cowls creak. I find a protein bar in my pocket. I eat it. I ball up the wrapper and drop it onto the decking, where it begins to twitchingly unfurl again. I feel the evening breeze coursing over the rooftops. I open my hand and hold it above me, letting the air play through my fingers. This is what I aim for: not the podiums or flowers or paychecks (or not only them), but the feeling of justified exhaustion, the satisfaction of having done what was asked of me. I hear some cats fighting, and somewhere far in the distance an emergency vehicle. The heavy door to the roof opens, clangs shut again.

"Hello," says Rafael. His hands knead each other. The satisfaction of the race finish must be wearing off.

"The pickup has been organized," he says. "I have spoken to Liz."

There is something I dislike in hearing Rafael use my wife's name. It's the same feeling I have had on trains, carrying B, chatting happily to him and yet encountering the glare of another passenger who appears not to think I respond to B's gurgles and demands as I should.

Rafael departs, and I stand and wait for the feeling of satisfaction to return to me. It does for a time, though the wind is now pulling up goose bumps on my forearms. I will see Liz, I think. I will see B. I leave the roof and close the door behind me. I walk back to the room, pleasantly giddy with my tiredness, with the thought of the two of them arriving so soon.

* *

Before I left for this race, Liz, Davina, and I had dinner at an Italian restaurant. Katherine watched over a sleeping B back at home. The high summer sun was still up as we were seated, and we sat at a table by the window and watched people leaving the park across the road. Liz and I talked about B, and our lives around him, and only when we had talked for some time did we ask Davina whether anything was new in her life. "I'm having an affair," she said. She laughed, pleased by the effect of saying it this way. She had met a man who worked for a commercial shipping company, she said. He lived in Newcastle and came down to London for work every couple of weeks. The two of them went to cheap hotels in the afternoon. "The logistics are difficult," said Davina.

"It sounds like work," said Liz.

"It's fun," said Davina. "The subterfuge. It makes you think people care." She laughed again.

I ordered pasta and when it came finished only half of it. "Is that all you're having?" said Davina. She herself was dismembering langoustines with great fluency.

I explained how important it was to come into the tour with no excess weight, half-starved, in fact. "You do this for sport?" she said. She laughed. She cracked a shell, tugged out white flesh. "It's insane."

"I know," I said.

"It's the doing," said Liz, "that is important."

"Perhaps," I said.

"Dr. Johnson wrote about seeing a man riding three horses at a circus," said Liz. "He said it was important not because of what the man was doing but because it increased our sense of human capabilities."

"That's good," said Davina. "I like that." She looked at me. "You're pushing our idea of what a man can do."

I understood, I suppose. I might use the anecdote one day. The sport I am engaged in is a game, but there is a level at which it surpasses that, at which the dedication, the logic and attention applied make it vivid, real, and meaningful. To cross the finish line first in one of those old storied races is not merely to have pedaled but to have played a part in a piece of theater, to have enacted a struggle, a narrative, from which conclusions about character and the tendencies of our age can be drawn. Liz's and my professions are similar in this way. We have small, specific goals, yet there is some implicit romance here: an unspoken claim that a deeper appreciation of life emerges from our focus, from our resolve to apprehend infinity not by cowering in submission to all that lies beyond us, but through meticulous reexamination of single things.

* *

For once, I am not rooming with Tsutomo, but with Fabrice. Usually Fabrice, as team leader, is entitled to his own room. Stage races normally have their casualties, and I suspect, though he hasn't mentioned as much, that Rafael has booked fewer rooms from this point in the race onward, expecting somebody to have gone home by now. Instead we have all hung on, suffering and giving mixed performances: something less desirable in Rafael's mind than crashing or burning out in a more single-minded pursuit of victory. Fabrice has been pushed into sharing.

As I pause at the door of my room, I can hear Fabrice clipping his toenails. He clips his toenails each night. To clip a day's growth seems impossible, so I suppose that he cuts ever further toward the cuticle. It's one of his many ceremonies of preparation. He likes the idea that he need not carry the crescents he cuts up the next day's climbs. I've asked him why he doesn't shave his head for the same reason, and he has told me that he has considered the idea and decided that the psychological drawbacks of coming to resemble his father would counteract any weight savings.

When I enter, he sits on the middle of his bed, contorted, given totally to his task, as content as a mystic at prayer.

I sit on my own bed. I watch him grasp a toe and position it for the scissors. There is a pressure upon him that I do not always bear in mind. Those of us around him—Rafael and the team—are not just sources of assistance but symbols of expectation. He pulls off a tiny crescent of nail. He lays it on a piece of open tissue on the bed. His big toe is vivid red, like the head of a newborn. He works on it with a nail file. "The rest day tomorrow," he says without looking up.

"It's great," I say.

"I have a good feeling about it," he says. "I'm going to rest like a champion."

Chapter 8

I am jolted out of sleep. There is someone in our room, standing between the beds. "Fabrice," he hisses. I recognize Rafael's voice. I sit up. Rafael nods at me in the half dark.

"What?" says Fabrice. He lifts his head from the pillow.

"You have to get up," says Rafael. He looks at me. "You too, Solomon." His voice is different so early: fragile and husky. "The dope man is coming in twenty minutes," he says.

Fabrice sits fully up now. "We're good?" he says.

Sometimes, if we are surprised just after a treatment, we may be forced to drink glass after glass of water so that traces of what we have taken are flushed through our systems. "You're as clean as the pope's pajamas," says Rafael.

He leaves the room. We climb from our mattresses and pull on tracksuits. Fabrice looks at his watch and then at me. "Ten minutes," he says. I nod. We return to the warmth of our respective beds. "The rest day," Fabrice says. He exhales heavily. "It's the rest day and they give us a six a.m. drug test."

In ten minutes' time I hear voices outside the room. Rafael is out there, and the Butcher. A phone rings briefly, then is silenced. There are footsteps down the hall. "Rafa," says a voice I do not recognize, that I take to be the tester. "How are you?"

"Henri," says Rafael. "I am working very hard. You know how it is."

"Yes, of course. You are very industrious. Your riders are ready, do you think?"

"Who knows?" says Rafael. There is something in his tone I know: a need to play, a compulsion to press his advantages for the sake of doing so. "They have just woken up. I think they might need to get themselves ready. I think they might need to drink a little before they can pee."

"By the rules, they should be giving their samples now," says the tester.

"Of course," says Rafael. "But they are in a stressful situation. We should wait for a little time."

"Hydration is very important, Rafa." The tester speaks primly, in jest. "Dehydration will impair your boys' performances. I would have thought you knew this."

"I do not know everything," says Rafael.

"This I cannot believe," says the tester. Both men laugh.

Rafael comes into the room alone. "Drink," he says.

"I thought we didn't need to," says Fabrice.

"No," says Rafael. "But we cannot give away everything so easily. We need to keep these men flexible." He goes out again.

The door to our room is opened five minutes later. We sit up in our beds. The tester is of average height, middle-aged, with brown hair and a side parting. To him, I think, already up and around this morning, the room must be stuffy, close, sour with sleep. He places his bag on a chest of drawers which sits between Fabrice's bed and my own. "I am sorry to wake you up, gentlemen," he says. Rafael and the Butcher stand in the doorway, watching. The tester squats between our beds, looks each of us in the eye. It is disquieting, his sudden closeness. He rummages in his bag. "Blood, then urine," he says. He takes out a syringe. "Who's first?"

When the tester has gone, we stay in our beds. I snooze. I am used to being up for breakfast already. My arm aches where the blood has been taken. At nine, I get a text from Liz. "Off the ferry," she says. "Driving. In the car of the tired and the tearful." I lie for a while, but I cannot sleep now. I get up, wearily, feeling my aches and pains. I shuffle around in the bathroom, waking up.

* *

At the breakfast table, the others are taciturn. It is as if the rest day, this reprieve from riding, is too good, as if it might disappear with our explicit acknowledgment of it. Everyone eats slowly. Near the end of the meal, Rafael comes over to where Fabrice and I sit.

"Did you get back to sleep?" he says. He doesn't wait for an answer. "I have a plan for you two."

"Yes?" says Fabrice. He chews a mouthful of banana. He takes a sip of coffee.

"An easy ride."

"Yes?" says Fabrice. It is obvious that we will ride today. It is said that our legs—half-sentient things, apparently—need to be *reminded* that they still need to cycle, that the race is ongoing.

"Yes," says Rafael. "With a guest."

We meet in the lobby of the hotel in the early afternoon. We will do the ride, I tell myself. We will eat again. Liz and B will arrive in town.

Sebastian stands in front of a rack of leaflets. He looks at brochures: for wine tours, for a cheese museum, for a water park, for a castle, for a crocodile sanctuary. "So much to do," he says.

"You want to go to a crocodile zoo?" says Rafael, arriving behind him. "Now things make sense."

"How is being a cyclist incompatible with going to a crocodile sanctuary?" says Sebastian.

"Would champions go to a crocodile zoo?" says Rafael. "Would your father?"

"My father is a boring and intolerant man," says Sebastian.

Rafael grunts, turns. "Are you ready?" he says, looking at Fabrice and me. We nod. "Good," he says. "Our guest is coming."

"Who?" says Fabrice.

Rafael points to the logo on Fabrice's jersey. "An executive of your sponsor. An important man."

"Nuggets?" says Fabrice.

"Nuggets."

"Can we ask him why we have brown shorts?" says Fabrice.

"No," says Rafael. "Brown is clean and natural, they tell me. It is about reminding the consumer that their chicken nuggets come fresh from the farm."

"My sweaty brown shorts?" says Fabrice.

"Brown is the color of environmental sustainability," says Rafael. "They have had certain image problems in the past year. Did you see that documentary about the chicken factory? The bootleg Bulgarian antibiotics? It's a wonder that all they're asking is that you wear brown shorts."

* *

The Nugget Man arrives in our team cycling kit, shoes and all. He has gray hair, lively eyes, and pristinely white teeth. "Comrades," he says, bearing these teeth in a smile.

Rafael greets him with an embrace, then guides the man to stand in front of us.

"Your riding companions need no introduction," says Rafael, "just as you need not be introduced to them."

"We're grateful for your sponsorship," I say. Fabrice nods slowly in agreement.

"I'm glad," says the Nugget Man. He is about fifty. He looks us up and down. "You've had some tough days." He grimaces and the tendons in his neck briefly reanimate the sagging skin around his Adam's apple. "Are you fellas well?"

"Yes," says Fabrice.

"I respect your dedication," says the Nugget Man.

"Anything to sell some nuggets," says Fabrice. Rafael gives him a reproving glance, though the Nugget Man is unflustered.

"I don't like to think of us as selling nuggets," says the Nugget Man. "Really, I like to say, we sell family mealtimes. Do you have children?"

Fabrice jabs a thumb in my direction.

"Isn't it hard to get them to sit down at the table?" he says.

"Mine's not even one yet," I say. "Sitting at the table is all he can do."

"We make baby food," says the Nugget Man. "I'll send you some baby food."

"Thank you," says Rafael.

The Nugget Man breathes deeply, changes tack. "We are a family company," he says warmly. "You play a role in that. Your dedication, your diligence—"

"Yes," says Fabrice.

"—you show us how to behave, how to get things done."

"I think of us more as a warning," says Fabrice.

"How so?" says the Nugget Man.

"I have not been to a party in five years," says Fabrice. "I am not a normal man."

"But you know it," says the Nugget Man. He is imperturbable. "That is important."

"Are you ready to take a ride?" Rafael says to the Nugget Man. "Don't go too fast for them."

The Nugget Man laughs.

"Seriously," says Rafael, looking at us but speaking for the benefit of the Nugget Man. "This guy is a proper cyclist. He could have been a pro, I think."

"Not quite a pro," says the Nugget Man. In his engagement with this claim I feel faintly embarrassed on his behalf.

Rafael leads the way out of the lounge, through tall glass doors, into the car park where the Butcher waits with three bicycles: Fabrice's, my own, and another matching model in team colors.

"Your bike!" says Rafael to the Nugget Man. "I hope it fits."

We pedal out onto the road. The Butcher follows us in the team car. Fabrice's open mood of last night is gone. I suspect he is annoyed by the Nugget Man's presence on this ride. Fabrice is accommodating until something encroaches upon his core concerns. Now he pedals sullenly, inside himself. He sits still on the saddle, his face set. The Nugget Man and I ride in front of him. The Nugget Man looks back at Fabrice occasionally. Fabrice's uncharacteristically dark mood works in his favor: he is the champion and a certain strangeness is expected from him. "He's so focused," the Nugget Man says.

* *

Liz asked me about Fabrice's romantic life after she had come to see us race in the spring. It seemed odd to her that I knew so little. He has had girlfriends since I've known him, but never for long, never apparently seriously. I have not met any of them. He has not confided to me a single thing about these relationships. "Is he repressing something?" Liz said. I told her that I didn't think so. My hypothesis is that he simply doesn't have the energy to give himself to loving. He is more of a fundamentalist than I, and he preserves all he can for racing. I think of my first months of knowing Liz, which felt so consuming to me. She exceeded human scale in my mind. I'd leave the house to cycle and trick myself into thinking I'd seen her passing in a car, or in the midst of a crowded shopping street, as I rolled along. The rides in those days were a torment. The possibility of her was everywhere. Her face seemed to dissolve in my memory as I thought of it, broken down by these misrecognitions. I began to fear I wouldn't know her if I were to see her, that I would pass right by her. Fabrice is not a man for that kind of stress, that disorder, that lack of control.

* *

Fabrice, the Nugget Man, and I roll into the car park. The Butcher takes our bikes and shoos us toward the dining hall.

The Nugget Man eats as we do, looking around him all the while, smiling like a boy at his own birthday party. No one talks. At the end of the meal, Rafael comes over to me, swinging a set of car keys around a bony finger. "Liz has just got in," he says. "Would it not be nice to go and see your wife?" He hands me a tracksuit. There is not time, it seems, to run up to my room. I put the tracksuit on over my riding kit. I take off my cycling shoes and my socks. I walk to the car barefoot.

We drive a short way around roundabouts, past supermarkets and DIY megastores. We pull into the car park of another hotel. "Here we are," says Rafael.

We walk across the hot asphalt toward the hotel reception. I like the sensation against my bare soles: something deeply felt, near to pain. Every now and then I tread on a bit of gravel and this gnarls my posture for a second. Rafael catches my expression at one such moment. "At least look glad," he says. "You being happy to see your family is our cover."

"I am glad," I say.

In the lobby Rafael asks for a surname that is not my wife's, not my own. He is directed to the third floor.

The hallway upstairs is quiet, lit only by the windows at each end. The carpet is worn and sticky. Rafael counts off the rooms. "This is the one," he says. He knocks and immediately after the knock I hear the sound of B's excited gurgle. Liz opens the door holding B. She looks well, despite the long drive. Her hair is mussed. She has a small mole on the right side of her nose, near the tear duct. It gives her glance a minor asymmetry, which I like. In those days when I worried that I would not recognize her, I clung to the memory of that mole.

I embrace her and B. Their scents mix: her skin, his, baby powder, deodorant, a tang of sweat.

Rafael steps back to find a view by which to frame our meeting. "Pretend I'm not here," he says. He waits awhile. "Behind every great man, as they say."

"Are you okay?" Liz says. "You look tired."

I nod. "Don't I know it," I say.

"He's a soldier," says Rafael. "Knock him down and he asks if it's all you've got."

"I'm glad to hear that," Liz says.

"I take care of my boys," says Rafael, "like they're my own God-be-damned family."

"We just got in," she says. "Do you want to hold him?" She hands me B. He is heavy, or I am tired, or both. I am gladdened by this surprise, though, and by his robustness, the way he shifts so much. There is a roving curiosity in him, a litheness antithetical to the self-possession of the tired, wary men I have been spending my time around.

"Look at that," says Rafael. "That's what it's really all about. That's why we do it all, isn't it?"

B looks up at me happily. His head is inclined upward. A filament of spit drips from the edge of his mouth. His fat hands clasp at my jacket.

"Wow," says Rafael. "What a sight. It warms the heart and all of those things. If only we could stay all day. I think, though, you have something for us, no? A little gift, shall we say, from a friend of ours?"

Liz turns and walks to the back of the room. We follow her. B's romper suits are spread around on top of a dresser, Liz's clothes folded and piled next to them. She unplugs a blocky machine by the window. She wraps its power cord around it and hefts it into a roller suitcase, which she zips up and drags over to Rafael.

"What's the machine?" I say.

"Portable freezer," says Liz.

"It plugs into the little cigarette thing in the car," says Rafael. "Amazing, no?" He looks at Liz. "You kept it on always?"

"Of course," she says. "I can follow instructions."

"You can," says Rafael. "This is true. But you'd be surprised how many can't."

They both laugh and yet I am outside of this joke, suddenly angry.

The freezer is needed only for blood transfusions. The blood is mixed with various chemicals so that the cells within it do not simply burst on being frozen. I think of the little freezer chugging away in the car for Liz's whole drive down here.

"You said it was just hormones," I say to Rafael. "You said you wouldn't ask her to carry blood." I shift my grip on B, who is surprised for a moment, though he doesn't cry.

"The specifics changed a little," Rafael says. "I talked to Liz. I realized she was capable."

"Why didn't you tell me about this?" I say to Liz. I am talking quietly for the sake of my son, my voice hoarse.

"I made the calculations," she says. "I made a judgment."

"Oh love!" says Rafael. "The trials and tribulations of true love!" He lifts his watch hand in a firm gesture and takes a sightless glance at it. "How nice it would be to stay, but really we must be getting on."

A toilet flushes in an adjacent room. A clattering of tortured plumbing reverberates through the wall space.

"You said only hormones," I say again.

"We needed the blood," says Rafael. "You don't want the blood?"

"Blood was not what we talked about," I say.

"I agreed to it," says Liz. "I'm a person. I make decisions. I've looked into this stuff. I've read how it works. I've been through the research papers."

"You're not pleased to work with your wife?" Rafael pretends to look shocked. "It has seemed to me such a happy marriage."

"I'm perfectly glad to work with *her*," I say. "I just don't want her involved in all this."

"You don't want her working with *me*?" says Rafael. "I did not expect to hear this."

I look at Liz. "Why would you do this?"

"I made a decision," she says. "I did it meticulously. I did everything he instructed to the letter."

"This is true," says Rafael.

"He paid well," says Liz.

"She speaks the truth," says Rafael. He points at B. "She is thinking about his future."

Liz takes care to catch my eye. "I was on your side," she says. "I was doing it right. I was watching out for you."

"It's done, anyway," says Rafael. He pats the suitcase. "It went well. All is fine. Why such a fuss about a cake that is already baked? It's done and now your beautiful wife and charming baby are here. Everyone can relax, no?"

B splutters in my arms. I take a tissue from the box on the bedside table and wipe at his face. He giggles. "That's the correct spirit," says Rafael. "What a lovely family." He smiles at Liz. "Stay here. Have fun. I will book you a hotel for after tomorrow's stage." He looks around. "A *nicer* place."

*   *

The room Fabrice and I share is full of bodies. Rafael and the Butcher are here, as well as Tsutomo, Fabrice, and myself. Rafael repeats his routine of looking behind the curtains and under the bed. This time he goes into the bathroom and taps at the air vent; he breathily sings "A Little Help from My Friends." My awareness of him is sharpened by my anger over the way he has drawn my wife further into our circle.

We drove back from Liz's hotel in silence. Rafael occasionally gave himself driving directions, responding too, murmuring, "That's right" or "I remember this." I do not think that in a million years I could change his mind about the smallest thing. Now he turns the television on and then off again. He presses a button on the room's smoke alarm and it emits a sharp beep. In the corner of the room the small freezer stands, unplugged and empty. The Butcher has long ago commenced defrosting the blood bags. He squirts in another liquid and then closes them again. He massages each bag. He lays them out on the table beside him.

"What a day for reunions," says Rafael. He looks at me. "First your wife, and now some of your blood."

I only nod. The blood is that extracted months ago by the beleaguered dope doctor. It was harvested at the height of our training and is rich in red cells. The blood in our veins, meanwhile, is ever more dilute, its capacity to carry oxygen diminished by the attrition of racing.

Fabrice lies back on his bed. Tsutomo sits next to him. Others on the team will be attended to later, in different ways.

I sit on the floor at the foot of the bed.

"Ready?" says Rafael.

We roll up our sleeves and lie back. Rafael takes a pillow from the bed and passes it down to me on the floor. I tuck it behind my head.

The Butcher locates a vein just beneath my armpit. He cleans the skin with a small piece of alcohol-soaked cotton wool. He inserts an IV needle into the vein. I incline my head to see my blood chasing up the needle into the head of the catheter.

"Keep still," says the Butcher. He goes back to the table on which the blood bags have been placed. Each bag of blood is numbered, and each number refers to a key Rafael has written in a small notebook he now holds. "Five hundred and forty-nine," says the Butcher.

Rafael nods.

"Give me some of Fabrice's blood," says Tsutomo. "I want to be really strong."

Rafael, unlike the others in the room, doesn't laugh. He takes Tsutomo to be sincere. "It doesn't work like that," he says. "You're a different blood type."

The Butcher connects a tube to the bottom of my blood bag. He palpates the bag, working steadily to get it to the end of the line. This tube is then attached to the top of the catheter. I feel a slight ache where this new blood flows into my arm. He affixes the bag to the wall above me with a piece of medical tape. "Now you just wait," he says. "Okay?"

When we are each connected to our bags, the Butcher takes off his latex gloves. He turns off the overhead light. He opens the door and slips out. Rafael stays sitting in an armchair, still as usual. There is a minibar refrigerator beside the bed. Tsutomo reaches down, opens it. "I can have a Diet Coke?" he says.

"You are joking?" says Rafael. "Those things are four times the price they should be." He snorts, points up at the bag taped to the wall above Tsutomo. "Is that not enough?"

We are silent then. I hear a phone ring in another room, the elevator arriving and departing, the patter of a child running down the corridor.

The annoying thing is that Rafael is not wrong about how welcome the treatment is. Though I usually prefer to look away from needles and blood, this time I keep looking at the tube and the bag connected to it. The blood coming in is still cool; it spreads a numbness through me, making the hairs of my arm stand on end. This discomfort makes me feel the efficacy of the treatment, just as bitter medicine feels more potent than sweet. The ritual of all of this is a comfort. It tells me that things will be better tomorrow. The therapy will work almost imperceptibly until I am on the point of collapsing, then I will feel that extra level within me. I will remember then that I am supported, that things have been invested in me. I am no fan of the danger of the process, but when I consider the way the team has got into me—altered my chemistry to my own advantage—I am grateful. Rafael and the Butcher understand, I think, and they act on this understanding. They try to help because truly, unlike the men with microphones, replica kits, or drug-testing paraphernalia, they know how much is asked of us.

I think of Liz in the slightly grubby hotel room, among the disarray of unpacked things. She has come all this way. She is here. It is done, as Rafael said. Perhaps she even saw more clearly than I that she could manage her task, that I would be glad of what she brought.

*　*

I didn't plan to end up near London. I had spent my early twenties living in northern France, racing there, chasing down a career. Just after I got a contract with Rafael, however, my father got sick. I went back to the South East to be with him. I wanted to get my fill of him. My mother was living up in Liverpool. She hadn't seen him for years. He was older than my mum, already middle-aged when I was born, and now he was an elderly man who regretted smoking. He wasn't fierce. He wasn't interested in my career.

Previously I had found myself wanting to orient him to the precise context of my achievements—that I was one rider in so many thousand, and so forth—as I am so reluctant to do at other times. But going back, I tried to let him be. He'd simply have preferred that I'd played football.

I read him stories about West Ham United from the sports pages of the newspaper. I read him one of those thick histories about the battle of Stalingrad. He did not have specific preferences as to the manner of his death. He just wanted to get through it. I went to him often, but I also kept training and racing. My days were stripped back. His body was slowly wasting, my own strengthening. Perhaps I was glad of this contrast, this chance to delude myself that in this divergence lay a chance to escape the fate he was suffering.

I stayed in my father's house. I cleared out a room at the back. I had clothes for cycling and clothes for going to the hospital in. Though it would be nice to roll out onto perfect roads each day, you can train almost anywhere. We may race in teams, but training is a private thing. You just need clear asphalt ahead of you or, failing that, a room in which to put a trainer, and a few hours to yourself.

I met Liz in the airport a month after my father had died. She was a reason to stay, her appearance an unbidden blessing.

* *

Rafael walks around the room looking at the draining blood bags emptying into our veins, each of us our own sort of timer. "Not long," he says. He looks at Fabrice. "This will help us in the mountains."

"Yes," says Fabrice. His voice is hoarse, quiet.

"One flat day," says Rafael, "and then the big hills, the time when the race really gets shaken up." He massages one hand with the other. Fabrice nods.

"You'll make time on the inclines," says Rafael. "No one can climb like you on the steeps."

"On my day," says Fabrice.

"We'll make it your day," says Rafael.

When the bags are utterly drained, Rafael makes one last circuit, flicking at them. "Every last drop," he says, "every single percent."

The Butcher returns to the room. He takes the needles out of our arms, stemming the leak of blood with a cotton pad we are to hold to our skin. He peels the blood bags from the wall. The medical tape, I notice, leaves the slightest glossy mark on the paintwork. The Butcher and Rafael bundle the equipment away, careful not to leave anything even minutely incriminating.

We file out of the room quietly. I feel chilled from within. We go out into the hotel's small courtyard, like hospital patients on a walk. We sit on a bench in the evening sun.

After some time, Marc comes into the courtyard. He asks if we are well, how our joints are bearing up. We give vague, clipped answers. We decline Ping-Pong. Eventually, he goes back inside.

I stay on the bench when the others leave. I think of Marc stalking the corridors of the hotel. I get a text from Liz. "We're unpacked," it says. "Shall we come over after dinner?"

* *

In the bike room at home I have a calendar of Yorkshire landscapes: windswept trees, old cottages in green valleys, meandering stone walls, the sun always fighting its way through the clouds. I mark things on the calendar in code, partly for secrecy, mostly to save time.

Liz and I have discussed Yorkshire. We took a holiday there before B arrived. I have a dream of buying an old farmhouse there. Setting up a country life. It is a joy to just say the names of the famous road climbs: Shibden Wall, Fleet Moss, Thixendale, the Stang.

I have considered woodwork. I am good with my hands; I have spent so many hours working on bicycles. I have the temperament. Liz is not sure. "Who makes money through carpentry?" she said, when I first brought the idea to her.

"I could do specialist jobs," I said.

"Yeah?"

"Restoration."

"And pay the bills?"

"Artisanal crafts are coming back."

"You're an artisan now?" She laughed.

"I could be."

"I don't doubt it, but it takes time to get that kind of expertise. Have you thought this through?"

"Of course," I said. "Have you?"

We could have the city and also space, I said, the chance for B to grow up as a country boy. Liz is suspicious of small villages though. "We'd be so isolated," she said. "Stuck out there, driving each other mad." I suggested that she could try for university positions in York or Leeds. "It's not that simple," she told me. "I have specific skills. There are only certain projects I could work on."

"You couldn't get a job at one of these places?"

"I don't know," she said. "I'm not sure it would be right for me."

"Because your work now is such a success?"

She looked at me, waited. We were sitting at the kitchen table. She stood, left the room.

This criticism was too close to hand, too clumsy. It was brutal but not smart. We each talked plenty about failures in our careers, yet each knew the seriousness with which the other approached their work. Between us we seemed to have agreed to never doubt the other's dedication, never to second-guess their commitment.

I was not sure about the carpentry plan, of course. I had wanted her to play along though, eager to toy with the idea that there were other options for us, different lives we could be living. The fantasy of the early days of our relationship—the sense that she could draw me out of myself—still turned over inside me, and though I had no right to hold her to the dreams I had conjured up in those days, I felt wounded when she pushed against the very thing I had thought she could facilitate.

Yet she had her expectations of our relationship too, I suppose. I thought of her favorable comparison of me with her friends: as a doer, as a taciturn, driven man; not the kind of person to give up on his prospects in favor of vain schemes, half-considered images of other lives.

*   *

In the early evening Liz comes to visit me at the hotel. I am sitting on a bench in front of the hotel when she arrives. I see her walking up the long street and know her—one tiny figure among others— without understanding how. She wears a blouse, white jeans. She looks elegant, happy, like a woman on holiday (as she is, I must remind myself). She carries B on her front. We go to the hotel café. Because of Rafael's fear that sex should destroy our racing form, he forbids private meetings with spouses during tours. "I do not want you to feel the temptation," he has said.

"We have to stay down here," I say to Liz.

"Why?"

"Rafael is scared we'll rip each other's clothes off in privacy."

"Of course," she says. She smiles as if in recognition of a proclivity of Rafael's that she knows.

Liz jogs B on her knee. His face shakes and his eyes widen.

A waiter brings us cups of herbal tea. Liz stirs her bag. The spoon tings against the cup. "It was crazy doing all that stuff for Rafael," she says quietly. "I'd make a good spy."

"I'm sure you would," I say.

There are a couple of journalists in the café. They watch us, recognizing me as a rider. I feel compelled by this to play a role, to be jollier than I feel inclined to be. Though I would like to retread the argument from the hotel, instead I take my time miming my pleasure, leaning forward, laughing. I let Liz's casual mention of Rafael's plan pass. I find myself loosening as we talk, no longer acting pleased but becoming so. I catch this slippage momentarily, tell myself to hold on to my grievance, and yet *why*? Liz tells the story of the fraught drive down the country with B. He was sick on her as she stood refueling the car. It is awful, vivid, funny as she recounts it. I chuckle and cough warm camomile tea back into my cup. I had forgotten this feeling, somehow. She watches me, smiles, shakes her head.

I am no longer considering the audience of journalists when a hotel guest, a tall man with gray hair and glasses, appears beside me to ask whether I could autograph a napkin. "Are you sure you haven't mistaken me for someone else?" I say. "A better rider?" He snorts at my joke.

This is new to Liz, I realize: this respectable man with his unlikely admiration for what I do. The gravity that the Tour affords is unknown to her. She has watched the grind of my training, the small races I do at home, but she has not seen this before. She is noticing the attention of others in the room behind me, and I feel this attention illuminates me, causes her to attend more closely to my gestures and speech. The waiter brings us more tea. For the first period of this long race I do not monitor my watch but allow myself to lose track of the time. It is B's tiredness that ends the evening: he is restless and must be taken back to their hotel. Liz and I hug. I kiss my son on the forehead. She walks with him out into the twilight, and I turn toward the elevator, taken with the gratifying thought that there are still new things I can show her.

Chapter 9

We drive to the start line through rain. I do not like rain: the sodden shorts, the up spray of dirty water against my face. It uses up much-needed reserves of forbearance as soon as we begin to race. Fabrice has told me before that he feels differently. He enjoys the weather, drawing his pleasure from the knowledge that it bothers others more than it does him. This is a difference between Fabrice and me. He cannot just endure but knows that his endurance is reliable and unique.

When we arrive, the Butcher and his assistants set up gazebos branded with our sponsor's logos. We hurry to them from the bus, seeking the middle of the shelters where the gusty wind will not blow sheets of rain toward us.

Shinichi stands by a barrier watching us. He wears our team jersey as usual, but over it a large see-through poncho. He looks cold. He appears so miserable that, though I must stand in the rain to do so, I go over to talk to him.

"Hello, Shinichi," I say.

"Hello," he says.

"Bad weather, isn't it?" I say.

Shinichi shakes his head. "No. Good weather. This weather is good for us. Tsutomo will show you today."

"We're a team," I say. "Tsutomo, Fabrice, me ..."

Shinichi looks at me. "You say he can't?"

"No," I say. "Well, maybe. We have priorities. Tsutomo will not try to win."

149

Shinichi shakes his head more vigorously now, loosening the raindrops that cling to the hood of his poncho, sending them running down the surface in rivulets.

"Maybe," he says, unwillingly. "Who says?"

"The stage is flat," I say. "We'll all finish together. There will be a sprint."

Shinichi looks disappointed.

"You just need to wait," I say. "His time will come."

"Wait?" He laughs now. "You think you only need to wait to have your time?"

I go back to the coach. It is dim, quiet. I sit rubbing Tiger Balm onto my legs, kneading my muscles. Other riders are elsewhere, warming up, going to the bathroom, doing interviews. I look up to see Liz moving down the aisle of the bus, holding B.

I smile. B beats his arms up and down. "Hello," I say. She shuffles into the seat next to me. She passes me B.

We sit for a time. I enjoy the smell of B's scalp. He grabs at me with his small sticky hands. We sit in silence. This is a kindness of Liz's. During her maternity leave, as I trained at home on the turbo trainer, she gave me space. My mornings were my own. I would sit in the little room with only the hum of a flywheel and the click of gears. Some riders listen to music or even watch films while on the trainer, but I need to feel the time. I waited it out in silence, studying the crack in the paintwork above the skirting board, the slight steaming up of the window. I relished the passing of these hours, sensing as they went by that I was accumulating something, gaining some second-order pleasure in my attention to this accumulation. Now, on the bus, I want to perceive the minutes ticking down until the race, to feel myself arrive slowly at the start.

Rafael climbs onto the coach. My heart sinks to see him approaching. "My favorite family!" he says. Liz laughs. "VVIPs!" he says. I resent the way that he can avoid the nerves I suffer. I know that he will feel the result of the race more intensely than I will, but beforehand he is ebullient, happy, patient in a way he is not usually, while I am the opposite. He stands in the aisle.

"You slept okay in that hotel?" he says. "I am sorry. I owe you an apology. That hotel was of poor quality."

"It was fine," says Liz. "I've stayed in worse places."

"I cannot believe that," says Rafael. He grins and gives a little nod. "But it is nice of you to say so. My colleague, the one we call the Butcher, is as you say in the doghouse for this. The one we have booked for you tonight will be better, or he will be in trouble. I will make him sleep outside."

"I'm not sure that will be necessary," Liz says. She grins. "But thank you."

He leans across Liz, touches my shoulder. "You are well?" he says.

"Yes," I say. "Fine."

"It is a happy situation," he says. He laughs. "Your family is here. The stage will be good, I think."

"Of course."

"It is raining, but what is raining? Are you a cat?" He looks at me with an intensity that suggests he expects me to answer.

"No," I say. Liz laughs at that. On my lap, B giggles too.

"Not a cat," says Rafael. He turns to B. "Your daddy is not a cat." B is glad to see the funny little man. Rafael widens his mouth in a manic grin, turns his eyes loose. B screeches with delight. I would not have expected Rafael to be good with children, but then he is a man who commits.

* *

In spring, I suffered insomnia. Liz speculated that it might be the drugs or the pressure that surrounds them, but instead I thought of a crash I had suffered in a race the previous year. I was descending through a village when a dog ran out in front of me. I pulled the brakes and turned the bars. I still hit the animal, though only softly, as the sudden deceleration had channeled my momentum up and over it. I came down on the road headfirst and lay there stunned at the edge of the village. A couple of spectators rolled me onto the verge and picked up my bike. My helmet had broken like a melon and drooped behind my head, attached only by the strap running under my chin. The dog was a Labrador and its owner blamed me. He attached it to a short lead and shouted that I should have been able to avoid it. The dog was fine. The man was scared by my condition, I think.

The team car arrived. The doctor, Marc's predecessor, shone a light into my eyes, holding my chin with his latex-gloved fingers. They checked my bike over and gave me a new front wheel and another helmet. They asked me some questions that I answered. I finished the race. Only later, in the shower, did I feel blood dried into my hair.

In March I had headaches and couldn't help but wonder whether that fall was the cause. I replayed the moment, again and again, the memory acquiring a definition and a coherence it could not have truly had. I have since thought often of the crash, wondered whether its effects have stayed with me. Probably the symptoms I suffered come from stress or from my new regimen, but there is some attraction in returning again and again to that stuttering image of myself going down on the road, to the drama and the idea that I was changed suddenly and by accident.

The insomnia passed, at least. Davina heard of my sleepless-ness through Liz and forced an herbal medicine on me. "You need to restore your natural rhythms," she said, as if the concept was in-contestable. My wife, loyal to her friend and interested in seeing an experiment conducted on me, made sure I took the pills each night. Despite my considerable skepticism, I found them effective.

I had other physical problems, after that, some so embarrassing I could barely tell Liz. My nipples became puffy, swollen, and sore. I rubbed Vaseline on them. I couldn't bear to wear a woven shirt. I de-veloped blotchy rashes. I only told Liz about the problem when I saw her studying my chest as I emerged from the bathroom.

Liz was sure it was the drugs. She speculated that it was one of the hormones, giving the body the wrong signals. She burrowed deep into Internet forums and the next day she handed me a set of pills. I took them nightly, and after a week the swelling had subsided. Liz told me they were the same pills she used to stop inflammation while breast-feeding. She found this very funny. She entreated me to call Rafael to offer news of this cure in case any other riders on the team were suffering similar difficulties.

*   *

Hans the mechanic passes me my bicycle. I mount up and ride out from the gazebo into the rain, ready to get wet and stay so for the next few hours. I have missed seeing Fabrice as I usually would. I feel out of sorts, rushed. Others are already ahead of me on their way to the line. My route to the start passes the bus. Liz stands at the open door. I pedal toward her. "I'm taking him to the hotel," she says.

"Yes," I say. I think of all Rafael's promises about the place.

"*We're* on holiday, at least." She lowers her chin to look at B. "We're going to have a bath, aren't we?"

Joe Mungo Reed

"I'm jealous," I say.

She looks at me steadily, silently urging me not to rush, to calm myself. "Honestly," she says. "It's good to be here. You're doing well."

I kiss her. I mount my bike. I roll off, and the spray flung up from my tires is already dampening my shorts. This is me, I think. I built this career, brought us all here. I am happy, for a moment, imagining the hushed, clean room that my wife and son will arrive in.

*　*

The start on rainy days is always muted. Fewer people are here to watch. They are in coats, under umbrellas. Groups stand back from the line, in doorways, waiting until the start is imminent. The commentator runs through his introductions. We riders all keep our heads down. Above the start line, flags wrap wetly around their own poles. When the starting horn goes, the fans rouse themselves to shout.

The hiss of our tires shedding water cloaks other sounds. Our plastic coats diminish our sense of others around us. Jackets cover numbers, jersey colors, familiar postures. It is hard to identify others in the peloton. Though cycling is a noncontact sport, one comes to relish smaller, locating feelings: the chittering gears of riders around you, for instance, or the feeling of air moving across your skin.

The topography of the stage is unremarkable. It is flat and fast and we all should end bunched together, sprinting down the high street of a southern coastal town, with Fabrice tucked in the wind shade, saving himself for the mountains the next day. It is a day to display the prowess of the peloton, to show that it is a machine which, when needed, can eat miles at little cost.

We sit and spin and take in the rain. Spectators huddle under umbrellas. Five riders have broken from the peloton and headed up the

154

road. As usual, they will be caught before the finish. There is a grayness to the sky and a misting across the landscape that make it hard to tell where the flat fields around us end and the sky begins. The route rolls endlessly through agricultural grids. Until one cycles and is forced into them, one forgets about these marginal landscapes, between the city and the truly pastoral countryside. When one cycles, one becomes aware that these areas are what mostly compose the world.

* *

At times I find it odd to be where I am, riding amidst the peloton. I have cause to check my own complacency. Selection for the big races is never a sure thing, after all. The squad is large enough that not all of us start the major events. At the outset of each season we are compelled to renew our claims for inclusion.

The training camp, earlier in the year, was a venue for competition in this respect. Ostensibly we were there to train, to get ourselves up to speed for the season, but we were also being judged. At the end of the week we did tests: physicals with the Butcher, power tests and a timed hill climb.

We sensed that our lifestyles were being monitored. Riders made defensive and offensive moves. Most of us kept to our rooms. Some played tricks. An anonymous rider called the hotel reception impersonating Tsutomo and had three burgers ordered to his room on the team bill. Someone else set a wake-up call for me at two a.m. the day before our biggest ride. Johan, lobbying to have more resources devoted to his sprinting in the coming season, took to oiling his thighs each morning. He would emerge from the hotel into the morning sun, his legs glistening, brown, as shiny as furniture in a stately home, his skin seeming to strain to keep all the muscles in their places.

On the last day of the camp, Fabrice and I went on a ride together. It was not necessary. We had completed all our drills and tests, and others were readying themselves to leave. There was no need to continue to impress Rafael. It was a bright day though, and Fabrice was eager to feel the winter sun. I said that I would ride with him because he appeared to want company and because I felt the need of some time to think, some moments away from the claustrophobia of the hotel. We took little food and not much water, because we would not be out for long. It was a pleasure to be so lightly loaded.

We climbed up out of the rocky, temperate landscape in which the hotel was situated, up toward truer winter. The road ran next to a river, which came down the valley, and was shaded in many places by broad trees. In the shade it was chilly, but the sun was hot on exposed skin. We rode fast to stay warm. Fabrice led most of the way up the climb. He had a spring to his pedaling motion. He whizzed along at a high cadence that seemed to deny all effort.

At the head of the valley, where the river steepened into small falls, the road peeled upward, ascending through the thin tree growth, nosing back and forth up the incline. We could see that above there was snow on the mountains. It was morning and there were still some small bits of ice fringing the slower-moving sections of the river. Fabrice pulled over, raising a hand to warn that he was doing so, out of habit. He had a puncture. "Don't stop," he said. "It's cold." He had his bike flipped over already, the back wheel nearly prized out of the frame. I had braked but stayed track-standing, balancing on my pedals. "There's a reservoir by the road, up there," he said. "I'll race you to that. You'll get a minute's start on me, maybe more." I released the brakes, lurched off up the road. He had the wheel in his hands. He began to work the tire off with his thumbs.

The training camp had not gone well for me. I had not found

my form over the week but felt heavy legged and awkward. We did a timed hill climb at the end of the week to assess our conditioning, and I was well beaten, not just by Fabrice (whom I would have expected to lose to) but by Tsutomo and men I should have easily surpassed, like Sebastian. Johan was not far behind my time. I supposed that I had choked in the hill climb test and never settled into enough of a rhythm. I sweated every stroke. I crossed the line at a crawl. Rafael was still to "process" our numbers over the coming days, and I did not relish the thought of this.

Still, I felt good that morning with Fabrice. I was glad of the chance to push into the incline, to play at Fabrice's little race. I stood on the pedals. The first switchbacks came and went easily. I felt better than I had all week. I had found my pace and felt that I could keep it. I stood, built a speed, rocked the bike beneath me. I did not feel that I could go any faster, that anyone could. A sign by the road declared that the reservoir was two kilometers away. The road crossed a bridge, then steepened. I pressed into the hill, stood, and pumped my legs to keep pace. I heard the sound of a gear change behind me. I looked back down the road and saw Fabrice on the bridge. When he hit the point that the road pitched up, he did not appear to slow. He came toward me surely, his eyes on me, his shoulders level. He came past me, and I tried to stay on his rear wheel. I was leaning forward over the handlebars, collapsing onto my bike, while he hovered, just touching the nose of his saddle, his legs spinning fluidly. His hands, with their thin fingers, were draped over the bars, as relaxed as those of someone resting on the armrests of a chair. The calmness of it all astounded me. We went past the reservoir and kept going. I struggled to stay in his slipstream.

We rode for five more kilometers until I eventually cracked. I dropped gears and sat back in the saddle. Fabrice carried on for fifty meters up the road and then turned and rode toward me. There was a lay-by next to us, and we freewheeled into that and set our bikes down. It was a sun trap, improbably warm.

I was spent. I clambered off my bike and doubled over. My lungs were torn up by the effort and the cold air. Fabrice stood, taking in the view. I laughed between breaths.

"What?" he said.

"You're a beast," I said. "You're a monster."

"What?"

"Riding like that after a week of training camp."

"Oh."

I took a moment to get hold of myself again. I walked over to my bike. I retrieved my water bottle. I went to stand next to Fabrice. We could see down the valley: the trees, the river, the rocks, flashes of the road we had ascended, in the distance the hotel. A car came down the road, rattling: a Fiat Panda, a farmer's car. "How do you do it?" I said.

"I love it," he said. "I love all of it."

I could see the reservoir below: a chunk of turquoise, clouds reflected across it. "I love the sound of a freewheel," I said. "I like the smell of the grease."

"That's not it," he said.

"I like feeling strong in a race," I said. "The sense that you have more strength than the others."

"No," he said. "That's not it. The thing in itself."

"The thing in itself?"

"The riding."

"You love the riding?" I said. "Every minute of it? All of it?"

"There is only all of it," he said.

"I'm good at it," I said. "I like parts of it."

"I love all of it," he said.

The Fiat had left a tinge of gasoline in the air. I coughed and spat.

"Love it and it will love you back," said Fabrice. He inhaled as if preparing to say more but then did not.

*   *

As we approach the town in which we will finish, the roads widen. The route coils, rising on concrete bridges, plunging down underpasses.

Here we finally catch the group of riders who broke away earlier in the day. The pace begins to increase, building toward a sprint finish.

Our team must again usher Fabrice forward, not seeking victory for him but trying to get him across the line in the first group so he loses no more time. Keen to avoid repeating previous mistakes, we begin to move him toward the front of the group. Johan, as usual, is lost to us in the hunt for another win. We form into a line as a team and Tsutomo leads, incrementally forcing himself into the personal space of the riders around him, worrying out a gap for the next of us to inhabit and pull Fabrice into.

As we get closer to the center of town, the roads narrow again. The turns become tighter. Warnings are shouted out amidst the peloton.

The town is incomparably noisier than the countryside. The crowds are thick here, and cries are contained by the tight layout of streets and buildings. We pass up a boulevard where baskets of flowers hang from streetlights. The regular transit of their bright colors through my peripheral vision marks our pace.

We cannot be picky about where our wheels land. Our trajectories are decided by the group at large. I crash through potholes and puddles, thump across drains and traffic markings.

I ride just ahead of Fabrice. I turn to check that he is on my back wheel. We pass under the five-kilometers-to-go banner and the pace jumps. The rain and wind are now coming from behind us. I think that I hear the sound of a ship's horn from the town's harbor.

"*On your left!*" goes up the shout, and we lean together, swinging suddenly left. We pedal through the corners here, maintaining our pace, leaving no gaps. The peloton accelerates again, up the straight, though the rain, and wind now cuts into us from our left side. "*On your right!*" comes the call. I pass it on myself. I hear Fabrice do the same. The riders in front of us dip away as they lean sharply into the turn. We lean ourselves, training our eyes on the exit. Then the rhythm is broken. I see a rider thrown out of the smooth movement of his colleagues ahead of me. Amongst the procession of bent backs there rises, for the briefest moment, the rear wheel of a bike, a flailing arm. Another couple of riders pitch forward in his wake.

A crash at this speed is like a bomb going off. All our momentum meets this tangle of bikes and bodies, going into or over it. I can steer neither right nor left because of the crush. I brake, take a quick breath. My front wheel hits something and twists sideways, as if snatched. I am flying over my handlebars, my feet still snagged in the pedal clips, dragging the bicycle behind me. I raise my arms reflexively. I fall toward a writhing mass of flesh and metal. Our bicycles have gone immediately from our mode of travel to sharp objects with potential to do us harm. I hit bikes and bodies and my hip contacts the wet tarmac. Metal and plastic scrape against the road surface. My feet release from my bike. An object flies over me. A wheel strikes my shoulder. Someone's trailing leg hits me. I am conscious of the smells of the wet asphalt and the oil of the road. I hear brakes screeching, people swearing. A final rider barrels into our prone group with a damp thump.

We lie cowering. We wait. Someone puts a hand on my back. We hear the television helicopter hovering above us. We hear those riders lucky enough to evade us zipping past. There can be no more, surely. There is a momentary stillness before we all try to stand.

Our standing is a trauma in itself. We are covered with each other's bodies and bikes. We push bikes off us and onto other people. We bump into each other and tread on still-prone riders as we climb upright. The pain too, begins to register. I feel the rawness of my upper right leg and an intense pain in my pelvis. I find my bike. Fabrice stands crouched as if trying to keep his weight off one leg. His left knee is cut deeply, blood flowing in lines around the kneecap. Tsutomo's arms are grazed and the shoulder of his team jersey ripped into tatters. We're each standing though, unlike others behind us. We have to make it to the finish, we know. We do not linger. Treatment, assessment of our injuries, can wait. The adrenaline of the accident can be used in our progress to the finish. This has happened before and will again. We remount our bikes unsteadily and begin to pedal. Our bikes click and complain, their gears having been knocked out of adjustment by our falls, but we are up and rolling. Around us, other riders struggle to do the same. A zombie peloton of cyclists, lacerated and bleeding, reforms for the last two kilometers.

At the line, Marc is a man transformed. We are battered and cut up and neither we nor Rafael can deny his help any longer. He awaits us at the bus. He bends his tall frame over and looks at each of us in turn. He puts on new latex gloves for these inspections and sheds them at the end. They pile at his feet like a glossary of sign language terms. He presses at our injuries. He asks questions. He talks to us with an off-handedness that his usual meekness would not permit. Marc makes calculations of urgency and risk. He attends to Fabrice first of all, and when he has done so, prompts our team leader to sit in a canvas chair, an ice pack pressed onto his shoulder.

My thigh hurts acutely. I see people looking at the point where my shorts have been ripped open. The strands of lycra curl away from the wound like a burnt outer layer of skin. Tsutomo stands silently next to me. The Butcher regards us. "I've got some job tonight," he says.

Johan comes past. "You look like shit," he says. He is changed into a tracksuit already. "Seventeenth," he says, answering my look. He shakes his head. "But at least I missed your shit show."

"That's a consolation," I say.

"Your man looks bad." He points to Fabrice, slumped in his seat. "You might not be working as domestiques tomorrow. You might have no one to assist."

"It's a bit early to be saying that."

"It's not all bad. They could let you off the leash." He reaches to pat me on the shoulder. "It's the mountains. Get in a break, get some camera time, try for a stage win."

"I'm here for Fabrice," I say.

"I'm just saying," says Johan. He moves off, back into the crowd.

Rafael emerges from the bus as I approach it. His hair is wet. The shoulders of his jacket are dark with rainwater. He looks at me and says, "And you a father?"

I nod.

He says, "You call that taking care?"

The crash didn't originate with me. I was hit by another rider and he, probably, by another before that. The TV stations will surely analyze the footage, seeking to find a culprit. Short of a truly egregious mistake on anyone's part though, we riders are as happy not knowing, remaining as superstitious as fishermen and attributing the crash to fate, to something in the wind.

I shrug. "They took my front wheel down. You've been in the peloton. You know how it goes."

"Just because somebody's been a chef," he says, "it doesn't mean they like spit in their soup."

"It was random," I say.

"You could have moved him forward earlier," he says. He stalks off toward Marc.

* *

The bus is overwarm even in this rainy weather, the windows fogged. I take a seat next to Tsutomo. The pain in my leg sears. I try to visualize it, to imagine it as a red shape slowly turning a cool blue. "Shit day," says Tsutomo. Rafael returns to the bus to speak to the Butcher, who sits just in front of us. Marc and the race doctors want Fabrice taken to the hospital to be x-rayed and CAT-scanned. Rafael is suspicious, convinced of neither the severity of the injury nor the notion that the hospital can do more good than he and the Butcher.

The atmosphere quietly intensifies. Around us other team buses depart. We are creatures of routine and we feel instinctively that we should be elsewhere. It is time for massages, for our return to the dim rooms of the hotel. The vehicle's engine is running to power the lights: a stultifying rhythm which promises progression but never builds.

My phone rings. It is Liz. "Hi," I say.

"You're alive?" she says. "That looked nasty."

"I'm okay," I say. "Torn up. Living, though."

"We watched all the replays on the TV."

"You know what happened better than I do."

"Perhaps," she says. "A rider went too wide around the corner ahead of you, hit a barrier."

"There you go," I say. "Rafael says we should have been farther ahead in the group, that we should have missed the crash."

"It wasn't your fault," she says.

"I don't know."

"It wasn't," she says. "We watched it again and again: the skid, the collisions, the ruck of you all going down. I watched it so often I'm surprised I don't have grazes myself."

* *

Eventually Rafael accedes. He directs the bus driver to return the rest of us to the hotel. As he is about to descend from the bus, he turns to Tsutomo and me. "You boys might as well come too," he says.

We walk toward the team car, past technicians dismantling the finish area scaffolding and rolling up the kilometers of wires required for broadcasting. A man deflates a giant yellow kangaroo—a promotion for an Australian energy drink—by stamping against its collapsing hide. What air is left in the inflatable causes the kangaroo's head to rise with each stamp, its large cartoonish eyes seeming to seek witnesses to this assault.

Fabrice is already seated in the back of the car, looking pale. "You okay?" I say. Tsutomo and I slide onto the rear seats next to him.

He holds out his hand, palm down, and flutters it. "Sore," he says. "You?"

I look at my own legs: the road grease, torn skin, and ripped lycra. Blood has run down my shins in thin lines, mixing with the dirt.

"Sore," I say.

Tsutomo nods in agreement. "Sore," he says, closing the circle.

* *

In the hospital Tsutomo and I are taken into different rooms and checked over. The doctor who examines me is a tall, slim woman. She tucks a graying strand of hair behind her ear as she talks. "A cyclist?" she says to me.

"Yes," I say. I look down at my leg, above which her gloved fingers hesitate. "A dangerous sport," I say.

"Tell me about it," she says.

"Do you cycle?"

"No," she says. "My son does."

"Seriously?" I say.

"He's ten," she says. "He's always falling off."

She scrubs at the cuts with cotton wool soaked in iodine, staining the skin around them. She closes up lacerations with stick-on butterfly stitches. "Let's check for major damage," she says. She has me lie back on the treatment table and moves my leg back and forth in a motion that reminds me of somebody removing a drumstick from a cooked chicken. "Does this hurt?" she says.

"Yes," I say.

She nods and moves onto the next leg. She asks again whether it hurts and I reply again that it does. "I don't think anything's broken," she says.

"I told you it hurt," I say.

"But you were not vehement," she says.

I leave the doctor's room and wait in a hallway with Tsutomo. We sit on a plastic bench. Farther down the corridor a janitor mops slowly, moving away from us, backward, erasing his own footprints. Tsutomo fidgets, jogging his knees and clicking his fingers. He too has had his cuts cleaned and been pronounced only bruised. "I don't like hospitals," he says. He shuts his eyes.

Rafael comes out of a consulting room and sees us. "Idiots," he says.

"Us?" says Tsutomo, opening his eyes again.

"No," says Rafael. "The doctors. They're encouraging Fabrice to abandon the race."

The Butcher appears behind Rafael. "To *consider* abandoning," he says.

"Why?" I say.

Rafael karate chops at his own shoulder in demonstration. "Fractured collarbone," he says.

"We can probably stabilize it," says the Butcher. "Then it's just an issue of pain management."

"We think they've underestimated him," says Rafael.

"And us," says the Butcher.

We are silent for a while. Rafael scuffs his shoe against the linoleum floor. "What about you boys?" he says.

"Soft tissue," says Tsutomo.

"My hip hurts like hell," I say. "The doctor wouldn't consider anything beyond bruising."

"Really?" says Rafael.

"She was quick and dismissive."

"Is that so?" says Rafael, interested. "She did not take her time?"

"No."

Rafael turns to the Butcher. "We should have directed Fabrice to that doctor. She sounds like less of a busybody."

The Butcher nods.

A doctor comes out of the room and indicates that Rafael should follow him down the corridor in order to talk discreetly. "He's a professional," I hear Rafael say.

"There's a lot of bureaucracy these days," says the Butcher to Tsutomo and me.

"They sound worried," I say.

"They're doctors," says the Butcher. "That's their job, just like mechanics find problems with cars. We just need to manage his injury for a day or two, keep him out of trouble, let him ride it off."

"You can ride off a fractured collarbone?" says Tsutomo.

"We'll strap it," says the Butcher. "Keep it still. We'll give him some tablets."

The doctor strides past us, back into the consulting room. Rafael wanders over. "Progress," he says. "They're letting us take him back to the hotel. I've told them we'll likely withdraw him."

"You will?" says Tsutomo.

"No," says Rafael. "But these people worry. They deal with ordinary people, mostly old people. They do not know what you riders can"—he searches for the word—"tolerate."

The doctor returns, followed by Fabrice. Fabrice wears a hospital tunic and has his arm strapped across his chest. He has on disposable paper slippers. His frail shuffle alarms me more than anything. I wonder whether it is pain or his sedation that causes him to move so deliberately. He smiles at Tsutomo and me, then shakes his head as if to say, *What can you do?*

"Over to us," says Rafael.

The doctor nods slowly, gravely. He is a neat man, his peppery hair styled with precision. He waits with his hands behind his back. "He's not going to sleep well tonight," he says.

Rafael wags a finger proudly. "This is yet another area in which he is unusual. He is very good at resting. Also, we are very good at facilitating our riders' sleep." He points to Fabrice. "This man has a special pillow probably worth more than your TV."

"This isn't a problem solved with feathers," says the doctor.

Rafael rubs his hands together. "Time to go," he says. He looks at the doctor. "You can get back to your patients." The doctor exhales and walks away, crossing the newly cleaned floor, taking a single weary glance back from the doorway of a consulting room before disappearing. Rafael moves to stand in front of Fabrice. "I know this is silly," he says, "but if you could look strong, that would help. There might be journalists or fans around. We don't want news spreading. We don't want your competitors sensing weakness."

Fabrice nods.

"How about we cover the arm?" says the Butcher. He takes off his team fleece and helps Fabrice into it, zipping the strapped arm inside the garment. It hangs in baggy folds around Fabrice's torso, disguising the bulge of his elbow.

"What about this?" says Rafael, taking hold of the empty right sleeve.

There is a box of tissues on a small Formica table beside the bench on which Tsutomo and I sit. The Butcher pulls a succession of tissues from the box, balling them loosely and stuffing them into the sleeve. He pushes the end of the sleeve into the pocket of the hospital pajamas Fabrice wears. This false arm looks spindly and unconvincing. Fabrice is a cyclist though, whose real arms are as useless as a snowman's. We all agree that the effect is good enough.

Chapter 10

I room with Fabrice again. When I come back from my massage, he lies in bed, the covers tucked up to his chin. He stares at the ceiling. His face is bloodless, that of a shop mannequin. He acknowledges me with the smallest movement of his head. I leave the room. His pain is more extensive than mine, something beneath which he has submerged himself, while the discomfort of my hip makes me itchy, restless. I have an urge to walk a little, to tease at the sensation, to break Rafael's rules. The corridor is quiet, lined with pictures of trees. There is an arboreal theme: a green and brown carpet, the walls painted dark red.

I walk and find my way down to the hotel business center. It's a windowless room, a square of desks running around the walls, six computers spaced between them, a large printer in the corner. Sebastian is the only person in the room. He looks up at me when I enter. He sits at a monitor, a long figure, a Modigliani, leaned back in his chair, his long right arm extended, stroking the mouse. He looks different in this situation. There is a grace to him, I think, when he is not contorted over a bicycle. He missed the crash, riding up ahead with Johan. "What are you doing?" I say.

He shrugs. "Not much. Financial news. I am learning about economics."

"Yes?" I say.

"This career doesn't go on forever, you know."

"I know."

"The Dow is up," he says. He turns back to his screen.

I sit at a computer. Its screen is dark. I do not turn it on but instead fiddle with the office chair, pushing the lever to lower the chair with a whoosh of air. Another guest comes through the door. He looks at the two of us. He wears a crumpled cotton suit and has a press card on a lanyard around his neck. "Are you riders?" he says.

"What?" I say.

"Cyclists?"

"We're businessmen," I say.

"Is it true that your team leader is retiring tomorrow?" he says.

"We do business," says Sebastian. "We just happen to be very skinny."

"The Dow is up," I say.

"It's a good day for us," says Sebastian.

The journalist shakes his head and leaves. I look back at the dark monitor.

A few minutes later, Rafael enters the room. "I've been looking for you," he says. He looks at Sebastian. "What are you doing?" he says.

"The FTSE is up," Sebastian says. "The DAX is down."

"Go away," says Rafael.

Sebastian stands and walks out of the room.

Rafael waits until the door of the room has swung shut. He sucks on his aniseed drop, swallows. He passes a hand through his hair. "I have some things to discuss," he says.

"Yes?"

"Not for the first time, things are fucked."

"I noticed," I say. "Will Fabrice be okay to race?"

Rafael flaps a hand. "Yes, yes," he says. "We just have to manage things correctly."

"Yes?"

"It is, as they say, hairline. Also, we can compensate in other areas. You can help us."

"I'm doing my best."

"Yes, yes," says Rafael. "In other areas too." He takes the chair at the computer next to me. He rotates to face me.

"What?" I shift in my chair and feel as I do a shock of pain from my hip.

He notes my expression, gives it time to pass. "We need more stuff," he says. "The situation has changed. The situation is not as we predicted."

"You're shifting," I say. "You said no blood, but she got blood."

"Yes."

"And now this?"

"It's not much," he says. "One extra treatment."

"No," I say.

Rafael shakes his head. His face is too close. I would give anything to punch it, but even now I am mindful of the consequences. He scratches his chin. His nail scrits against his slight stubble. The odd thing is that I believe he is aware of what I am thinking: both my desire to hit him and my inability to do so.

"Your wife makes a little trip, meets someone, sees a little more of the country," he says.

"No," I say. "Why us? Why not the others?" It is like a dream, I think, speaking with Rafael, the kind of dream in which one cannot move as one wishes, in which one is trapped in the wrong kind of body.

"You can do it," he says. "You're proven. It went well before."

"The one time," I say. "The one time because it was essential."

"Exactly," he says. "You are flexible. You can adapt to conditions.

And now things are critical. We are unable to be losing Fabrice, to be dropping out of competition in the general classification. Fabrice is in the top ten. Perhaps he can even hold this position. Maybe I am wishful. I believe he is a little magic." He sighs. "Our sponsorship situation is precarious; our world ranking is not a certain thing. We have three days of mountain stages coming up. I cannot tolerate a rider who does not do his best to prevent negative consequences."

"We won't do it," I say.

"We'd microdose," he says. "A twelve-hour glow time. You've been tested just two days ago. The risks are negligible. These things are for recovery, to give Fabrice a little assistance in this tough time."

"It's too much."

"You've had your moments on this tour. You've surprised me. Don't think I didn't see that spell out front you took. You're on form. You could be someone important in this race. It would be a shame to see you fall away for a lack of preparation."

"I don't want my wife involved," I say.

"I am no expert on love," says Rafael, "but it seems you are very often talking for Liz. She has her own motivations. She knows her own capabilities."

"She is being dragged into this stuff."

"She told me you would react like this."

I wince again. Rafael notices. He lets it pass. "You talked to her?" I say.

"Just now," he says. He smiles. "Your son has been—what did she say?—grouchy today. She is at the loose end. She is a clever woman. She needs stimulation."

"I need to talk to her," I say. I stand from the computer chair with difficulty.

"Exactly," says Rafael. "That is what I would suggest."

* *

I climb upstairs into the lobby, pass by the polish and the tile and the glass, the hard public voices ringing around the space. The pain in my hip stabs. I feel my grazes abraded by the bandage. I walk out of the sliding doors into the early evening and pace the asphalt of the hotel car park, waiting for my phone to connect. The sun is still up, the air warm, the sky clear of cloud.

"You spoke to Rafael and didn't tell me?" I say.

I have gone too quickly and she takes a beat to register my anger, to reply. "He said he was going to talk to you after the call," she says. Her voice has a gummy, tired quality. "The man has momentum."

"He's full of shit."

"But I know that," she says. "Do you not think I know that?" She sighs. "I did well last time. We got paid. You're in his good books. We're here."

"This new thing is so sudden," I say. I walk past lines of parked cars. I brush my hand against the body of a black BMW, warmed by the sun, the temperature of a living thing.

"He's explained the plan. It's not even blood. I can manage it," she says.

"But you don't have to."

"If I pass, he uses one of his own men. The man I met at the motorway stop, who gave me the freezer, had the worst comb-over. He was picking wax out of his ear as he talked to me. I could just see a policeman taking interest in that kind of man."

"Maybe he will just give up," I say.

"But I think he's right that the team needs to finish strongly," says Liz. "Your world ranking is dodgy. The sponsors will not be happy. The team finances are not exactly balanced."

On the other side of the car park, a van reverses, bleating out a warning as it does so. I wait for the sound to cease. "How do you know all this?" I say.

"I talk to people," she says. "I work this stuff out. I am interested. They need the finishing bonuses to pay you all. They need to get Fabrice across the line. This is a decision that affects the whole team: Sebastian, Tsutomo, the funny little guy with the beard. This isn't such a simple decision."

"You don't need to be concerned by all that," I say.

"Why not?" she says.

"This is Rafael's business."

"And so yours, and so mine."

"But we don't have to be involved in it."

"I'm here," she says. "Just know that. I am eager to help you."

I wait a second. Though the day's rain has dried off the car park, the smell of damp earth comes from the flowerbeds that surround the asphalt.

"He called you?" I say.

"Yes," she said. "He called and tried to exercise charm."

"And what did you say?"

"I listened."

"You believed him?"

"I am not unaware that he can be manipulative."

"Yes."

"I'm coming to see you," she says. "Let's talk about this face-to-face."

* *

When I return to the room, Fabrice is still in bed. He sits up, propped up with pillows. His arm is in its sling. He watches me enter the room. "Okay?" I say.

He widens his eyes in silent laconic response.

I think of his shuffling toward the team car in the hospital car park earlier in the day. "It hurts?" I say.

"It's bearable," he says. "The Butcher is coming."

I change into clothes that do not bear the team name or logo. I pull a pair of jeans over my wounded legs with some difficulty. I look at Fabrice sitting in bed. He looks dazed. He feels my eyes upon him. He flinches back into alertness. Perhaps Rafael is right, and Fabrice will be able to hold on until the end of the race.

Yet that scant possibility is not what Fabrice has trained so long for. I think of dull days lived not for their own sake but for the light that will be cast back upon them by success, of rituals, exercises, and personal strictures justified only by victory. Success or failure can bleed through time, making periods of our lives good or bad after the fact. The past year has run away from him in a moment, and I see this fact on his face, in his uncommon stillness, in his hollow gaze.

"I'm going out," I say.

He nods stiffly. "Yes," he says.

I close the door quietly behind me. I ride down to the hotel lobby in the elevator. I stand outside the hotel and wait for the family car to loom out of the dusk.

* *

We park on a shuttered shopping street. We seek a bar instead of the hotel café, for reasons of privacy, and subtlety and distance. The first bar we try is too busy. Patrons and staff turn their interested faces as we enter. The bar on from that is also crowded. The Tour is felt here, inescapable, a frisson to a Tuesday night. We carry B in his car seat. We walk toward the old town center, down narrower, cobbled streets; past the town museum, town hall, and church. Here the restaurants seek tourists. A man standing outside a bistro, smoking a cigarillo, waves. "Come in," he says. "It's a good place."

Liz shifts her grip on B's seat. "We're not eating," she says.

He shakes his head. "It's a good place. It's perfect."

He is improbably correct. The bistro is empty. I watch Liz, try to gain a sense of her mood, take a cue from her. The radio is playing loudly: eighties hits, ballads, drive-time, Yamaha synths. "I make it quieter?" says the waiter.

"Please no," says Liz.

He looks puzzled by her vehemence. She wears a summer dress and a red woolen cardigan. She wears a dark lipstick I would not have expected her to put on. We both order glasses of wine which we will not drink. She reaches across the table, holds my arm, and rolls up my sleeve to where my elbow is grazed. She is precise in her movements, yet gentle. She studies the broken skin silently. "Does it hurt?" she says.

"A little," I say.

"You have been strong," she says. "You've looked good this tour."

"Did Rafael tell you that?"

"This is me," she says, quietly. She begins to roll down my sleeve again, taking it slowly, being careful to not drag my clothing across the graze. "This is me talking to you. I'm doing it for you. Maybe for myself, a little, but no one else."

She lets go of my arm, sits back. The music thumps on. The waiter moves toward our table. He looks at our untouched drinks. "It's okay?"

"It's okay," says Liz. The waiter leaves. "You're not having much luck on this tour," she says.

"No," I say.

"I could pick something else up for you." She winks.

"What?"

"A shipment of horseshoes? Four-leaf clovers?"

Her expression hangs suspended. I laugh. She does too then. I laugh more than the joke could possibly justify. I am giving up something, letting go. I feel tired by this laughing. B beats a chubby hand against the side of his baby seat. The waiter regards us with satisfaction from across the room.

I have worried about Liz being beguiled by Rafael, by his claustrophobic certainty, but perhaps his power over others is as much a projection of mine as anything. For her he may be just another silly man, obsessed with this small strange sport. She is too sharp, I think, too tuned to the absurdity of this world.

*   *

B sleeps in his seat in the rear of the car when we drive back. I think of the pleasure of journeys in childhood, when I would arrive somewhere late at night, snoozing in the back, barely waking to murmurs and streetlights and my mother's hands, redolent of cigarettes, lifting me from my seat. Liz stops and drops me at the hotel. There is no moon. We say good-bye in whispers. The car drives quietly back into the night.

I pass through the lobby of the hotel. The restaurant area is empty but for the Butcher. He sits at a table with a coffee, surrounded by papers. Around him, the hotel staff are already cleaning up, spraying disinfectant onto tables, counting out pieces of cutlery for breakfast. A waiter turns off a bank of ceiling lights, and now only the Butcher's table and the two next to it are lit. He sees me. "You want to see the profiles?" he says. There are papers in front of him: printouts of highways, photographs of roads, elevation maps. He is studying the terrain of the coming stages.

"Why not?" I say.

He passes me a couple of the elevation profiles and a map. The route is marked in red on the map: a line squiggled through the mountains, calligraphy in a script I do not know.

"A hard couple of days," says the Butcher, "coming up."

"Yes," I say.

I scan the elevation profiles as a musician might a score, looking for patterns, difficulties, places where I might excel. The climbs are mostly steep, staccato, not the longer, more gradual ascents on which I tend to do well. I feel them in my stomach. I consider the climbs, the point at which they will begin to feel unbearable. I think of the creak of cranks, the whisper of a tire rolling over a patch of gravel. I wonder how I will feel tomorrow. My consciousness roams around my body.

"Are you ready?" says the Butcher, as if he can hear my thoughts. I nod impulsively, but following that comes the sense that this assent is true. I am not beyond cracking under pressure, but also, just occasionally, I have found myself racing without doubt, pushing unencumbered to my limit. I feel that that will be the case in these coming days. It is so simple, after all. It is just a question of riding as fast as I can, of closing down concerns. I imagine standing up on the pedals and beginning to move away from other riders, pushing into the hill and hurting those who try to follow me. For a moment, the image seems more vivid than this dark café, the grumble of the commercial dishwasher in the kitchen, the car lights raking the windows.

I am not like Fabrice. I do not love it all. That is not me, and I have come to know it. I am another type of person. I like results, and I am good at deferring gratification. I am good at waiting, at directing my energies. This is my temperament, and it has forged me as surely as all of Fabrice's zest and energy have made him. I know that minutes

I do not enjoy can be built toward moments that I do. That is all. My career has been built incrementally, through schedules and planning, by faith in my preparation.

I hand the Butcher back his maps, leave him sitting in the empty restaurant with half a cup of cold coffee. I walk out the front door of the hotel, into the night—the chirp of crickets in foliage, the night wind, the sound of a car horn—and call Liz. "You should do it," I say.

"You want me to?" she says.

"Yes," I say. "I do."

Chapter 11

In the morning I listen to Fabrice in the bathroom. I hear him cough and retch. Normally I would not be so attentive to these noises. We each make a rough job of putting ourselves together each day. Today, though, I am eager for signs of Fabrice's health. He comes out of the bathroom shirtless. His shoulder is strapped with blue medical tape; he has grazes around his elbow. He holds his arm against the bottom of his sternum. He smiles at me, and I sense the effort behind this smile.

"Did you dream?" I say.

"Yes," he says. "I dreamt."

He goes over to his open suitcase and stands, studying the kit folded within it.

"You're riding today?" I say. I know the answer to my question, but I want to hear him affirm it.

He smiles ruefully. "It's the mountains," he says. "Today was always going to be painful."

I think of something he said when I was riding my first race for the team. It was an early-season event and I was struggling. I was blowing off the back of the group, and then, unprecedentedly, Fabrice appeared next to me. I complained about not having the necessary fuel in my legs, about not being ready for the day. He listened. "Consider only *how* you feel, not *why*," he said. He stood on his pedals and accelerated toward the head of the race.

I hunkered into my bike and tried to really pin down the nature of my discomfort and weakness, and, as I imagine he had suspected,

181

I found that I could not. There was just the race, the road, and those ahead of me. There was nothing to prevent me from staying with those men, only the worry that I would not be able to do so. I retreated from the bleating of my own consciousness. I hung on, made it to the finish with the main group. The technique has not always worked for me, but it did then.

Now Fabrice sits on the edge of his bed in his boxer shorts. He looks at the wall ahead of him. "I'm going to breakfast," I say.

"Yes," he says. He does not shift his stare.

* *

The breakfast room is at the rear of the hotel. Outside, a man on a large lawn mower is trimming the grass. He steers with the heel of his hand on the wheel, swinging the mower around with a fierce fluency at the end of each run. The lightest flotsam of cut grass is cast over the gravel paths.

I arrive earlier than the other riders. A waiter carries a tray of pasta from the kitchen. He looks at the pasta and then back up at me, as if I am the sole cause of such a culinary-temporal abomination.

As the waiter moves away, I approach the buffet table and smell in his retreat a faint odor of cigarettes mixing with the scents of banana and cut oranges, and in this a memory of my parents: the morning, the old hanging lamp over the kitchen table, my mother washing dishes, my father talking loudly as he hurried to leave the house.

I mix muesli, fruit, milk, yogurt, pasta, and scrambled eggs in a large bowl and take a solitary seat at the table.

When I have been eating for a couple of minutes, Fabrice walks stiffly into the room. He gives a brief smile. He pulls out the chair opposite me. He sits himself down gingerly. "Have you heard about Eric?" he says.

"What?" I say.

"Slovenian Eric," he says, "who rides for the bankers."

"Right," I say.

"They say," he says, "that he has been taking performance-enhancing drugs."

"Who are they?"

"The news channels, the journalists, the race stewards." The news animates him. He leans forward, despite himself; a wince betrays his shoulder injury, his momentary forgetting of it.

"How do you know?"

"Rafael called me when I was leaving the room. You had gone." He points to the jumble in my bowl. "You were mixing this up."

The waiter returns to place a coffeepot on the table.

"It's shocking and saddening," says Fabrice.

The waiter leaves again.

"Are you worried?" I say.

"I *am* shocked. The bankers are diligent." He has an energy he didn't have up in the room. The intrigue, the game of it, has given him something.

"Do you know the substance?" I say. "Do you know how they got him?"

Fabrice exhales. "That is not for us to worry about." I hear the ding of the arriving elevator. The doors of the breakfast room open and a number of the team enter at once. The Butcher and Rafael are conversing together. Rafael looks up, feeling our gazes upon him, and winks.

* *

On the way back to my room I see Marc. "Have you heard?" he says.

"What?" I say.

183

"About the guy taking drugs."

"Sorry?" I say. Marc is the kind of man that even I can lie to.

"A guy on the German team was caught taking drugs," says Marc. He reaches a hand up and fingers the thinning island of hair at the front of his head. "I don't think he is necessarily the only one."

"Really?" I say.

He leans toward me. "Trust me. I have my suspicions."

"I suppose we'll have to wait and see," I say. He touches the bandage he wrapped around my forearm the previous day. "It needs to be changed?" I say.

"No." He keeps his eyes on it. "It's good."

"That's good to know."

"A pleasure to be of assistance," he says.

When I return to my room, Fabrice is elsewhere. The news is playing at a low volume on the hotel television. There is a picture of Eric, then footage of the Germans riding together in the race. I put my personal things, my clothes and vitamins, into my bag. I have time to really consider the news then. Across town, in another hotel, another man is packing up, his career possibly at its end. His name will be struck through on starting rosters, removed from the classification. The dope men have come for him, and then Liz, today, will do what she has promised Rafael. I pick up my phone and call her. It runs to voice mail though, and I end the call.

I go to the bathroom, and when I return, the news has moved on. The price of milk is at an unprecedented low. It is unclear whether the minister for the interior will resign after having been caught offering government contracts for personal gain. I try to find comfort in the quickness with which the world can swallow our misdeeds.

* *

Rafael mentions the disqualification in his morning speech. "I'm shocked," he says, as the bus huffs and sighs through traffic toward its parking space. "Truly. I have always had respect for that team. I always thought that they were professionals. But to fail a test in such a way? That is a real shame. It has not just harmed them, but all of us. We are all hurt by association. I have already had a call from our sponsors." He tuts in an exaggerated manner.

At the start line the journalists are more agitated than usual. Fabrice and Rafael are immediately cornered by television crews.

I follow Fabrice. He gives a rueful smile. I watch him from behind the camera. "So," he says, "I am out in the wind and the rain, riding myself into the ground, while I find that this guy prefers to just take a trip to the pharmacy. It leaves an unpleasant taste in the mouth."

It is only later that I find Rafael sitting on a bench near the perimeter of the starting paddock. He holds a small cup of espresso, sniffs at it. "I'm worried about our plan," I say, "given recent developments."

Rafael looks up at me. He drinks the espresso. His nose twitches. He slides along the bench and indicates that I should take a place next to him. He waits for me.

"We can't do it now," I say.

"What?"

"The plan."

"You think I have not made these calculations?" says Rafael. "The bankers' situation is a decoy, if anything. The heat is on them. They have been very foolish. I do not like to say this, but they let this happen to them. Nobody wanted this to happen. They have been very sloppy." He taps his empty espresso cup on the cast iron arm of the bench. "The plan was good before. The plan is good now."

"It doesn't feel good."

"What is most dangerous about descending?" Rafael says. He

185

studies my expression. "Braking suddenly. Chickening out. Hesitation."

* *

I walk back to the bus. I watch Fabrice. He slips his team tracksuit off slowly, every movement cautious, his expression vacant. When he has stripped to his riding kit though, he steps onto the trainer and begins cycling as smoothly as he ever has. He does not wince or work his way into his pedaling. He simply starts. That is Fabrice, I think. He can draw lines in his experience, choose to leave behind disappointments and discomforts. Where I would feel fate pressing heavily upon me, he can, with an act of will, decide things will be well.

I am called to warm up. I strip off my tracksuit. I start riding on the trainer next to Fabrice. He turns to me. "Two parachutists leave a plane," he says. "One thousand meters above the ground, one of them asks if maybe they should open their chutes. 'No,' says the other, 'wait.' At six hundred meters, the first man asks the same thing. 'Wait,' he's told again. At two hundred meters the answer's still 'Wait.' At fifty meters it's the same."

"Right," I say.

"Finally, at ten meters from the ground, the first man says, 'Surely we should open our chutes?'"

Fabrice stops pedaling. The flywheel of the trainer fizzes. "'Why?' says the second man. 'We've been doing fine so far.'"

* *

I find a chair and sit for a few minutes trying to compose myself. People move past me, mounting their bikes, grabbing energy gels, water bottles, or good luck tokens before they leave for the line. I will do this race, I think, and then I will return home with Liz and my son.

I think of the house, of that back room of mine, of the summer only half done.

My phone rings. It is Liz. I hear the sound of a car in the background. "I'm going there," she says. "I have a missed call from you. Things are okay?"

"Yes," I say. "I suppose."

Perhaps I want her to pick up on my reluctance, but she does not. She is focused, and maybe this is for the best. "Did you call me for any reason?" she says.

I pause. "Not particularly," I say. I could tell her, I think. I could say. But why?

"You'll do well," she says. "I'll do well."

The Butcher arrives holding a plastic tray. We put our personal items into the tray, which is then placed securely onto the bus for the duration of the race. He looks at me and shakes it. The objects in it rattle together. A photo of a young child, smiling on a sunny beach, shifts amidst watches and jewelry. I say good-bye to Liz and drop my phone into the tray. "Good luck," says the Butcher.

Before we head toward the line, Rafael puts his arm around Fabrice, who stands on his bicycle. He whispers something into Fabrice's ear. He looks at me and Sebastian. "Hard to believe," he says, "but I envy you boys."

* *

Despite concern for Fabrice's health, there is an anticipation among our team at the start. We are into the last set of mountain stages, those that will decide the race at large. There are only so many of these days in a career, and today I have the sense that others are ruminating on this fact. We are nostalgic in real time. I see Tsutomo looking at the assembled fans as we wait to set off from the line. There is a slight smile on his face, and I think I have some idea of what preoccupies him. To get to this place, we have needed to have such focus upon our sport, and yet even a long career will be just a fraction of any ordinary lifespan. I am not blind to the absurdity of this job, to the inessentiality of all this carnival. And yet in the years after this, whatever I choose to do, I will be lucky to win a tiny part of the acclaim I enjoy now, to experience even a small portion of the excitement that I feel coursing around this gang of skinny men of which I am a part.

Since I first held B in my arms, I have wondered what I will be to him. I will be done with this career by the time he is grown. I can visualize him in fifteen years, say, as a slight boy with a mop of Liz's hair and that same acute expression of his, and yet I cannot put myself into the picture.

Perhaps the fact is just that this point will be approached step by step, that I will not change suddenly but remake myself in increments. That is, after all, how I have lived with B so far.

In those first months in which Liz returned to work, when I would train early in the morning and then care for B for the rest of day, we would often ride the train into the city. I would carry him in a pack on my front. I learned to move differently with him, warned by the looks of strangers when I rushed too quickly through a crowd or jumped onto a train just before the closing of the doors. I took him to churches, not because I am religious, but because they were calming places, because his wide eyes seemed to predispose him to appreciating monumental structures.

I took him, for instance, to the church of Saint Stephen Walbrook. We cut through the lunchtime crowds on Cannon Street and then up a smaller alley, to the doorway into the church. We went up the steps and then into the great space inside that was disarmingly empty. There was just a single elderly woman standing in a waxed jacket and gazing up into the dome. She looked at us and I carried B forward as I lifted him a little in his harness so he could truly see. The quantity of light that Wren's design could draw from the gray London sky astounded me. The shapes of the arches and details of the dome above appeared as if they'd grown from bone. I considered what effort it must have taken men working with their hands, what attention they must have exerted. The old woman made that kind of face people make for babies, and B gawped, happy in that moment. Then she looked back at the dome and then back at me, in a manner that seemed to ask, *Aren't we lucky to be here, now, just the three of us?* I looked back silently in agreement, filled with that renewing pleasure bought on by a place so apart from its surroundings, a wonder found so close to home.

* *

The start of the race is announced over the PA system. We riders shift into a position to begin, pedals at ten o'clock, calves flinching. Then the horn sounds, and we set off. We climb away from the start line bunched together. Television motorbikes ride in front of us, pulling ahead and then dropping back with coughs of their exhausts. The helicopter has peeled off to put us in context against the sprawl of the town we have just left.

The pace settles. At first we talk about Eric. The bankers ride in a group at the rear of the pack, conferring among themselves, monitored with interest by the rest of us (though not necessarily without sympathy).

We descend for a time, and on the first bend the whisper of applied brakes arises, as coordinated as any orchestra. I ride next to Fabrice. I ask how he is. He nods at me, looks forward, his face empty.

As we begin to make our way up a valley though, people pull

alongside Fabrice and offer him their anxiety dreams. He plays his part. He is deliberate. What I see as discomfort, other riders regard as calculation. A rider from an Eastern European team asks about a dream in which he wished to go out cycling but couldn't find any shorts. "Inadequate reasons conceal unconfessed motives," says Fabrice. Another rider wants to know about a dream in which he was trapped in a thick snowstorm walking endlessly toward a light that moved as he approached. Fabrice thinks. "You want to lead your team," he suggests. One of the bankers even arrives and describes a dream where he prepared an elaborate dinner for himself. "This is an innocent dream," says Fabrice. He spits high into the wind above the peloton.

When I am able to talk discreetly with Fabrice, I counsel him to preserve his energy, to not give too much of himself away with all this speculation. He tells me that he is in control, however. He says that holding court as he is doing can only serve to communicate his confidence to his rivals.

The stage has four high passes and a mountaintop finish. As we begin our ascent of the day's second climb, one of the other team leaders, a climbing specialist, sprints away from the group. Fabrice, needing to preserve his proximity to the leaders, is compelled to join the chasing group. Over the radio, Rafael tells me to go with Fabrice. Tsutomo also makes the break with us, moving away from all those riders behind who are set on grinding up these mountains, merely enduring the stage.

"Enjoy it, boys," Rafael says.

*　*

On the inclines we are silent. Our lungs need ever more air and our legs fill with heaviness. The crowds shout us rabidly up the hills. On the busiest parts of the climbs, hands extend from the side to pat our backs, to push us a little, or merely to make contact. Our small group of chasing riders works together efficiently. Each rider is guarded now. When I do talk to Fabrice or Tsutomo, I sense our companions taking note.

Fabrice eats pills: painkillers, anti-inflammatories. He is dosed heavily. He pedals in leaden circles. His eyes show little. I myself have taken pills provided by the Butcher, though fewer than Fabrice. My skin still feels ragged. I can still sense where my bandages rub against me.

"How do you feel?" I say to Fabrice.

"I feel almost nothing," he says.

"You're a perfect cyclist," I say.

"Maybe," he says, "but a certain amount of pain in a race is important, like scratching an itch."

"When they wear off," I say, "you'll get your pain."

"I know," he says, "but that is not the right way. I like to accumulate it."

* *

We all know the young man out ahead of us. He's a media darling: short and skinny with slow, gentle eyes. He has a propensity for ill-fated breaks from the peloton, which is one of the elements of his appeal. He likes karaoke and has attracted publicity with this predilection. It is only in front of the microphone and in the mountains that his facade of gentleness is broken. He seems to believe he is better suited to the hills than anyone else, and though we know that he has previously overestimated himself, the rest of us are wary of the day he will achieve what he has set out to do.

At a flat section, I pull back to the team car to collect water. The window buzzes down. Rafael begins the slow charade of passing bottles. I stop pedaling and my freewheel mechanism hums. "How is it going?" Rafael says. The Butcher is driving. Rafael waits.

"Okay," I say. I put a bottle into the pocket of my jersey, take hold of another.

"We've been running calculations," says Rafael. "You're going to make the catch in the next hour. Present conditions persisting. At the pace he's going it's impossible."

"Physiologically impossible," the Butcher adds with satisfaction.

We climb up another bare mountainside. Ski lifts loom on the horizon. The fans around the road here have slept in tents and caravans and then waited all day. They wear baseball caps thrown out by the parade of sponsors' vehicles. They ring cowbells.

The sun is intense. I take a bottle of water proffered by a fan and pour it over my head. Fabrice chews on his lip. Ahead of us, the television motorbikes sound their horns to clear fans from the road.

We catch the stage leader just before the summit of the climb.

When he turns to see us on the road behind him, he slows to let our group catch him. However, he does not let us leave him. He sits and pedals smoothly, staying in the midst of our group. He is wearing no gloves and a chunky golden ring on his little finger. Fabrice nods at him, and the man nods back cordially with an expression far more relaxed than his time out ahead should allow. Fabrice looks at me, a pantomimed surprise in his expression.

We freewheel down into the valley, through villages. People stand pressed to the side of the tarmac, against the walls of their houses, to accommodate our velocity. Dogs bark from gardens.

We do not pay much attention to anything but the wobbles of our front wheels beneath us. We think about cornering as smoothly as possible. We think about the positions of other riders behind and ahead of us, seeking to prevent our paths from conflicting.

The road flattens. Other teams push up the pace. I ride with Fabrice. His jaw is set. His legs move steadily. I note the slightest tension in the way he holds his handlebars. The fingers of his healthy left hand grip the bar tape firmly. His nails are tiny ellipses on nubby fingers, emerging from fingerless gloves and pressed until red against the grips. I see the way he places the heel of his right palm on the bars, not gripping around them. There are shouts ahead, warnings conveyed with waved hands. Fabrice swerves around a pothole. A pain squirms through his posture as he does this. It is so subtle that I do not think anyone else sees it. "Good?" I say.

"Good," he says.

The agricultural machinists move to the head of our small group: four of them. Three of them take turns on the front. The fourth man, their leader, sits just behind in their slipstream. They are pushing toward the base of the penultimate ascent, trying to tire the rest of us before we are even climbing in earnest. "An offensive move," says Rafael over the airwaves. "Endure it."

The road begins to steepen. The crowd is denser and louder. The machinists still work, infernally rotating. Logically, of course, they will have to crack before the finish. Struggling to stay with them, however, witnessing their coordination, I feel this is impossible. Fabrice rides behind me. We move at around thirty kilometers per hour, but I think, most of all, of my location in relation to his: his front wheel rolling along the road, moving in tiny increments toward and away from my own rear wheel.

Ahead of us, one of the machinists reaches his limits. He pulls off from the group, drops a gear, and sits back on his saddle as we pull past him. I am pushing through my lactate threshold, toward oxygen debt. "Red," says Rafael through the radio. "You're going red."

I hold on. I do not look at Fabrice. I feel him behind me. He is following, hanging on himself.

The pace rises again. The group of three machinists splits. Two more drop from the front. Only their leader stays at the head of the pack, just behind new pacemakers from other teams. Looking back at the men dropping off, my eyes move onto Fabrice. He is pallid. He sits lopsided on his saddle. He reaches into a pocket, pushes something between his lips. "Good?" I mouth. He just nods. The road straightens. I can see it stretching ahead of me, then far away twisting into a steep corner. I stand on the pedals, change a gear, then shift again. I sit. I stand. For the immediate future, these small changes put off my collapse. They will not for long, however. I have no idea how much Fabrice feels.

The space between the rear wheel of the rider ahead and my own front tire increases by a couple of centimeters. I look to my right to see Fabrice standing on his pedals and moving past me. He knows before I do. I feel bile rising in my esophagus. I am done. I cannot hang on. Other riders pass me: the leaders, the climbers, only a few domestiques. The back of the group approaches. Gaps between riders increase: centimeters, then meters. The last of the group struggle to keep pace. They dangle from the mass of riders, flutter fitfully in its wake. Then I am passed by the last rider of the group. He will also be dropped, but for an instant he too stands in one final, futile effort; he straightens his back, rocks on the handlebars. Then, tiring, he slows, pushing his pelvis forward, locking his arms, seeking some position in which to rest his muscles. I am behind him now by twenty meters. I will not win this distance back, even against him. "Keep it up, Fabrice," says Rafael over the radio.

I ride alone. I am passed by other riders. Eventually I settle with a small group who ride determinedly toward the finish. I stay with them up the last climb. Through my earpiece, I hear Rafael all the while encouraging Fabrice. Without injury, this might have been a day for Fabrice to make gains, but I can hear in the way Rafael talks that he is now expecting something else: only that Fabrice does not let his rivals get any further away. "Close this out," he says. "Do not let the fucks fuck with you."

At the last some riders attempt to break from the leading group. They go, one at a time: bursting, being caught, bursting again. I surmise all this from the cries of Rafael through my earpiece. Fabrice is left grinding on. "A little more," says Rafael. "Just a little more." I hear the roar of the crowd at the finish up above me as the leading riders fight for victory in the stage. Fabrice loses only twenty seconds. I still have a couple of kilometers to pedal to the line. I keep making my way up amidst others who have been dropped. I pass fans on the last corner before the finish, who hold a large sign that reads "Drug takers go to hell." I am riding with one of the bankers, and these fans jeer him in response to all the business of the morning. They cheer loudly for those riders coming behind us though. Their voices are hoarse from all the shouting they did as the leaders passed them, from their thrilled reaction to all those improbable final surges.

* *

At the bus I am told Fabrice is already inside, getting an impromptu massage from the Butcher. Rafael stands on the steps, looking over the small car park, surveying the detritus of a finished stage: bikes, camping chairs, piles of dirty kit.

I deposit my bike with the mechanics. The air smells of WD-40. They are already working on Fabrice's bike. A mechanic polishes the frame with a tan chamois. My attention is drawn to the top tube of the bicycle. I count the little line of wings: five. There is another one since the morning.

Rafael sees me looking at the sticker. "You did well," he says. "You are getting closer." He goes back inside the bus.

On the ride home, I sit next to Johan. "How are things?" I say.

"I hate mountains," says Johan. "I'm sick of being dragged up hills. I'm tired of staring at Sebastian's behind."

"It's tough," I say.

"It's the time of the tiny little men," says Johan. "They can barely climb the steps of the podium. How can you compete against men who will do that to themselves? Do the podium girls want to be kissing those men?"

"I don't think they want to be kissing any of us," I say.

"How are you a professional sportsman?" he says.

We make our way down the mountain to our hotel, lurching around switchbacks. Johan falls asleep, his chin on his chest, his head rolling left and right with the motion of the bus. The sun, still high, cuts through the forest around us. Bars of shadow rake through the bus, caressing the faces of resting riders.

My phone rings. I can see from the screen that it is Liz. I am glad, eager to share the successful stage with her. "A solid day," I say.

"Hello? Sorry?"

"The stage."

"Oh." She pauses. There is a different impulse within me then, a sudden sense of dread. I have gone too quickly, I think, neglected my earlier concern. "I . . . I have news," she says. I know it. I know it as she is saying it, and feel I have brought it upon us in that very moment of complacency. "I'm detained, Sol," she says. I wait. "It's about the contents of the car."

The bus judders into another turn. A water bottle skitters down the central aisle. "They have something on you?" I say.

"The police apprehended me." Liz's voice is steady but fragile. She talks as if someone else is listening to her. "They looked in my car. They found controlled substances for which they say I have no legal use. They have taken me into custody."

I pause. Next to me, Johan still sleeps perfectly peacefully.

"Where's Barry?" I say.

"He's here," she says. "He's sleeping. They haven't put us in a cell. Having a baby counts for something."

"Where's the police station?" I say.

"It's near the Spanish border," she says. "In a small mountain town."

"You had to cross the border?" I say.

"Yes," she says.

"You didn't tell me that," I say.

"No," she says. "I didn't."

"This is terrible," I say. "Getting caught crossing the border."

"Apprehended," she says, brittle. "Apprehended on suspicion."

"I'm sorry," I say.

"I wasn't apprehended at the border anyway."

"I'm just trying to work out what has happened."

"I was speeding," she says. "That's all. I was confused, very nervous. I gave them cause for suspicion, I suppose."

"Yes?"

"They asked to search the car."

"And that was that?"

Someone says something in the background. I hear movement. The phone is put down. Liz speaks just out of reach of the receiver. She returns. "They don't want you to ask so many questions," she says.

"Why?"

"We are not to discuss the ongoing investigation," she says.

"Why?"

"In case we corroborate," she says, exasperated. "In case we get our stories straight."

"Right."

"I couldn't get through to Rafael. His phone was engaged."

"You've been trying to get him before me?"

"Of course," she says. "This is his business. What they are alleging."

"But you'd tell him before me?"

"I'm in a police station," she says.

"Yes, but . . ."

"This is not the time," she says. She laughs an exasperated, mirthless laugh. "Just talk to him, please."

I stand. Johan is asleep. I push past him. He does not wake. He wrinkles his nose and shifts position.

I make my way down the bus toward where Rafael sits. He is leaning across the aisle, in conversation with the Butcher. Rafael looks up at me. "What?" he says.

"My wife is being held in a police station."

He looks at me, thinks. "Really?" he says. His tone is light. "Why?"

"Activities on your behalf," I say.

A glare betrays his irritation at my speaking so openly. "No," he says. "This is a confusion."

"I just talked to her," I say.

"She is in an unfamiliar country. She does not know the language so well. I can assist, of course. Your family, my family." He joins his hands in front of him. His eyes are still fierce.

"It's serious," I say.

"Calm," he says. "*Please.*" He looks at the Butcher, then back at me. "Find a seat on your own. Relax." He rises from his place and turns to look behind him. He sees Sebastian three seats back. "Get out of the way, Sebastian. Find another place." He turns back to me. "Go and sit. I will work on it. I will talk to some people."

I call the police station, and I am told that Liz is not available. I ask for an explanation, and the policeman says only, "Not now." He puts down the phone.

I sit. We are in the valley now. There is a river to our left. The road clings to a steep hillside. We move in and out of tunnels. To our right one can see rock walls stretching above us. I feel totally blank now. Others around me sleep. We go into an illuminated tunnel and the body of the vehicle is suddenly flooded through with yellow light. I study the stitching of the seat in front of me. I feel a nauseous emptiness, a yawn at my center. We emerge back into the open air. Time passes. I look to the front of the bus. Rafael's head is moving, a phone clamped to his ear. He throws up a hand as he says something.

We stop at the hotel. The other riders wake, oblivious. They take some time disembarking. They pass down the aisle bleary-eyed. I stay in my seat, and no one seems to notice this.

The Butcher goes to help the riders to their rooms. The driver gets off the bus to begin unpacking gear from beneath it. Only Rafael is still on the vehicle. He rises from his seat, walks back toward me. "I'm in contact with a lawyer," he says. "I'm making up a strategy."

I nod. He walks back to the front. He begins a call as he does so.

* *

Marc is in the reception when I get off the bus. He guides me to my room. "Somebody is a little exhausted," he says.

When I enter the room, Tsutomo is sitting on the bed, staring ahead of him. His bags and mine have been stacked by team helpers against the wall. Next to them, the bathroom door is partly obscured by jars, placed like an old-fashioned supermarket display. There must be two hundred jars of baby food.

I lie on the bed. Our son is in a jail, I think. Will he be picking up Liz's panic? I think of walking through London with him on my front, the sense that he was this little feeling thing—alternately excited, fearful, grumpy, overawed—a small absorber of the emergent temper of the city. Tsutomo, on his own bed, has taken one of the jars of baby food and begun eating from it with a hotel teaspoon. He looks at me with sympathy but does not ask the cause of my discontent.

There is a rap on the door. I open it to Rafael. "So . . . ," he says. He beckons me out.

We walk down the corridor. Rafael frowns, unready to embark on what he has to say. "Your room is suitable?" he says.

"Fine," I say.

"Good," he says. He clucks his tongue. I can smell the aniseed on his breath.

We reach the end of the corridor. He opens the door of a room. "They think I am important," he says.

"Who?"

"The hotel people. They have given me the honeymoon suite."

The room is four times the size of mine and Tsutomo's. There is a large bed piled with cushions against the right wall. There is a minibar next to the bed. The other side of the room is mostly empty, as if whoever designed the room ran out of things to put into it. Two high-backed armchairs have been placed in front of the window, facing each other obliquely. Rafael gestures toward these. I pick a heart-shaped pillow from the seat before I sit down. Not knowing what to do with it, I hold it in my lap. Rafael takes his place in the other chair.

"I have contacted a lawyer," he says.

"And?" I say.

"He is on his way." Rafael shrugs. "They have twenty-four hours to charge your wife. The policemen are a little bit, shall we say, confused by what they have found. It will take a little while to play out."

"How long?" I say. "She's in prison with my son."

"Jail," he says, "technically." He has his normal composure. He does not respond to my tone, my anger.

"How long?" I say, again.

"They will do tests on the materials, determine their origin, their status as controlled substances. When they know what they are doing, they will put her in front of a judge. We will know more after tomorrow's stage."

"*After* the stage."

"Of course."

"I will race?"

"Of course." He leans forward and studies my face.

"That's all?" I say.

"That's the plan. The lawyer is good, I think, and not too expensive."

"Why would you say that?" I say.

Rafael thinks. "I am a straightforward man," he says. He stands. "Let me get you a drink." He points at the minibar behind him. "The drinks are highly priced, but considering the circumstances . . ." He shows me his open palms. "You would like some carbonated water?"

"They're not just disposable," I say. "We're not talking about a dodgy doctor. This is my wife and son."

"Yes," says Rafael. "What do you mean 'disposable'?" He walks toward the minibar. He squats, out of view, in front of the built-in refrigerator.

"This is my family, in detention."

"They have procedures for this situation," he says. "This is not a totally barbaric country. That first hotel your wife was in was poor, unfortunately. Her location tonight is quite similar but, well, operated by the gendarmerie." He rises above the bar, back into my sight line. He holds a bottle of Perrier. He smiles in what I think he might intend to be a sympathetic expression. I feel shame, I realize. I am here with this man, and I do not know what to say. He ambles back across the room, cradling the glass bottle. He cracks the seal, hands it to me. "Please," he says. "Enjoy."

I wait.

"Hydrate yourself," he says. "You will feel better."

I drink, and the water is cool, welcome. This in itself feels like a defeat. "It is good?" he says.

"I don't believe this," I say.

"Quite understandable," says Rafael.

I think of B and Liz in an institutional building, unfamiliar, chilly, the sounds of doors opening and closing, no sense of what is occurring, of what should be occurring.

"You said this wouldn't happen," I say.

"I suppose I am not infallible."

"Shit," I say.

"Yes, it was a disappointment to find this out for me also."

"What are you talking about?"

"It was a joke," says Rafael. "I was feigning ignorance."

"My wife and child are in prison."

"Jail. I was trying to leaven the mood."

This time yesterday I was speaking to Liz on the phone. "I am not unaware that he can be manipulative," she said. Our downfall is in that: in the sentiment, in the mannered way she expressed it, as if it were all a game.

"We have had a hard few days," says Rafael.

"I'm going to go to the jail," I say.

"But that won't help anything."

"I'm going to go though."

"You have a strategy?" he says. "A daring jailbreak?" He looks at me as if I am a prodigious child, his eyes playful. The thing I feel more than anger is humiliation. We have given ourselves over to him, Liz and I, to this look of mild amusement at our plight.

I stand from the armchair. I walk around the room. The sun is low, the evening beginning, the sky turning. I am aware, again, of the tiredness of my legs. I sit back in my place in the armchair.

"I can't talk to her on the phone," I say.

"Not now the lawyer is involved," Rafael says. "That is the priority, is it not? Getting her out?"

I don't know what to say to this, how to productively resist him. Rafael strolls over, faces me.

"For now, you are most useful riding, doing your job, letting the lawyer do his thing." He stands over me and extends a hand toward mine. "Dinner is soon being served," he says. "You have done a lot to deserve it, and you will need it. There is a big day in the mountains coming up." He looks at me in a funny way. There is a pity there. His eyes are unusually quiet. He waits patiently. My wife and I are small to him, so much less than we imagined. This was clear for both of us to see, and yet we did not attend to it. We thought our assent to his plans worldly and pragmatic, when really it was the opposite. He has always been sure we could be moved to his will.

He is right that I cannot help Liz, perhaps correct that to race is the rational thing to do, though of course he has his own motives, another game. Yet is to consider his agenda—even to consciously reject it—to let him trespass into my reasoning? There is one thing to do, one correct choice to be made. She is pragmatic, I think, had called Rafael first. She wants me in this job, wants me successful in this life. She will guess my reasoning. I think of our conversation discussing the drugs, as we awaited B. "Don't put a face on for me," she had said.

This is our characteristic even now, I tell myself—the resilience that others do not have.

Maybe I also want her to feel her share of the shame I feel in this room, here, with Rafael: the smallness, the searing sense of having been so easily taken in.

"This is some very bad luck, my friend," he says. He is waiting. I take his hand. He leans back. His built-up shoes ruck the carpet a little. I rise to a standing position. I take my own weight. "Dinner," he says, turning. "Then a sleep. Then a ride. Then things will look different."

Chapter 12

Sometimes, in this life, I arrive in a town and realize that I have visited it before. Routes overlap each other. We are transported to regional races and training camps without much idea of where we go. We drift into and out of familiar landscapes. We are forever coming upon sections of previous courses, passing back through towns we once flashed by. Occasionally I will turn a corner and I will find myself recalling the features of the road the way one might recognize a passage of music.

There are the famous climbs, those which one has no doubt one is repeating. But more striking are the minor coincidences: the way a veteran rider may realize that he is traversing a roundabout he went around fifteen years ago, as a junior; the way one might descend a road one climbed previously. Our histories, in this sport, are spread over minor roads used most of the time for nothing more than the simple acts of living.

I come to a realization in the town square from which we will start this morning. I climb down from the bus, and look at the town hall and the café on the corner and the war memorial, and know that I was here many years ago in one of my early amateur races. Back then I arrived in a borrowed car with a couple of other aspirants. I adjusted my own gears, stuffed my pockets with energy bars, the wrappers of which I had made small nicks in so that they might be opened easily during competition. There was no team bus then, no support car, few journalists. It is tempting to wish for a return to those days, to harbor some kind of retroactive sympathy for my younger self who left them, who could not have imagined my predicament this morning. That would be too easy though, because that man was hungry, and that past era seems good to me now only because of the way I fought my way out of it, the way I came to satisfy this hunger and to know this sport to its full extent.

*   *

I slept badly last night. I woke to some news from Rafael, passed to him through the lawyer. The lawyer was at the police station, I was told. An early morning meeting had been arranged. Katherine was on her way to the small town.

Meanwhile Rafael is intent on supressing the news. My teammates do not know. Tsutomo, with whom I roomed, and whom I probably disturbed with my sleeplessness during the night, does not know. Rafael is considering Liz's predicament in terms of press coverage. He is worrying about keeping her case out of the papers if she is charged.

For now, I sit on a canvas chair in the start area. I drink coffee. I fidget. I try to come around to the task ahead.

Last night I thought of what Liz must have been enduring. I wondered whether the cell was warm, comfortable, whether the food she was served was good, whether she could care for B as she needed to. Without contact, I have struggled to keep faith in her understanding, in the extent of her endurance, or in my own reasoning. I wondered whether she thought of where I was and whether she could have imagined that, as she sat in her cell last night, Fabrice, Tsutomo, and I still had injections: syringes that were supposed to contain microdoses of anti-inflammatory hormones but, because those substances sat in an evidence locker, actually held just water and glucose.

Amongst our trio, only I was aware of the lack of efficacy of these treatments. I submitted though. I offered my assent to the notion that they should make us stronger today.

*   *

To first know Liz, in those early weeks after we had met, was to think of space in a different way. We would arrange to meet, and I would head out on my bike to train. Yet all the while I would wonder where she was, what she was doing. I would be out riding and a storm would come in, and I would wonder whether the rain had reached her down in the city. She would tell me she was going to visit her mother, and my attention would be on those roads up into East Anglia. I think of those signs one finds at landmarks that state, through fanned-out arrows, how far it is to major cities. I felt myself to be attuned to where Liz was, like such a signpost pointing to only one other location.

When B arrived, suddenly there was another point in my conception of space. Three of us: enough, any mathematician will tell you, for one to locate oneself with knowledge of one's distance from the other two.

*   *

Fabrice comes over to where I sit. He smells of sunscreen. He smiles a smile he did not have in him yesterday. "How are you?" he says.

"Fine," I say.

"Good for you," he says. He wants something. He moves the right arm, the one attached to his damaged shoulder. He'd like me to ask about this surprising range of movement, the apparent comfort with which he makes circles with his elbow. "We're going to do it," he says.

"You're going to hold on to your placing?"

"Perhaps more," he says. He winks. "Though maybe I am crazy."

"You're feeling good?"

"I'm up in the clouds," he says. "The Butcher found something that works for me. It suits my constitution. I respond to it."

"I'm glad," I say.

"Hey," he says. "A giraffe goes into a bar and orders a beer . . ."

He stops, then. He waits for some signal to continue from me. I cannot do it, I realize, though I do not know why just listening to him for a few seconds should be too much. "I have to fetch something from the bus," I say.

"Really?" he says.

"Yes. Sorry."

He touches me on the elbow. I make my way slowly away from him, past the mechanics and through a crowd of support staff. Voices drift over from the group Fabrice has gone to join. "Why did the giraffe *want to* go into the bar?" I hear Sebastian say. "I think this is the question."

I spit onto the cobbles of the square. I try to collect myself. I look around the paddock. The bus of the French farm-machinery team is parked next to ours. The team's riders, all known to us, wait together near their vehicle. There are a couple of press trucks facing our bus. Retired riders walk about, serving in so many capacities: as pundits, organizational staff, team leaders. It is a small world. One can live one's whole life in it. Rafael came in as a young rider, for instance, and has never left. There are whole families created from this tight mix. Riders marry team administrators, journalists, masseuses. I sometimes expected my own life to be conducted within this space: an assumption drawn from what others around me intended, what others before me had done. I had thought of working in administration, planning stages, perhaps doing journalistic work. Only with the arrival of Liz into my life did I really think that I could be done and walk out of it, into the world beyond. I am grateful to her for this. Though like any creature accustomed to a certain life, I have sometimes felt this latitude to be a fearful thing.

Rafael has been standing beside me, I realize; I do not know for how long. He squeezes my shoulder, then walks away silently.

* *

I begin the stage removed from those around me, separated from their giddiness, their attention to the stakes of the day. I pedal near the rear of the group, letting other team members drift ahead of me. Tsutomo rides next to Fabrice. The pace is high but steady.

Teams are stocked with experts who are able to explain our riding as the conversion of so much potential into so much motion. They predict our limits, work out how many calories we might burn through. We riders, though, do not think in this way. We think about rhythm. There seems to be a perfect pace, at which we could ride forever. Things stack together: breathing, pedaling, thought. In this zone you become a sort of passenger within your own body.

This morning, despite myself, I find a rhythm. We pass around a roundabout on which a policeman stands, waving a flag to give advance warning of the obstacle. He looks ahead, moves the flag evenly, does not flinch in response to the proximity and speed of riders going by. There is something impressive in seeing a man diligently doing so mechanical a task. To lose oneself in an act like that, in a perfectly repeatable motion, can be a joy. It is one I find in my own riding on this late morning. I know the policeman's satisfaction as I pass him.

I find myself creeping through the peloton. I arrive next to Fabrice, who wordlessly takes a position behind me, who follows me forward through the press of riders, into the foothills of the first mountain of the day. The gradient rises. The peloton stretches. I welcome the burn in my thighs.

* *

As the climbs go on, the better riders move to the front of the group. They do not lead or set the pace but hover behind those riders who do, wary of others breaking away. If any of the main race competitors jump ahead, the others are ready to cloak the attack, tagging behind them, preventing gaps from opening. I think of our group as some single-celled organism: stretching, compacting again, shuddering, never quite splitting.

We ride and watch each other. "Eat, Fabrice," says Rafael through the radio. "Eat and drink." This is the time in which essential acts become forgotten.

"You're riding with the big names," Rafael tells us over the radio, some relish in his voice. By this he means the leaders, the climbing specialists. And though these riders are to a man short and skinny, I cannot help but turn the phrase through my head as I pedal, imagine these men around me as bigger and more solid than they are, credit them with the gravity of something larger than themselves.

I ride ahead of Fabrice as the pace starts to increase. He has drawn himself into an unfathomable blankness. He pedals. He eats on command, reaching into the pocket on the rear of his jersey, sucking an energy gel, or chewing a sugary fruit bar.

* *

When the main group passes over the second peak of the stage, it is already diminished. All day the pace has slowly risen.

The descents offer some respite, but today more is ventured even here. People take corners quicker, pushing tires to their limits. Fabrice and I find ourselves pedaling hard on downhill straights to keep pace with those in front. When not pedaling, we tuck ourselves down into our handlebars, our stomachs on our saddles, seeking the most aerodynamic profile. We barely touch our brakes.

The mountains here are shunted next to each other, packed in and steep. As soon as we finish a descent, we begin to ascend again. In this region, Sebastian has told me, people hid from religious tyranny in former times. They built churches as visible and as high as possible, warding off charges of heathenism. Now these churches look down on us from mountainsides. Bell towers pick out the network of villages through which our route will climb. Sometimes the descendants of these fleeing peoples ring the bells in these churches as we appear, encouraging our own flight from the valleys.

* *

I stay with Fabrice. I pace him. I feel light, able to accelerate, to shift, to mark the other competitors around me.

I am riding as well as I ever have, I think, and in this I realize a change in me: I am not nervous. I do not have the normal sense that I must ration my energy, the usual dread of the sudden plunge that will come when my reserves are spent. I have what I have. I am doing what I am doing.

I taste the smallest quantity of blood in my throat. A wind blows up the valley. A fan showers us with water, holding his thumb partly over the top of a plastic bottle, waving fat drops from it.

I pull back to the car often to retrieve bottles. The Butcher passes them out to me. "There are some painkillers in this one," he says. "Tell Fabrice that this is the stuff he likes."

I nod in reply. The Butcher smiles, as happy as I have seen him.

Fabrice receives the bottles without comment. He concentrates. All the team leaders are now on edge, seeking to identify weakness or confidence and to react accordingly. We riders study each other. We consider fingers itching against gear shifters. We regard tensing calves and wonder if they aren't preparing for a burst of speed or suffering the first stages of cramp. We look at others' faces—blank faces, pained faces, happy faces—and wonder what they really mean.

We ride and we wait for a move, and time does not seem to pass. Yet the road rolls beneath us. The landscape changes. We cast empty water bottles from our bikes.

* *

With three-quarters of the race gone, we approach a mountain pass: the final ascent of the stage. Rafael has warned us that this is where crucial seconds will be won or lost in the overall race. The road climbs from fields, through trees, past barren slopes that in winter would be ski pistes, and up into windswept emptiness.

From the start of the ascent, the skinny little men start raising the pace. The fans cluster on the road ahead of us and part as we approach, a human bow wave. Some of them run beside us. In front the motorbikes sound their horns. Voices rise in response.

The karaoke singer, the same man who was out ahead for hours on the previous stage, goes at the third turn. He does it craftily, just after another couple of riders have lunged into a break and been chased down. He sets off where the road pitches up more steeply. We are not ready to pursue him.

I accelerate to the front of the group. I stand, begin to really chase the little man. Fabrice is behind me. He says, "Not *too* hard."

Tsutomo takes a turn at the front. We let other teams, keen to pull their own riders back into the pursuit, do their share of leading.

When I can, I turn and look at Fabrice. He breathes evenly. He pedals smoothly.

The chase slows a little. I push to the lead of the group again.

On the front, I feel well. Rafael now has a reading of how far out ahead the karaoke singer has pulled himself. "Forty seconds," he says through the static.

I press the pace a little more. I am tiring, but I do not really care. This is the last climb of the day, and when I have pulled Fabrice back into contention, my work will be done.

"Thirty-five seconds," says Rafael.

The corners come and go. The route is fully lined with fans. We are in trees, and the smell of wood and moist earth is around us.

I feel the slightest spasm of a coming cramp at the back of my knee. I want to coast for a couple of strokes of the pedals. I move out of the racing line and Tsutomo arrives immediately to lead. "Thirty seconds," says Rafael.

A message for Fabrice is whitewashed onto the road:

GO

FABRICE

GO

We accelerate around the corners, where the road flattens. We push right into the inside of turns, brushing into the fans. Fabrice, behind us, still seems content.

"Thirty-seven seconds," says Rafael.

This panics me, the fact that the gap is no longer dropping.

"Steady," says Fabrice.

I take the lead again. I will the cramp to hold off just a little longer. I stand on the pedals.

"Thirty-six seconds," says Rafael. I think we should have made up more time. I take a drink from my water bottle and throw it to the side of the road.

Tsutomo moves ahead of me again. The other teams seem resolved to ride behind us, to let us do the chasing. I would normally be annoyed by this. Today, though, I push and do not worry about holding back.

I take a turn. I stamp on my pedals. My hamstrings ache. They are completely empty of strength, close to cramping. There is an ecstasy in this exhaustion. It is the kind of heedless tiredness that I remember from summer evenings in childhood.

"Twenty seconds," says Rafael, and I see the singer up the road. We approach him so quickly that this time estimate is obsolete as soon as it has been issued.

The singer disappears around a corner. I feel shaky but push on. My breathing is a mess. I want to finish this. We turn the corner ourselves.

I dig my fingernails into my handlebar tape. We are so close. There is bile in my throat. The singer looks back, seeing that he will be caught. He puts in a burst of speed just to test us. I ride a little faster. I pray that this is a bluff. I am an instant from collapsing when he drops his pace again. He sits down in the saddle. He lets us make up the ground toward him. We come past. I ready myself to peel off the pack, to leave Fabrice and the other main contenders to scrap out the rest of the day.

As I am about to slow though, another rider puts in an acceleration, passing us. I flail after him. Fabrice is behind me. I am a meter behind the rider seeking to break. He keeps pushing, but I hold my pace somehow. I can hardly breathe. My vision is nearly gone. He looks back. He gives up. I catch up to him and in the same motion I swerve from the racing line and begin to slow. Fabrice glances a grateful hand against my back as he passes me.

I simply stop. I double over at the side of the road and start vomiting. The radio turns on. "Good job, Solomon," says Rafael's voice. "That was what we needed." A man wearing swimming trunks and hiking boots comes over and rubs my shoulders as I stand hunched over the front of my bike puking onto the verge.

* *

My hands are on my knees and my knees are shaking. My field of vision is returning to normal. The air smells of pinecones and warm tar. I have done all I could. I couldn't have set Fabrice up better. I stand. The man rubs circles on my back. It does not come to me, though: the regular feeling of having executed a plan, the suffusing rush of exhaustion to an end. I still feel a numbness to the stakes of the day. There is a weight in my stomach that all this effort has not reduced, that has lain waiting beneath the simpler pain that overlaid it.

The riding has been less than it was, and in this easier. I have wanted nothing more than to use myself up. Maybe I should have always raced with such lack of interest. And yet, of course, had I always felt about racing as I do today, I would never even have begun this career. I could not have discharged my duty so effectively today without the desire to be done with all this.

I clamber back onto my bike. I make two unsteady strokes. The man in the swimming trunks pushes me, and I am going again. Stragglers pass me—not Johan and the other sprinters, who ride in a bunch even farther behind, but better, more tragic back markers, who expected more from this day and now seek vainly to get themselves back in contention.

I struggle to stay with any of these men though. I cannot hold them in my line of sight. It is not until a domestique of the German banking team passes me that I find someone riding at a pace that I can sustain. I tuck behind him. He looks back and nods.

The team vehicles come past then, moving up the road to be just behind their leaders. When the car of my team goes by, Rafael stares straight ahead. The Butcher waves.

After some time, the banker wriggles an elbow to indicate that it is my turn to ride ahead. I step up on the pedals. I bear my stint setting our pace. Unlike the leaders, we are not shepherded by motorbikes or race referees. Spectators swarm around the road as we ride. My skin is pricked with the spittle of fans. I can feel their warmth and taste the sourness of their breath. I lead for as long as possible and then pull out of the racing line.

When the banker edges past me, I seek to settle behind him. I sit down in my saddle. I change the position of my hands on the bars. Sitting alters the muscles I use to propel myself. In this new position, however, I am just as weak. Usually in exhaustion I can pump my thighs at a low cadence. Now even this ability is gone. The space between me and the banker stretches: a hand, an arm, the height of a whole person.

* *

I am alone but for the groups of fans I pass through. Life rolls back over me now: the police station, the lawyer, the investigating judge, my wife and son entangled in the middle, Katherine making her way across the country to assist where I have not.

I inch toward the peak. I stand to force my pace. The difficulty of any given activity, I suppose, is no guarantee that that activity is not selfish.

Two fans run beside me: a couple of men, one of whom is wearing a comically outsized pair of sunglasses. The crowd shouts words of encouragement, though I am sure that they do not know my name. They spray water at me. Some of them even reach out to clap me on the back.

I consider Fabrice's advice about physical pain and try to pin down what hurts me.

The radio channel crackles open. "Push, Fabrice. Push," says Rafael.

Beads of sweat run down my nose. The television helicopter is thumping up near the peak, a few kilometers away. I wipe my face with the back of my glove. I try to change gear. The chain chatters, misaligned. I wiggle the shifter and it jumps into place.

My lips are crusted with sunscreen and grit and salt. My mouth tastes like tin.

The crowd is all around me, encroaching onto the road. They wave flags, they bellow me on. They mug for a photographer coming past me on the rear of a motorbike.

I do not believe in this, I think. I do not believe, and realize in coming to this conclusion how much I did. I do not feel the necessity of these people being here, the sense that I do anything special. It feels like some assumption in the logic that has brought me here has given out: an assumption buried, assumed secure, like the foundation pile of a house, ignored until it crumbles. And yet what exactly this assumption was I do not know. I cannot work back to it. I am the same man, the same body. I stand on the pedals. I haul on my handlebars. And yet it is gone.

*   *

I come around a switchback and there, improbably, is the banker who just dropped me. I approach him gradually, wondering whether he is slowing or I am accelerating.

He looks back, grimaces. I am on him, then. I pass him. I ride ahead.

I take a sip from my bottle. The sugar of the drink catches in my throat. I cough and spit.

Rafael's voice prickles through the team radio. "Okay," he says, "down, down, down." He addresses Fabrice, who is already over the peak and beginning to descend toward the finish. "No gaps," says Rafael. "Keep it tight."

It's a surprise, somehow, to be reminded that the race continues with such intensity ahead of us.

"Hey," says the banker again. He clicks up a gear and overtakes me. "Keep a pace," he says. "Wake up."

Chapter 13

We head toward the peak, over which the others have already gone. A couple of riders pass us. The fans, as usual, think us dispirited. They offer the standard affirmations of our ability, entreaties to push onward.

As I stand to force myself over the last meters of the climb, the radio channel opens. "Crash," says Rafael. "Crash on the descent." I look to the banker, who seems to be getting the same notification in his own earpiece. He nods. He slows a little. Then we are passing under the inflatable arch that marks the summit, tipping over into the descent.

The banker settles onto the drops of his handlebars, covering the brake levers with his forefingers. I do the same, tucking into his slipstream. He looks back at me. There is no need for us to go too quickly. We are no longer playing a competitive role in the stage, after all.

The banker swings around a left switchback and then a right. We do one bend and then another, and I find myself seduced by the action, loosening. Riding as just two of us, I need not worry about cutting off others behind me, nor being caught up in the crashes of those just ahead. Riding becomes a work of geometry.

The route drops into trees and begins to twist more sharply. We leave the dome of the peak and nose down into forest. The road coils. Just occasionally a view opens out and we can see into the yawn of the valley to our right. It is car-commercial scenery. Spectators, where they observe this section at all, stand in ones and twos on the inside of turns. They cannot really see us, so quickly do we pass, and the inessentiality of this descending to the spectacle of the sport makes it feel truer, cleaner.

The banker rides ahead. Just occasionally he looks back to check that I still follow him. My bike moves under me, shaken by minor mechanical asymmetries, jogged by cracks in the road.

Despite ourselves, we are speeding up. We take a sharp right hairpin and I wonder, in that moment, at the improbable hold of my tires to the tarmac. Finding a rhythm, we both rise out of that turn and immediately set ourselves for the next leftward switchback. In shifting the lean of the bike from one side to another there is a moment of lightness, a brief levitation. Then we are tucked down into the corner, traveling around it, coming out to a view of the valley below.

It is as the road opens up ahead of us that we see the lights: red and flashing up the road, initially hard to locate, the flickering seeming like afterimages or the play of the sun between trees. As we approach, we see the race referee's car pulled over, its lights going, motorbikes stopped, cameramen and journalists standing in the road. There are four team cars parked on the verge. My own team's is there, the bankers', a couple of others. I cannot pick out Rafael and the Butcher amidst the group. The helicopter is overhead, thumping a nervous pulse onto the scene. The banker and I slow to avoid all this. I can make nothing out of the hubbub arising from the men busy at the outside of the corner. Past the activity, fans are already walking up the hill to see what is going on, uninterested in myself or the banker.

We carry on rolling, because we don't know what else to do. We take another corner, and another after that, not flowing as we were before but maneuvering our way around, our engagement with the descent no longer instinctual. Then the banker slows further.

He looks back at me, expecting something. I stare ahead, trying to shake off his glance and what it could entail. After an eternity, my own radio channel opens, carrying the news that the banker must have received already. "We're at the crash site," says Rafael. "Fabrice has gone off the edge of the road."

I pull on my brakes. The banker nods to me as he continues away. He's in no hurry but has no reason to stop. The bike comes to a halt, and I stand. I look back up the hill. *Off the road,* I think.

I feel shaky. I wonder whether what has been said can be true. There is a moment of dislocation from my surroundings. I look at my hands gripping the bars. I open one hand and turn it over, surprised, momentarily, to see my body respond to my will. The palm of my glove is grubby; my fingers are grease stained. On the back of my sense of shock arrives a rush, a desire to act. I am able to, I think. I have a seasick notion with it that perhaps I have waited for a moment like this. An old man walks up the hill from where he has been watching the race. He looks at me intently. I turn my bike until it faces back up the incline. Something is asked of me, I think. I step on my pedals and begin to ride up the hill.

*   *

I pedal the wrong way. The support cars of other teams pass now. Other riders, behind me in the race and now coming down past me, do not pay me any notice. They are closing in their focus, trying to ignore those events they do not have the time to interpret, as I was until so recently. Perhaps they do not even see me.

I am driven by a nervous energy. The fans I pass do not know how to acknowledge me. Some nod, some of them quietly applaud.

The helicopter hovers near the crash site, and I can measure my progress up the hill by the intensification of the sound of the rotors.

I think of Fabrice and imagine him, for some reason, lying on the road.

All of us, I think, have our images of *the* crash: the one we fear will take us down permanently. For me, these revolve as nightmares. For other temperaments, I think, there is some theater about this scenario, some redeeming glamour. Though most would deny it, we have all found ourselves in darkened rooms, late at night, pawing at laptops, seeking coverage of the worst accidents: lifeless bodies laid out on the road, blood leaking from a head wound and spread by the last motion of the prone rider, like the mark of a large paintbrush dragged lazily. "The head is where the blood is," the Butcher once told me, when he patched a weeping graze I had acquired on my temple. While I ride back up, I find myself plugging Fabrice into my own imagining. Hence the road, I suppose, and the doctors surrounding him, one of them pumping vainly at his chest. In my vision Rafael is there leaning in, trying, perhaps for the last time, to exert his influence on the endurance of his rider.

As I approach I see, of course, that this is not the case. There is no Fabrice, just other people standing, looking over the side of the roadway.

The Butcher busies himself retrieving something from the back of the car. I lay my bike down and walk over to the group at the edge of the road.

The sight stops my breath. It is a cliff edge. I can see the far bank of the river a long way below, a little scrub and rock above that. For a couple of meters beneath our feet there is steep, rock-studded grass, then the terrain drops right away, utterly invisible from where we stand.

"He went over here?" I say.

A man in overalls, a mechanic or an ambulance man, nods.

Then I hear Rafael's voice, addressing someone else. "You do not know," he says. "You do not yet know."

Two men study the terrain right at the edge of the road. They kneel on the tarmac, look at where the dirt falls away.

"Excuse me," says Rafael, to no one in particular. "Does anyone have a fucking idea what they are doing?"

Radios crackle—not our own team radios but the bulky black things carried by emergency workers and the race organizers. Stewards stand near the vehicles speaking tersely into these devices. I sense that their activities offer an answer in the affirmative to Rafael's question.

I hear the whirr of freewheeling bicycles, the application of brakes, and the multilingual warnings of a large group of cyclists approaching an obstacle. I look up to see a bunch of about thirty riders. I imagine being in the wilderness and being passed by a body of fleet-moving creatures. Having adjusted their course past us, the riders do not give our group any further attention. When one is descending, hazards are beyond concern once one is upon them. A good descender thinks not of where they are but where they will be in three seconds' time.

Amidst the spectators is a stout man in a short-sleeved checked shirt. He glances around with curiosity. He has a gray mustache. His hair is an artificial shade of black. He catches my eye. "Right over there," he says. "I saw him go right over."

"What?" I say.

"I was watching from there," he says. He points across the road, to the inside of the corner. "He came down in a group. He took the corner a little wide. He tried to brake, I think." I examine the man, as if that will give me a clue of how to take what he is saying. He shrugs. "It was a terrible thing to watch," he says, though I do not think from the way he says this that he regrets having witnessed it.

"Mother of God!" says Rafael. "Am I going to have to climb down the cliff myself?"

He stands next to me, among the men clustered around the edge. We are doing nothing. We stand where we do merely because it has some place in the story of what has happened. The coordination of the event—the rescue? the recovery?—is happening elsewhere. "Does anyone understand the urgency?" Rafael says. The pitch of the television helicopter above us changes and I see it peeling off, away from the mountains. I wonder whether this is a bad omen. "He's down there," says Rafael.

A man wearing a polo shirt embroidered with the logo of the Tour organizers turns to Rafael. "You have to understand," he says, "it's a long fall."

"Don't think I don't," says Rafael. "Don't you misunderstand, either. It takes a lot to kill a man these days." I am surprised that he can say the word "kill," that he can speak already of what I can barely think. He looks around him, picks out and focuses upon me. "He is a man who can surprise you," he says.

The sound of rotors returns. We look up to see a different aircraft, a red mountain-rescue helicopter. With this sight there is a change in the body language of those around us. Their helplessness in the face of the catastrophe is validated. There is nothing they can do but watch. They stiffen their postures, no longer shrinking in their impotence, ceasing to will their own invisibility. The helicopter hovers over the gorge. The rotors pummel the air. This close, I feel their movement in my stomach. The tufts of grass around the lip of the cliff are blown back toward us. Dust is thrown up. We shield our faces. Through fingers, we see a man emerge from the helicopter, hanging from a rope. We watch him descend ahead of us and then down out of view.

When the man has been deposited in the gorge, the rope is dragged back up into the helicopter. Another man descends, and after that, a red lozenge-shaped stretcher is lowered.

We at the top of the cliff wait. The men at the end of the rope already know things that it will take minutes or hours, perhaps days, for the rest of us to find out, that may, in fact, remain unspoken forever. Does Fabrice lie crumpled over rocks, in the bushes? Could his fall have been broken by foliage? By a plunge into deep water?

I walk over to the car and to the Butcher. He nods, acknowledging me. We stand silently together. "It's hard to watch," he says after some time. He cannot keep still. He touches his face, his neck, his chest.

I am still standing next to the Butcher when the sound of the helicopter changes in tone. We watch the paramedics winched back up, steadying the stretcher hanging next to them. This sight, I suppose, confirms nothing but Fabrice's continued existence in the world. I feel it in my chest, however. The thought that he, in whatever condition he is in, is there, within my line of sight, has some power. I feel intensely my relation to Fabrice in these moments. I think of him in the helicopter, and then as it departs I count his movement away from us in my imagination: one kilometer, two, three. It feels like this can do something, as if my bearing his situation in mind can somehow help him. I imagine the hospital staff waiting for him: somebody on the helipad looking into the distance for the approach of the helicopter; gurneys, machines, and surgeons prepared for his arrival. When I attend to the process, break it into steps, into increments, it feels that there should be no space for him to slip away.

I am drawn back to the moment of holding B for the first time and the shock I felt at having in my arms a new living being. He had been nothing, and then had come to exist. It seemed wondrous that suddenly here should be life: magic hiding plainly in the middle of a world which, since childhood, I had been assured held no such thing. I feel this in some inverse way about Fabrice. I know life ends, can end, and yet I cannot understand it in this context, this moment.

* *

The silence after the helicopter's departure is broken by the approach of more riders: the large group of sprinters and back markers. They stream past, seeking to keep within the time cutoff, to avoid being eliminated from the race.

Sebastian and Johan peel off from the back of the group.

They stop by the team car. They place down their bikes. They stand. They look around. They clump over to the Butcher and me in their stiff cycling shoes.

"Hey," says Sebastian. He reaches a heavy arm around my back and pats me on a shoulder. His size makes this gesture awkward, yet there is something touching in its gracelessness.

"How is he?" says Sebastian. The Butcher looks at him, and he gets it. "Right," he says. He nods slowly.

We stand and look out into the gorge.

Rafael is still moving around with great intent, trying to learn what is happening from officials who are in contact with the helicopter, seeking to get a better idea of the specifics of the crash. He looks up and sees us, and I sense a relief in his realization that he can turn his energies upon us.

"Ride," he says. He waves his hands around.

"What?" says Sebastian. "Keep racing?"

"No," says Rafael. He sighs. "Just ride. Get out of here. Do you not think I would, if I had a bike?"

We move then, unthinking really, obeying Rafael as sheep respond to the bark of a dog. It is the thing that requires the least thought. There is nothing we can achieve standing on the road. Fabrice is gone. There are only these other stunned people.

We fetch our bikes, mount them, point them down the hill. "Get out of here," says Rafael. "Honestly."

We set off. We roll up to speed. The three of us string out. Sebastian leads and Johan and I trace the same path around the corners. This is the kind of thing we have repeated innumerable times at training camps.

The three of us find a rhythm. I return to the pattern I went through with the banker: lifts and plunges, dipping in and out of the turns, the dreamlike motion.

The gradient begins to slacken and the road flows out ahead more loosely. There are fewer corners and the trees have given way to fields. We no longer ride in the shade, and the atmosphere is warmer. We press into the heavy, hot air of the valley.

In this final straight section of the descent we do not tuck ourselves down into the bikes as we would in competition, but sit up on our saddles as the air thumps into us. The eddies grab at our clothing, blow back the hair on our arms. Something about the air, the violence and unpredictability of it, brings me back into a bodily sense of myself.

We pass into the town and go under the banner signifying the start of the final five kilometers.

We drop into a cobbled corner, then take a leftward arc around a roundabout. We pedal up a tree-lined boulevard toward the center of town.

* *

People are cleaning up around the finish line when we reach it. I wonder for a second whether we should check that our arrival has been registered. Stewards are already working at the finishing arch, getting ready to dismantle it. They remove the large digital clock under which we pass each day.

The three of us dismount. Johan and Sebastian walk off, wheeling their bikes. I wander my own way. The first person I recognize is Shinichi. He leans over one of the crowd barriers. He offers a small wave. I go over. "Hello," he says.

His eyes are reddened. I realize that I wait for him to offer some commiseration, and further that he is not the man from whom to seek this. He is struck by the shock of the event himself, I realize. He feels it has happened to him.

I find I have no energy with which to speak. Instead I raise a hand in parting and walk away.

I see other riders now, other members of staff from other teams. The atmosphere is muted. People come to me and say that they are sorry. I do not feel able to ask them exactly what they are sorry about. I turned my radio off at the crash site. I have not turned it back on. These sorrys pile up, form the shape of something. No one says it, though. Perhaps his fate is not known, and it is the indeterminacy, the worry, that causes all these grave looks.

At the bus one of the mechanics, Hans, works slowly on the bikes. It is Hans who gives me the news, just like that. "He passed," says Hans. Hans, who lives in Belgium, who listens to nineties rap as he works, whom I hardly know. "I'm sorry," he says. I stand there. This moment, I think, will last for both of us. I have almost never talked to Hans, and suddenly here he is, telling me this. It is as if the interaction both justifies and explains our presence to each other in this world; as if he has existed all this time just to give me this news; I, for him, to receive it. Perhaps I will never so much as talk to him again, but I will remember this, the way he said, "He passed." I hand

Hans my bike. He takes it, turns, leans it against Tsutomo's bicycle. He turns back. "I'm sorry," he says.

*   *

It is only when Rafael returns that the full story is told. He stands in the aisle of the bus, the same position from which he gave the morning's race briefing. This day, more than any other of his career, has proven him powerless, and he is not insensitive to the way that a precise retelling of events gives him back the slightest measure of control. Dead on impact, is his conclusion.

I want to know, then, the role of the rescue, the frantic trip to hospital, the medics, the beeping machines. It makes me angry to think of Fabrice, already dead, submitted to these vain indignities. I raise my hand from the rows of seats. "What?" Rafael says.

"Did they not know?" I say.

"There was a possibility," he says. "Apparently there was a possibility."

I find it strange to think that the whole of my descent off the peak, my turning back, that ride to the line, all happened in a world of which Fabrice was already not a part.

Next to me, Tsutomo weeps, wipes at his face with the backs of the cycling gloves he still wears.

Chapter 14

The hotel is the same as so many we have stayed in before, and yet of course everything is different. In the reception, other guests view us cautiously. The staff look into the middle distance with expressions of studied blankness. These vacant looks cover an interest in our arrival, I think, a desire to detect the marks of the tragedy upon us.

The Butcher lists off the numbers of the rooms in which we will be staying. His voice is steady. There is an effort behind it, a care he would not usually exert. We step forward to collect keys. Riders leave the lobby silently, one by one. And yet I stay behind. I catch Rafael's eye. His telephone is ringing from his pocket but he does not acknowledge it. "The other business?" he says.

"Liz," I say.

He flinches, as if annoyed at my vocalizing what he had merely implied. "I'll come to your room in fifteen minutes," he says.

* *

I am sharing a room with Tsutomo, and he is inside when I arrive. He lies on his bed with his clothes on. He lifts his head to look at me when I enter, and this look is something different from the gazes of hotel staff or fans or the riders from others teams whom I met in the finish area. There is none of the inquiry those glances held. There is an understanding of this day, I realize, that will always exist between us, that others will never quite be able to approach. He closes his eyes again, lies back.

The TV on the chest of drawers in front of the bed is on but muted. There is footage of a large building, a bus parked outside, and I realize slowly, dumbly, that it is our own hotel. I go to the window and part the curtains, and there, across the street, are two television vans; a reporter is standing in front of a camera, gesturing behind him. I look back at the TV. The footage runs a couple of seconds delayed. The window from which I look is too far away to make out in the picture. This event is escaping us, I think, already gaining its own momentum. I leave the window. I go to sit on my own bed. The TV pictures cut to footage of the corner where Fabrice left the road, where I and others waited just a couple of hours earlier. There are plastic-wrapped bunches of flowers there already. Fans are placing cards and photographs. A woman kneels and tries to light a small candle. A man behind her is putting down another bouquet. What brought them there, I wonder, with such certainty that there would be others? Where has all this grief emerged from? Another man talks to the camera, red eyed and fervent in whatever he is saying. The picture cuts again to a woman with a toddler, the two of them examining the tributes left at the verge. I realize that I am envious of these people. There is a sureness in their acts. This death has given them something, I think, and despite themselves they are grateful. I recall the way the fans watch us riders as we pedal uphill, searching our expressions, seeking a breaking point, some elemental sense of our being. There is so much in this sport that is hidden from them, and yet in Fabrice tumbling into the gorge they have an undeniable truth, a point of calibration amidst all the other uncertainty. The magician has been felled by a bullet he did not catch, and his act, therefore, has been proven true. The camera focuses for a moment on a sketch someone has done of Fabrice and left by the road in tribute. The television picture draws out again to take in the woman with her young child. She dabs at her tear ducts with her little finger.

"They can never get enough," says Tsutomo. He has opened his eyes and is watching the screen.

"They have come out for him though," I say. Tsutomo sighs. I think of the way he hurries past Shinichi each morning.

"They are so hungry," he says.

* *

I wash my face in the bathroom. I drink from the tap. When I come back into the room, the news has moved on to another story: footage of a factory, of a cashier in a supermarket. There is a rapping at the door, and when I open it Rafael is outside. "We'll go to my room," he says. We walk down the corridor silently. His phone rings. He takes it out of his pocket and rejects the call. He opens the door of his room and beckons me in.

"She is out?" I say. "She is on her way?"

Rafael closes the door behind him. He comes around to face me. The room is dim. The curtains are drawn and no lights are on. "She was apprehended in a very small town," he says. "The police there— how shall I say it?—are not your Sherlock Holmes." He waits for a reaction. I have that sense I had watching the Butcher reading out the room numbers: that I am seeing someone working carefully, trying to lose themselves in a habitual action. I think of Fabrice starting to pedal on the trainer in the morning. "They were very confused about what they found. There is a provision in the law for a case that is complex. They are able to hold a suspect for another twenty-four hours."

"Are able to?"

"Are able to and have, I should say."

"She is still not out?" I say. I feel a vertigo, a sudden nausea. Yet this reaction is not from the bluntness of a surprise but from the feeling that I should have known this, that in some part of my mind that I did not attend to was the expectation of this betrayal.

"Yes, yes," says Rafael. "You understand."

"But you said you had this in hand."

He steps back a little. He is unused to my tone, my intensity. "I am not all-powerful. I think today you have seen this, no?"

"She is in prison still with our child!"

"Your mother-in-law is there. Your mother-in-law has Barry."

"You said you were looking out for us, and yet you fucked us."

"In this, I think you are not being impartial," says Rafael. "I understand you have a reason to be upset."

"You are a slug," I say. "A worm."

"Yes, yes," he says. "We are all not ourselves this evening."

"I am done with you," I say. "I am done with this job."

"She will go in front of the judge tomorrow morning. We are very sure that she will be released for now. Whatever charges they throw at her, we have a plan to help her, provided, of course, that she works with us."

"Sorry?" I say.

"We will make her imprisonment just a memory."

"What do you mean *work with* you?"

Rafael steps back another pace. "It is important we have a straight story between all of us," he says. "These prosecutors are tricky people. Also, there is now a man at the center of this who cannot protect himself."

"What are you saying?" I say.

"I am saying what I hoped I would not have to say out loud." He kneads his brow. There is an anger in his words now. "Fabrice has just been killed." He waits a second as if I am receiving this news for the first time. "There are certain things your wife could say which would damage the way our friend is remembered. You understand?"

"I know what you are implying."

"It is that simple," he says. "We will not be racing tomorrow. We have forfeited the race. The organizers will not punish us for this. The other teams will ride tomorrow's stage only symbolically. There will be a silence beforehand. Everything is changed." He glowers, and I realize that for once this does not worry me.

"I would not ride if you told me to," I say. "And whatever Liz wants to tell the police I will corroborate."

"There are certain bits of information that would really damage the reputation of Fabrice," says Rafael. "If things have, shall we say, the wrong *emphasis*. I would just like to be sure that Liz shares these concerns."

"She will be telling the truth," I say. "There is only the truth."

He spits air. I smell aniseed. He looks at me as if I am making the most rudimentary mistake. "There are facts," he says. "I will give you that. But whether the facts make a truth is another question. You know, I had an uncle who once died of a heart attack at a brothel. Do you think they mentioned that at the funeral?"

"This is not the same," I say.

"They told everyone just that he died in bed," says Rafael. "Do you know why?" He slaps his own thigh. There is an unsteadiness to his way of speaking now, an uncharacteristic lack of control. "He went to the brothel irregularly. This was not, in his heart, the man my uncle was. However, the thought of him dying beneath a prostitute would have been difficult to dislodge from the minds of people." He pauses for a moment. He stares into space. "There is a truth beyond truth," he says.

"If people want to understand," I say, "they will understand."

"No."

"As we do."

"They are not us. They do not have our perspective. They will not take the time," says Rafael. He fixes his gaze on me. "This man was like your brother and you do this to him." He strokes his hands together as if rubbing dust from them. "You would not be here if it were not for him."

Rafael would say this. This is all within his method of working. And yet the image comes to me of Fabrice, easing past me on that climb at the end of our spring training camp. I realize he must have had to argue for my inclusion in this race.

Love all of it, he had said. What to do with that? Where to put it?

"It's just a sport," I tell myself. "A game."

I am surprised to hear Rafael answer, to realize that I have spoken aloud. "For you," he says, "it is not possible to believe this."

I feel a shudder, the lurch of having fallen in a dream. It works through me. Rafael is right, I think. I did not admire Fabrice just as a man who played a game.

"You were not good this winter," he says. "I did not want to bring you to this tour, but Fabrice was insistent."

I glimpse again Rafael's strategy, his compulsion to press his points. It is this that rallies me, gives me back my resolve.

"I'm going to go," I say.

Rafael steps back. He shakes his head. "I am going to see the body soon," he says. He looks at me pleadingly, as if he wishes me to corroborate the horror of such a necessity.

"Right," I say. I push down the thought of Fabrice as a corpse.

Rafael exhales. He sits on the hotel bed. He looks at me sadly. He is surrendering, or choosing the tactic of seeming to. I realize he is not wearing his built-up shoes, which lie thrown off by the door. "He was a man totally dedicated to one thing," he says. "He gave himself up to a task. He was not a man of our age in this way. Who really believes in something bigger? Who really gives themselves up these days?" There is something pleading in these questions. He knows, I suppose, that he is not reaching me. My anger lessens to a numbness. Probably it has always been this simple to step beyond his grasp. This realization does not make me feel strong though, but weak, like someone seeing a billowing sheet in the daylight that had scared them nearly to death the night before.

"You cannot control everything," I say.

He glares at me. "But I will do him the decency of trying," he says.

I shut the door. I leave him to himself.

*   *

I take a taxi to the small regional airport, where there is a car rental franchise. I arrive just as the rental counter is closing. The woman serves me quickly, without interest. I get an anonymous silver car. The sky is white with cloud, the air warm. It is a calm evening. I still have not eaten since the race and I am running on a strange reserve. The world is made oddly luminous. I take a toll road, then turn off toward the mountains. The evening is coming in, peaks casting their shadows across the valleys. I pass alpine villages, factories, reservoirs. Electricity cables span the valley above me, blinking lights hung on the wires to mark them out to aircraft.

I stop at another hotel. Katherine comes to greet me. She holds B. She takes charge. She seems more watchful though, less assertive than I have known her. I have a sense that things are suspended, that she is waiting for clarity. We take the elevator to her room. B's crib is there. She puts him into it. She notes the way I am looking at my son. "You need to wash yourself before you look after him," she says. "You need to eat."

We walk out into the corridor. "I am sorry," I say.

Katherine looks at me with a certain amount of distaste. "You're apologizing for what?" she says.

I shrug. I shake my head.

"You don't know?"

"I suppose not."

She sighs. "It was her choice?" she says.

"To carry the things?"

"Yes."

"She volunteered," I say.

She looks at me wearily. "I thought so."

"It was just bad luck," I say. "We did not expect this."

"Naturally."

"She is meticulous, always."

"Yes." There is an unpleasant sternness to the way Katherine concedes this.

"You should be proud of her," I say. "I have never met anyone so able. She is like you."

Katherine watches me a moment, as if seeking a signal of my seriousness. "Do you think I want her to be like me?" she says.

She points me in the direction of my room then. She tells me to shower. She has a bowl of pasta brought up to me when I have finished washing. I eat, and when I am done, Katherine brings in B. "How was Liz?" I say.

"I saw her only briefly when I went to collect him," she says. "It was not a proper visit."

"And how is she?"

She thinks. "You will have to wait and see," she says. "My seeing her is one thing. You two being back together another."

* *

B is glad to see his father. He pulls at my sweatshirt as I hold him. He cackles. I put him on the floor and he waves his hands. He bounces on his bottom. It is all this joy that slays me: his belief that I am so unequivocally good. He does not doubt me but revels in my arrival, and this pleasure undoes me completely. I weep as I watch him play on the carpet in front of me.

I cannot give such faith what it deserves. I pick him up, but he wants to be on the floor. He has energy. He cries out when I have held him for a minute. I put him back down.

Later Katherine and I bring in his collapsible crib and assemble it, and then I put B to bed and go to sleep at nine. He wakes only once, and I wake up myself and go to him quickly. I hold him, rock him. I speak to him in a soft voice; the act of paying him attention is some block against the rushing back of the past day, the return of all that self that comes with waking.

* *

In the morning I feel a soreness growing in my throat. I will get a cold soon. The body always knows when it may collapse, when one is finally done with racing. At nine the lawyer calls. He tells me that Liz will soon be going in front of the judge and that after lunch I will be notified of when she will be released. I eat breakfast. I tend to B. Katherine stays in her own room.

I turn on the television to watch the start of the day's stage, the moments of tribute that will precede it. The television helicopter films from above, taking in the people who fill the square from which the stage will begin, the trees and lampposts and bus stops marooned within a seething sea of bodies. They have the special certainty of a crowd. Once more I wonder where all this grief comes from. Is it just for Fabrice? Is it channeled and repurposed from other incidents in these many lives? There are so many versions of him, I think, so many perceptions. I think of what Rafael has said about the effects of the revelations that Liz and I will make. I leave the TV for a moment. I go to the hotel window and look out at the ordinary midweek street. This moment of tribute is happening, I tell myself, and nothing I do in the future will change that. Yet even as I indulge this thought, I am aware of its refutability, because what have I been watching in the memorializing of Fabrice but the process by which some large event will color the understanding of all that led up to it, the extent to which the past, as we carry it within ourselves, may be changed? He is a tragic hero now, his racing life, his stunted successes a prelude to this state.

When I return to the TV, the silence has begun. I watch my teammates in their matching tracksuits standing ahead of the other mounted riders. They are different, on the screen, these men I have spent so much time with. Unlike those fans the camera picked out, they look uneasy. Only Sebastian does not stare at the ground. A church bell sounds. The TV speakers crackle as the broadcast microphones strain to convey the deep reverberations. Then the commentator begins speaking in low tones about Fabrice. The silence is over. My team moves aside, and there is a flutter in my stomach at the thought that I will not return to the bus with them, will not have a plan placed ahead of me. What I said to Rafael now hits me: I will never again be part of that team, that half-thinking thing. They will go home. They will rest. Together they will build a context, a bearable story around these days. They will return to racing in time, fortified and excused by the idea that what they do is what Fabrice would have wanted (as if he could have really considered such a thing).

The broadcast cuts to archive footage of Fabrice. He is young at first, in saturated video from the youth world champs. Then there are clips of him riding for his first team, then his second. After that is an image of him standing next to Rafael, and then him in the team kit that I have ridden so many days in: speeding up a mountain pass two summers ago, coming to the finish in a spring classic. For an instant I catch a glimpse of myself watching him from the background as he moves through the crowd at a finish line. I look at my own face and feel for that man in that moment as if I am witnessing a swimmer caught in a current.

* *

It is a nothing moment when Liz comes out of the police station. The media have chosen to ignore her imprisonment: a favor extended to us because of Fabrice's death. "You should be grateful," said Rafael when he gave me this news over the phone. I could hear the interior of the team bus in the background: the rattles and whines of a vehicle in motion. I did not bother to protest.

I stand on the west side of the building, the car parked beside me. There is a blank wall, a single door near the dustbins, a collapsing fence, a van with a flat rear tire. The door opens. A policeman emerges. Liz comes out following him. She wears the red cardigan that she had on three days ago when I last saw her at the bar, when she dropped me outside my hotel. She holds her hand over her mouth. I am the only person waiting. The policeman nods at me. He moves to the side, allows her to pass. She walks across the asphalt toward me. She looks back briefly in response to the sound of the policeman closing the heavy door behind him. She turns slowly back to me again.

I move forward to greet her then. We embrace stiffly. We hold on to each other for long minutes. We are each waiting for the other to move. She is the one who draws away eventually. She opens the door of the car, climbs into the passenger seat.

I take my place at the wheel and begin to drive slowly through the car park. I glance across at her. She looks straight ahead. I want time to examine her, to seek differences, to gauge the effect of these past days on her. She looks at me briefly, if only to shake off my glance. There is the mole at the side of her nose, a rawness to her skin. Yet I cannot draw upon a true picture of her from my memory. I have that old fear of being unable to hold an image of her in mind. I could study her for years, I think, and still not recognize the precise ways she has changed.

We pull out onto the road in front of the station. There is no traffic. We drive in silence. I know that I should talk but I cannot. She lowers the window, and I can hear the burr of the air, the reverberation of the engine bouncing against the buildings we pass, rising and falling like a crude sort of sonar.

She is the one to speak first. "I need a shower," she says.

"I can imagine," I say.

"Can you?"

We stop for traffic lights. Now she is looking at me, and it is there in her look, I think: I should have gone to her. This will be a fact to live with, as solid, I realize, as Fabrice's fall. I knew, of course. I have been waiting, I realize, for this rebuke: a bodily anticipation, curled within me, beneath reason, beneath thought.

She presses the button to raise the window. She begins with the practical information. She is being charged with "importing medicines dangerous to health," she tells me. The investigating judge, she says, was not impressed with the defense mounted by Rafael's lawyer. Rafael and the Butcher will be called in for questioning in coming days. "I'm going to get my own lawyer," she says. "I'm going to give the judge everything as it really happened. I think that this is the best strategy, having been there and—"

"I will back you up," I say. I cut in.

She looks at me.

"I will tell them everything also," I say.

It is as if she is still waiting, seeking an explanation as to why I have interrupted her.

"I'll corroborate," I say.

"Yes."

"I'm quitting," I say.

"Yes."

"I'm going to support you."

"Yes," she says again.

We stop again at a junction. I look at her. She glances back. I am waiting for a reaction, I realize, waiting for her to understand what I have said.

The road is clear. I pull away. I glance at her again. She does understand. And yet she does not feel a need to remark, to make a show of receiving the news.

It is a small thing, this promise that I have presented to her as if it were a gift. It hits me only then how much hope I placed in this gesture of renouncing the team. It is the minimum. It is the smallest measure of support and she takes it as her due.

And yet I thought that it would change things. I thought that I could just say it. I have an image of Fabrice tumbling into the gorge. "I am letting him go," I want to say, but that is not her story, not ours. I am gripping the wheel of the car so that the tendons stand white across the back of my hands. She seems to be waiting. "You were saying?" I ask.

She shakes her head. I slow to allow an old woman over a pedestrian crossing. I release my grip on the wheel. I take hold of it again.

In a playground to the right of the road four boys are kicking a ball against a fence. I think of all I have done to become only a moderately successful racer. I think of having B. There should be a word for the moment at which one realizes what a task truly entails, comes to see how little one has really understood what is required to reach a goal. We navigate one junction, and then another. I follow the signs for the hotel. Perhaps there is already such a word, unknown to me. We pull in to the car park. There is a van outside the building. Men are collecting laundry from the lobby, carrying bulging white bags of bedding on their backs as if they are ants. I come to a stop in the row of spaces farthest from the doorway, facing a block of flats. On the first floor an old man is tending to plants in a long window box. It is an utterly ordinary day.

I cut the motor. The man looks up from his watering, sees us, then returns his attention to his plants. He spreads the leaves of a fern with one splayed hand, pushes the nozzle of his can toward the soil. I watch his careful work, gladdened a little by it. He wears a loose white shirt; a small straw hat balances on the crown of his head. He straightens, turns to hunch over a rose. It is his lack of interest in us that gives me a tiny lift, I realize. We are ordinary in our graveness, our desolation. Some hope in that, perhaps. The question is not how to do what is remarkable, as it has been for so long, but to do what is sufficient, to know what is enough.

Liz is quiet beside me, watching the man as I am.

We are just a couple in a car. Could we allow ourselves to begin with this?

We do not move. The engine ticks as it cools.

"So, here we are," she says.

Acknowledgments

Thank you to Amelia Atlas and Amanda Urban, for believing that this novel could be published, and for the work and vision that allowed its publication to become a reality. Thank you to my editor, Jonathan Cox, whose insights and suggestions have improved this book immeasurably. I am deeply indebted to other readers who have given advice: Lindsay Norville, Emma DeMilta, Matt Grzecki, Simone Richmond, Grady Chambers, Richard Cohen, and Steven Koteff. The Syracuse University Creative Writing program gave me the time and space to finish the first draft of this book, and the teachers I had there—Dana Spiotta, Arthur Flowers, George Saunders, Mary Karr, Chris Kennedy, Christine Schutt, and Bruce Smith—will be an influence on my writing as long as it continues. Thank you to José-Luis Juárez-Morales and his colleagues for taking the time to show me around your laboratory and having the patience to answer my questions. For too many things to mention, thank you to my partner, Jenny Brown, and to my mother, Nicola Bennett.

About the Author

Joe Mungo Reed was born in London and raised in Gloucestershire, England. He has a degree in politics and philosophy from the University of Edinburgh and an MFA in creative writing from Syracuse University. His short stories have appeared in *VQR* and *Gigantic*. He is currently living in Edinburgh. He is working on his second novel and pursuing a PhD at the University of Manchester.